The PEOPLE UPSTAIRS

DAVE LOPARDO

PublishAmerica
Baltimore

Softcover 9781462696215
PUBLISHED BY PUBLISHAMERICA, LLLP
www.publishamerica.com
Baltimore

Printed in the United States of America

CONTENTS

DEDICATION

To Alissa and Thomas Dzis, and Reese, John, and David McGowan:

This is the me you never knew about.

FOREWORD

Who *are* these people, and where did they come from? I honestly don't know. They were up there, though. They awoke me on many occasions, usually between three and four A. M., living their subconscious lives. I caught them in the act and wrote it all down, usually after an encore performance.

A question: do *they* awake from their daytime slumber and spy on *me*, to perform their interpretation of it at night?

I am more discriminating in my words and actions these days. As anyone knows who lives in a multi-level dwelling, it is best to stay on good terms with the people upstairs.

Bob,

Best Wishes,

David D. Lopardo

"NOVEMBER AGAIN"

For eleven Novembers I waged a yearly battle with the leaves dropped by our two maple trees.

Last year, I bought a mulcher mower designed to eliminate raking and bagging. In two half-hour sessions, it roared through the yellow carpet with a vengeance, turning leaves to mulch the size of potato-chip crumbs. Instead of blisters and aching muscles from several hours hard work, there were two brisk marches up and down the backyard. All that remained was a brownish-yellow sheen glowing from the newly-mulches leaves.

When I surveyed the result, and thought of how I was free from this hated task, I felt an exuberant boldness overflowing.

In this venturesome frame of mind I cast about the surrounding territory for new worlds to conquer. My neighbor, Louis Young, was digging a hole in his backyard, in the same location I had seen him dig each of the three Novembers he had lived next door to us.

By nature I am not inquisitive of people whose lives are contiguous to mine, but Louis was an exception. He dug that hole each November, covered it with planking, and filled it in each spring. I had turned it over in my mind many times, my theories ranging from some type of yard improvement, to some mysterious cult ritual. I had never come right out and asked him about it, though. There was something in his bearing that seemed to preclude a little neighborly questioning.

All my wife and I had ever been able to piece together about Mr. Young was that he was a widower, retired, had an old hound that would occasionally appear in the yard with him, and liked gardening. We had never exchanged more than a few polite hello's and some common gripes about the weather. Yard work and gardening seemed to be his only visible interests. That, and digging mysterious holes in the ground.

Mystery aside, and made bold by my triumph over the leaves, I approached the row of small shrubs that separated our property.

"Mr. Young!" I called out.

"Didn't see you there. How do?"

I had surprised him, and he lowered his shovel and looked straight at me. It may have been the first time we had spoken without one of us coming or going from one point to another. He was of average height and build, thinning gray hair, and bright, piercing blue eyes. He wore his usual flannel shirt with olive-green work pants and work boots. He bore a slight resemblance to the actor Ray Walston, from the 60's sitcom *My Favorite Martian.*

Ordinarily, this conversation would have petered out with a quick but polite capping of remarks about nothing in particular. My recent leave conquest had left me looking for new horizons, however. I was hoping to steer the conversation around to the topic of those maddening holes he dug each November.

"You know, Mr. Young . . ."

"Call me Louis."

Aside from my first real close-up look at him, I took notice for the first time of the sharp, clipped tones of an upper New England accent, something we don't hear a lot in western Connecticut. "All right, then, Louis, I'm Richard . . ."

"Saw your name on the mailbox, Richard."

He had a calm, but businesslike expression, as though he was saying to himself, 'We have names. Next topic.'

"Louis, my wife and I have been meaning to invite you over for cake and coffee, you know, just to say 'hello.'

"That's nice of you, Richard. Let me know when it's a good time for you, and I'll be glad to drop in."

That was it. He went back to digging. The hole, about eighteen inches wide, three feet long, and two feet deep, seemed to be about the size of the previous two. It was in *exactly* the same location. I didn't feel as though I'd broken the ice enough to risk prying and further, despite my original intentions. Besides, he had accepted the invitation. That would have to be enough new horizons for one day.

That evening, during dinner, I recounted my conversation with Louis to my wife. She raised her eyebrows in surprise.

"What's he like?" she asked

"Typical old Yankee, sort of. That accent. You know."

"Ayuh," she replied, with a teasing grin. "Did you ask him about the hole?"

"No, I thought maybe we could work our way up to it when we have him over."

"I don't know, Richard. Some of these 'typical old Yankees' can be a bit touchy about their habits."

"How touchy can he be about a hole he digs in plain sight of half the neighborhood, " I asked.

"I just don't think it's a good idea to make friends with him to satisfy your curiosity. It probably has something to do with his gardening, anyway."

"Cathy, where do you get this stuff? He's lived there three years and we barely say hello to him. Admit it, you'd *love* to know why he digs that same hole every November and fills it in every March."

"Not necessarily. I'm surprised at you. For someone who values his privacy so much to go probing into someone's personal life . . ."

This went on for ten minutes, and while I wouldn't classify it as an argument, it was definitely a "conflict of agendas." Cathy and I struck a compromise: we did it her way. She was free to invite Louis over for cake and coffee, and I was free to keep my fat mouth shut about his peculiar backyard diggings.

Two days later, she gave me the go-ahead to invite Louis to our house. When I got home from work shortly after five, I looked him up in the phone book. Not surprisingly, there was no listing for him, so I trotted over and knocked on his front door. A loud howl arose from inside, and I remembered the old dog he had. When he opened the door, the dog was by his side, but had stopped howling. He seemed to recognize me, his tail wagging slightly.

"Louis, Cathy and I were wondering if you would be free to come over tonight around seven."

"Fine as any. Hope old Butch here didn't scare you none. He still sounds the alarm when someone comes a-knockin'."

"No problem. We'll see you at seven, then?"

"I'll be there."

So ended yet another enlightening conversation with our neighbor, Mr. Young. Walking back to my house, I was already thinking of ways I could get him to reveal the hole mystery without directly mentioning it, thus keeping to the deal made with Cathy. There had been no answers supplied by my brief glimpse into his kitchen. It looked much like any of a man alone in his sunset years.

He came over exactly at seven, as promised. It was not the same Louis Young I had observed and whimsically wondered about for the past three years. His backyard uniform had been replaced by black dress slacks, a white-striped shirt, and black shoes. He seemed friendlier, more relaxed, and held up his end of the conversation without any prodding or prompting. It was as if the man we had seen was a character he played, and we were now seeing him off-camera.

At about 9:15 he politely announced that it was getting late for him, and that he was needed at home. "I best be heading out," he said. I usually go to bed early in the colder weather, and Butch gets uneasy if I'm gone too long." He thanked us again, and promised to return the invitation soon.

It turned out that Louis was conversant on just about any topic, and seemed to have moderate, common-sense views on politics, current events, human nature, or anything else.

He had led a full life. Born and raised in a New Hampshire town of nine thousand, he wanted to quit high school and join the army during World War II, but his parents wouldn't sign the enlistment papers. The war in Europe ended before graduation. "And there I was," he said wryly, "stuck with a high school diploma."

He had married a local girl, Alma Winters, and had one child, Francine, who now lived in Florida. Most of his working years had been spent in sawmills and nurseries. He and Alma had moved twelve miles from here seven years ago to be closer to his older brother. Since then, both his brother and wife had passed away. "Had to get out of that house after that," was his only explanation of how he ended up next door to us. Butch, the basset hound, had been around since the late New Hampshire years.

"My mind was set on a shepherd, but Alma fell in love with the little cuss, and that was that," he told us. Butch was now twelve going on thirteen, and aside from an occasional call or letter from his daughter, was Louis's only real comfort in his retirement.

"Have you ever thought of moving to Florida to be with your daughter?" I had asked him.

"After Alma died Frannie was after me for a bit to go live down there, but Florida's not for me. Besides, there was Butch to think of."

After Louis left, I noticed that both Cathy and I seemed quite upbeat and refreshed. But I could see something else on her face, something I wasn't sure would necessarily help me in my need to know about the hole Louis dug. Cathy had lost her father when she was nineteen, and I was sure had never fully accepted it. She had never known the warm, nostalgic mystique of an older man's stories and wisdom. Louis had captivated her, somehow.

In the meantime, I received credit for not having hinted about the November digging, but in reality I had been too caught up in the pleasant aura of the visit to follow my original plan. I could see the hole from our second floor bedroom window, and I confess, it bothered me more than ever.

With Thanksgiving approaching, Cathy asked me to invite Louis. I magnanimously agreed, secretly balancing it against "future considerations." He politely declined, explaining that since his brother's death, he had spent the holidays with his sister-in-law and her family. Even old Butch was included in the festivities.

The day after Thanksgiving found Louis at our front door, and true to his word, he returned our invitation. There had been a small turnout at his sister-in-law's, and she had sent him packing with enough leftovers for a second Thanksgiving.

"Always seems to taste a little better the day after," he remarked, as the three of us sat around his kitchen table, our appetites overwhelmed for the second day in a row. It was obvious that holiday leftovers were a special treat for him, and here he was, giving most of it away. I was impressed at his generosity, and Cathy seemed entranced by his down-home hospitality.

As Butch made one of his strolls by the table, looking for handouts, Louis reached down and scratched the dog's head. "He's getting' on quite a bit," he said. "Slowed down a lot the last year or so. Figure I owe him a final resting place close by. That hole out back, that's in case this old guy checks out when the ground's froze."

I had my answer, and on one level it made sense. He simply wanted to be able to bury his old friend. On a more vocal level, however, it gave me the creeps.

"Louis, doesn't that bother you to dig your dog's grave every year, and then have to *look* at it all winter?" I was sure that Cathy had tried to kick me under the table but had hit the leg of my chair.

He thought a moment, and said, "Richard, it's November again. That time of year. Time to be gettin' ready for winter. New Hampshire winters can make you hard." He paused, and looked down at Butch. "Always felt bad when my dogs died. Always buried 'um myself. It's the way of things, Richard. The old habits die harder than anything."

I could see his point to an extent, but for the most part it seemed ghoulish and unnatural. I had intended to good-naturedly take issue with him on it, but Cathy was giving me a furious look, so I let it drop. My wife was no fan of death, funerals, digging graves, or anything remotely related. Although Louis had volunteered the information, I knew from past experience that somehow I would end up shouldering the blame for it.

When we got home, Cathy skipped the anticipated scolding, and went directly to the silent treatment. "Cathy," I pleaded, "I didn't say a word to him about it. He brought it up himself."

She squinted at me, considering. I knew I was about to get another dose of "Cathy logic."

"You *would* have brought it up, though," she said.

. . .

That hole was wrong. I knew it was none of my business, and that Louis meant well, and it shouldn't have any effect on our friendship. It was not the way to approach life—or death, in my opinion. It seemed to be an affront to life itself. I repeat: I knew it was none of my business and Louis was only trying to do the right thing.

Looking back now, I firmly believed that *I* was doing the right thing when I set about trying to get Louis to fill in the hole. I had to be sly about it, because there was Cathy to deal with, and I had to be subtle about it, because there was Louis to deal with. He held the home field advantage, so to speak, because it was his hole, and was already dug. Plus, I did not want to jeopardize what I considered to be a warm, budding friendship.

In the ensuing days, I made use of every chance encounter with him to pass the time of day, converse pleasantly, and then casually mention something that would swing the conversation around to Butch, life and death, or even the hole itself. Twice, I had him over for a neighborly visit. It was no coincidence that Cathy was out of town on both occasions, Christmas shopping with her sister.

I'm not sure if Louis was on to me. At times he would tilt his head and nod and seem to be considering my point of view. Other times he seemed to ignore me, politely. Once, when the topic of death happened to come up, he mentioned how longevity did not run in his family. "You know, Richard, if I live two more years I'll be the second-oldest one in our clan." It was a sobering thought.

The name 'Young', apparently, was a grim reminder of the family history. His father had died at fifty-three, his wife at sixty-two, and his brother at sixty-six. Only his mother had ever made it to age seventy. I wonder now if that was his way of telling me he'd rather not hear any more about it. As the days passed, however, I persisted.

Things with Cathy had smoothed over. She had no idea what I was up to. On one of her shopping trips, she bought Christmas presents for both Louis *and* Butch. The hound was getting dog treats in holiday shapes. For Louis, she had found a beautifully-detailed ceramic New England sawmill. On the underside she proudly pointed out a tag which read "Made in New Hampshire." She spent as much on that as she usually did on *both* my parents. I didn't complain, though, balancing it against "future considerations."

Of course we invited Louis over for the Christmas holidays. He informed us he and Butch would be at his sister-in-laws for Christmas Eve, and would be staying overnight. Cathy seemed disappointed, but we agreed to visit as soon after as possible.

On Christmas Eve, Cathy and I visited a host of aunts and uncles, then returned home for our traditional gift exchange. I got her a topaz ring, and she gave me an all-weather dress coat.

Christmas morning found us laughing over all the cute, useful, and odd stocking stuffers. That afternoon was the big

Christmas dinner, to which we had invited Cathy's mother and sister, my parents, and my brother and his wife. Everyone was in their best holiday mood. The weather, oddly, seemed to heighten the festivities. For the past ten days there had been a pronounced warming trend, with the temperatures the highest recorded in thirty-seven years.

I had never seen Cathy happier. Inwardly, I wiped my brow and counted that my *real* Christmas present.

When Cathy's sister Jannine left shortly after ten, we had the house to ourselves, and were basking in the afterglow of a perfect day, when we heard a car door outside. We assumed it was Cathy's mother, returning for her oft-forgotten purse. Looking through the window of our inside front door, I saw a car pulling away from Louis's house as he and Butch ambled up his sidewalk.

"It's not your mother, Cathy, it's Louis."

"It's only 10:15, Richard, let's bring him his gift so he'll have it on Christmas." There was a childlike sparkle in her eyes. I half expected her to jump up and down and tug on my sleeve.

Within two minutes we were knocking on Louis's front door. It opened with Butch still howling. Louis was standing there, his coat on, holding a large, mound-shaped package. "Merry Christmas, come on in," he said. "Saw your lights on, so Butch and I were about to come over. Looks like you beat us to it." Cathy looked as though Santa himself had answered the door.

"Merry Christmas, Louis," I said. "I see you made off with quite a haul at your sister-in-laws." Several white boxes were piled on his kitchen table.

"Did all right, I guess. My usual new gardening clothes and a book on raising exotics." We all removed our coats and sat down while Louis offered us some Christmas cookies from his in-law's. "Don't know if you folks could use this, but I hope so," he said, handing Cathy the package he'd been holding.

She handed him the box containing the sawmill. "Merry Christmas, Louis."

Butch, meanwhile, had been very restless, giving the gift-wrapped box of dog treats I was holding several pokes with his long snout. "Is that for Butch?" Louis asked.

"Yes."

"Just give it to him, he'll unwrap it himself."

To our delight, the old boy did just that, at which time Louis confiscated the box and tossed several of the treats in his general direction. Butch was beside himself with a rare display of excitement, not knowing which to pursue first.

Cathy unwrapped our gift, while Louis watched appreciatively. It was a luxurious combination fruit basket and cheese platter. I thanked him, commenting that it was the perfect holiday gift, while Cathy fawned over it as though it were the crown jewels.

As Butch settled down by the table and bit the head off a dog-biscuit Santa, Louis unwrapped the package and removed the sawmill from its box and protective sleeve. It was obvious he was time-travelling, a wistful, longing look in his eyes.

"Do you like it, Louis?" Cathy asked, nearly breathless. "It was made in New Hampshire."

"Sure do. Worked in three sawmills back in my younger days. This one looks like Old Man Delaney's place. Spent nine years there till it folded. Thanks, folks." He quickly looked down at the sawmill, obviously overwhelmed with emotion. Cathy wore an expression of serene satisfaction. Some mission, on an agenda known only to her, had been accomplished.

Cathy and I both knew that our gift from Louis was, for him, a very giving gesture. He was, after all, a man who had been raised in a small, clannish circle of relatives and life-long friends. We, apparently, had touched him equally. Ordinarily, I don't think he would have cared that much for a ceramic collectible, but the building evoked such pleasant bygone days, I knew that he was quite moved.

He filled in the hole the next day. For the second time, I had accomplished my covert goal without having to take definitive action. He was waiting for me when I came home from work, and led me around back. I was both pleased and surprised. Had my subtle persuasiveness been that effective?

"I told you Richard, the old habits die harder than anything, but I been knockin' heads with death too much lately. My wife, then my brother." He shook his head. "Thought I was doin' right by the old boy to have a spot ready for him when his time come, but it just don't seem right anymore. I'm sixty-five now and pretty much alone, but you and your wife reminded me that you got to live *life*, not live death."

We stood on either side of the filled-in hole and shook on it. It was a handshake that embraced life, and life only.

Winter came to her senses three days later, and eight inches of snow fell on the former hole, while the earth within began to freeze solid. The remainder of winter followed suit. Temperatures dropped, snow fell, and the ground froze hard . . . harder than anything.

I made the mistake of trying to ease Cathy's mind by telling her Louis had seen the light and filled in the hole. Naturally, I omitted any role I might have had in his decision. Who was I kidding? Cathy exploded.

"Can't you simply *leave . . . things . . . alone?*" she shouted. I should have, too.

. . .

Butch died on February 27th, of acute kidney failure and pancreatitis. Louis, for all his previous winter planning, had to have the vet dispose of the body. There would be no burying. Nothing short of a flamethrower and backhoe could dig, now.

Cathy wouldn't talk about it, and in fact wasn't talking to me at all. She wouldn't come over with me when I spotted him by the former grave that day. She and death remained on very bad terms.

"Louis, we're so sorry about Butch," I said, standing by the spot where we had spoken the previous November.

"He just plain wore out, Richard. It's the way of things. Old dogs die, and old men cry. You were right about the hole, though." He paused, and gave me a hard Yankee stare. "Just wish now I didn't listen."

In the months that followed, Louis remained polite and cordial, but I could see him wrestling in his mind with something. It was no big surprise when he put his house up for sale in mid-April, and moved to Florida at the end of June. His daughter had found him a cozy, furnished unit in a retirement community two miles from her.

He came over one night in June and said that things in Florida were day-to-day, so he'd say his goodbyes. I tried to rekindle some of the old friendship, but Louis would have none of it. What we saw that night was the Louis I met digging the hole last November, that day when I felt so bold over cheating the leave-raking with the mulching mower. That damn machine.

He was gone the next day. We haven't heard from him since. I talked the real estate agent, an old friend, into giving me his forwarding address, but I remembered Cathy's words ringing through the kitchen. *'Leave . . . things . . . alone.'* I threw the paper away.

. . .

Here it is, November again. That time of year. I drained the gas and oil out of the mulching mower. It's season is over. I still held that machine partially responsible for me sticking my nose where it ended up not belonging. I guess it's just the way of things.

I stood on the spot where I had that conversation with Louis a year ago, my shovel in hand. Making sure Cathy wasn't looking out a window, I jumped the shrubs onto the neighboring lot, still unoccupied these five months.

I dug Louis's hole, Butch's grave. I was willing to risk Cathy's anger if she caught me. There was unfinished business here. From my back pocket I took Butch's collar, which I had also talked the real estate agent into giving me. Whether Louis had forgotten it, or didn't want it, I'll never know.

A knock sounded from our bedroom window. After everything that had happened, had I actually thought I would get away with this? My only hope was that Cathy had five months to let this settle, and that she would realize that I was doing this for Louis. It was a soft knock rather than a pounding one, so I thought there was a chance.

Looking up at her, I was able to gauge that she wasn't angry, merely confused. I held up Butch's collar. She stared at it, and gradually I could see her face soften until at last it wore a tender smile. She nodded slowly several times, opened the window, and rested her arms on the sill. There was nothing that needed to be said between *us*, but there *was* something that needed to be said.

"Old dogs die, and old men cry," I whispered, and dropped the collar into the hole. I quickly filled it in, Cathy watching from the bedroom window the entire time.

Jumping the shrubs, I headed back to my garage. There were leaves to be raked.

"TIMEKEEPER"

Denny Watson flipped the handle on his father's lawn mower to the 'Off' position, and as the engine wound down and died, walked it back across the grass to the alcove between the front porch and the cellar doorway.

"Lawn's done, Dad," he said, in his usual indignant tone, and went inside. His father Carl, who remained outside with his trimmer, nodded to his older son and regarded him, as always, with ambivalent feelings. Denny was so bright, so perceptive and creative. On the more disturbing side was the perpetual annoyance and anger that seemed to fuel his eleven-year-old son.

Denny grabbed a dishtowel and wiped the perspiration from his face, neck, and arms. He walked down the hallway to his room, opened his closet door, and under a pile of comics and assorted odds-and-ends, took out the large two-hundred page red notebook he called "The Timekeeper Book." Opening to the current page, he made his latest entry. *May 17th—mowed lawn, 35 min. (Dad).*

Denny Watson had many such entries in this notebook. An examination of the book might have led one to believe that Denny, a bright and precocious boy, was merely keeping an honest account of his labors and time worked.

A more careful examination would have revealed various entries that gave away its true purpose. *April 8th—visit to Aunt Karen and Uncle Gus, 2hrs. 15min. (Mom and Dad),* or *Nov. 27th—listened to complaints about roaming dogs and neighborhood noise, 6min. (Mr. Sliva).*

More than a third of the entries in Denny's Timekeeper Book did not involve chores done for his parents, or watching his eight-year-old brother, Ben. They involved minutes and hours of his day involuntarily spent in the company of others, mostly relatives and neighbors.

Denny's train of thought regarding time had somehow switched onto its own private track. Denny regarded every minute not in school or asleep as *his* time, *all* his. Selfishness with time had developed to the point where he divided the entire world into two groups: Denny Watson, and "You People."

He was grateful to a few of "You People" for opening his eyes to things. Social Studies had been the giveaway. All those rich, powerful, and famous people had all died eventually. Their time ran out. Time, he reasoned, was obviously the most important thing in the world. Without time, you had nothing. The rest had been given to him by Mrs. Norton, a reading teacher who wrote children's books. She had visited his class back in October as part of a school-wide writing program. She told them that her ideas came from observing children and keeping a daily journal.

Denny decided he had to keep a journal of "those people" who were stealing his time. Someday, when he was a famous author, he would have a clear account of who owed him. They would owe him "big time." He had also reasoned that successful authors didn't have regular jobs. They were their own bosses. No one took their time away.

For his birthday, a month later, he asked for a large notebook, one of those five subject types. His parents got it for him, and still believed that he was using it to write down story ideas. They had agreed that it should be confidential. Denny was able to write in it without fear of discovery.

School and sleep were beyond his control, he thought. Everything else is *mine*. Anyone who takes even a minute will

get written up in the Timekeeper Book, and would owe him .
. . big time.

There was a quick knock on his door, and his mother poked
her head in. "Denny, we're going over to see Grandma now.
Get cleaned up a little. We'll be leaving in a few minutes."

"Do we *have* to?"

"Denny, she's your grandmother. You haven't seen her since
she left for Florida." Marjorie Watson looked with tempting
curiosity at the large notebook which Denny instinctively
tilted toward himself. "Got another story idea?"

"Yeah, Mom, another idea."

"You've been writing in your notebook for six months now,
Denny. When will your father and I get to hear some of it?"

"Don't worry, Mom. When the time's right, you and Dad
will be the *first* to hear it." He smiled oddly.

"Good," she said, unaware that a deep part of her
consciousness had detected a dark undercurrent in her son's
answer.

She closed the door, and Denny began making a new entry.
He had to do some quick math first. "Let's see, twenty minutes
drive, times two, plus a two-hour visit, that comes to . . ."

Denny's mother announced the visit to her younger son,
Ben.

"Really?" he squealed. "Do you think Grandma brought
me home some oranges?"

"Maybe, but don't you go asking her the minute we get
there."

"I won't. I promise."

Opposite reaction, she thought, relishing Ben's excitement.
They were virtual opposite in almost everything. Ben had her

fair coloring and her husband's mild disposition. Denny was darker like his father, but seemed to live in some perpetual state of red alert.

Marjorie and her husband had noticed that Denny was becoming more self-absorbed, but what alarmed them most was his extreme selfishness. They could never get him to share even the most insignificant trinket with Ben, and had given up forcing him to. The brooding aftermaths were more than they were willing to endure. They conceded that one of their sons was intelligent, but selfish.

Writers, however, were often dark cauldrons of emotion, and they were sure that Denny had the talent and drive to become a successful author of adventure books, which he had announced several months back. For his birthday, they had gotten him a large red notebook with which to record ideas and observations. He had kept true to that wish, forever jotting down short entries in it. He *had* demanded that it be private, and had yet to share any of it, but then, that was Denny.

. . .

Marjorie drove her two sons to school, leaving Ben off on his side, while Denny got out and walked around to the other side. Denny hung out with the guys from his class before school and at lunch. He thought they were usually okay, except when they wanted to borrow stuff from him, or waste his time.

Lately there had been too much of this girl stuff. Some of the sixth grade girls *were* pretty, but *his* time was too valuable to waste on them.

The guys were sitting in a corner of the school entryway, and as Denny approached, he heard enough to know they were at it again.

"She's cool."

"Who?" Denny demanded.

"Linda's cousin. She just moved here from California," said Craig Taylor.

"Her name's Brittany," added Rob Swenson.

"What's her last name, 'spaniel'?" asked Denny with disdain.

"Got a problem, Watson? Don't like girls?" asked Craig Taylor, squinting accusingly at him.

"What's wrong with you people?" Denny asked defensively.

Craig gave a sidelong look at the others. "Elementary, my dear Watson." The other boys laughed expectantly. "We aren't interested in the same old things. What's wrong with *you?*"

Denny spun around and looked back over his shoulder. "I go to school with idiots, that's what!"

Craig watched him march away and shook his head. "That kid gets stranger all the time."

In the teacher's room after school, Mrs. Woodson, Denny's teacher, conversed with Ms. Faine, his teacher from the previous year. Ms. Faine habitually asked about the progress of her former students. "How did Dennis Watson perform this year, Grace? He showed so much potential in my class, aside from a few social problems."

Grace Woodson had reached zero-tolerance for all the euphemistic terms educators used to describe anti-social, dysfunctional, and plain old rotten behavior. "If you're referring to the fact that that Denny Watson is the most self-absorbed, selfish child I've ever taught, then he *still* has a few 'social problems'."

"I'm thinking it's just a phase he's going through, Grace."

I'm thinking you should talk to his parents. He's been in this *phase* for eleven-and-a-half years, now."

"Oh, my."

"Barbara, the boy is positively brilliant when he applies himself, but he has such a mean, anti-social streak in him that I don't know how he's avoided serious trouble." She reconsidered. "Yes, I do. His mother told me he rarely socializes outside of school. He goes off in the woods by himself, or writes in his journal. He's positively cruel to his younger brother, too."

Barbara Faine struggled to digest this indictment of the boy who had so fascinated her the previous year. "Aside from that, though, he *is* doing well in school."

. . .

Marjorie Watson drove her sons to school even though they lived only a few blocks away. This was to avoid tardies, as Ben was a bit methodical. Denny had been instructed many times to wait for him, as Marjorie did not want the boy walking to school alone. Denny usually bolted ahead and left Ben crying. They had taken him to task for it, but he complained that Ben walked too slowly and made him "lose time." Marjorie surrendered and drove them.

Going home was another matter. Because of the time of day and number of kids, it was relatively safe for them to walk home, ideally together. That seldom occurred. Ben meandered along at his usual pace, while Denny covered the distance like a combat infantryman on forced march. By the time Denny had gotten home and changed to go off to the woods, Ben was just arriving.

"Slowpoke." Denny grunted.

"Going down to the woods, Denny?"

"That's right, jerk."

"Can I come, too?"

"That's wrong, jerk. Don't follow me, ya hear?"

As Ben hung his head and went inside, Denny made a quick detour to the corner store, bought a quart of grape soda, and headed into the woods across the street for one of his adventures.

His favorite adventure was to go down to the small pond in back of Hubbard's property and catch a frog in his bare hands. The fun part was deciding its fate. Denny never knew what he would do to his captive until he actually did it. He could kill it, torture it, release it, bring it home, or play "Fatemaster" with it. That involved taking the frog and throwing it as far and as high as he could, then following its flight on foot to see if it had been killed, injured, or was unharmed.

The day was hot, even for mid-May, and after ninety minutes without a capture, a slightly frustrated, overheated Denny Watson sat on his favorite rock, gulping the sweet grape soda.

"Get any frogs?" It was Ben, standing unassumingly on the path that led through the thicket of blueberry bushes back to their house.

"Wadda *you* want? I told you not to follow me, jerk."

"These aren't your woods, Denny."

"This pond is *mine*. I claimed it."

"Can I have a sip of your soda, then?"

"Sorry, Benny boy. No soda for you. I bought this. It's *mine*. This time I don't *have* to share."

Ben's mouth and eyes watered from the anticipation, and Denny's cruelty.

"Please, just one little sip. Then I'll leave."

Denny smiled. "Nope." He chugged the remaining soda, capped the bottle, and tossed it out into the middle of the pond.

He smiled generously. "All right, Benny boy, you can have the rest. Don't say I never gave you anything, jerk."

Denny ran around him back toward their house. By his reckoning, Ben had stolen twenty minutes of potential pleasure from him at the pond. It was time for another entry in the Timekeeper Book.

Ben, although accustomed to these rebuffs by now, cried the simple tears of a hurt eight-year-old. He spent the next ten minutes throwing stones at the empty soda bottle until it smashed and sank. Like Mrs. Woodson, Ben had reached his own zero-tolerance point. For once, he hurried home, an intent purpose in his stride.

Ben had not yet arrived at the dinner table after being called twice, and Denny had to be reminded not to begin eating until all four of them were seated. It was one of the few rules still enforced by his parents. Denny made a mental note of the time being wasted.

When Ben finally entered the kitchen, he looked slightly confused, but angry. He held Denny's Timekeeper Book open in both hands as he walked, like some make-believe religious procession. Denny's astonishment and rage rendered him speechless.

"What are you doing with Denny's journal, Ben?" Carl asked angrily.

"You little creep!" Denny jumped up to grab the notebook from Ben, who ran around the table and shoved it in the protective custody of his father's lap.

"This isn't a journal, Dad. Denny wrote our names in there, and Grandma's, and Mr. Sliva, and Craig . . ."

"What are you talkin' about?" Denny shouted. "You can't *read!*"

The absurdity of the remark froze everyone. Even Denny was amazed. So wrapped up in himself, part of him still thought of Ben as some annoying four-year-old.

Carl, angry at Ben's invasion of Denny's privacy, now directed that anger at his older son. It astounded him that he was raising his voice to Denny, but that anger, hidden there for years, pushed through the crowd of confused thoughts to the forefront. "Your brother has been reading for *three years,* if you stopped for one second to think about anyone but yourself!" He began to glance at the pages, flipping them back and forth with disbelief. He couldn't have looked more disbelieving if he had uncovered a plot by Denny to overthrow the government. "What the heck . . .does this *mean? What* is a Timekeeper Book?"

Denny stood at his place, defiant. "It's a record of all the time you people stole from me! It's *my* life, and I need all my time to do *my* stuff, not yours. You're using me *up!* I need *all* my time!"

"'You people'? Is that what we are, Denny, 'you people'?" Carl's face now carried disbelief to a new level. Denny looked at his mother for help. There was sadness and disappointment on her face. He realized there was no chance of winning this confrontation, and was looking for a merciful end to it. His father provided one for him.

"Dennis," he said, swallowing the majority of his new-found anger, "go to your room while your mother and I discuss this. "Ben, you too. I'm glad we found out about this, but I can't condone you taking Denny's book without permission. You may take snack trays and bring your dinner with you."

Denny stormed down the hallway to his room. In the background he could hear Ben taking out a snack tray and setting it up. "Still got an appetite, huh Ben?" he whispered.

"Enjoy it while you can, jerk. You're gonna pay *big time* for this one."

When school let out the next day, Denny made no attempt to leave Ben behind. He was confined to the yard for two weeks, so there was no point in hurrying home. His parents had the Timekeeper Book in their bedroom, were in the process of reading it. Sitting on his bed, he heard the front door slam. Ben's round, happy face appeared at his window.

"See ya, Mr. Timekeeper."

"Get outta here!"

"That's what I'm doing. Bye." Ben performed his own version of sibling torture, turning every three steps and waving goodbye.

Denny would have preferred to spend his punishment in his room. His parents, however, seemed to find a new resolve from this episode. They made a list of chores around the house to be completed in the two week period, or another week's punishment would be added on. Denny had no choice but to leave his stronghold. On one of his trash takeouts he saw the pages from the Timekeeper Book in the plastic garbage bag, ripped and crumpled. He thought of salvaging them, but first looked at the kitchen window. His mother was watching him and shaking her head.

"You people," Denny muttered.

By the fifth day of the punishment, Denny was looking for an opportunity to escape to the woods. With Ben off playing somewhere, his father at work, and his mother dozing on the couch, he took the chance. He slipped out of the yard and across the street to the woods.

He had big plans for any frog he caught. He would pretend it was Ben. Moving around the pond methodically, taking extra care to be quiet, he was about to pounce on a large leopard frog when he heard a rustling of the blueberry bushes.

"Mr. Timekeeper, I *see* you," came a high, taunting call. Ben stood by the edge of the pond, next to Denny's favorite sitting rock.

"You better not *tell*, jerk!"

"Ha ha, you're in trouble, Denny," came the teasing reply.

Denny made a mad dash along the edge of the pond at Ben, who immediately started running. Ben's second step was on the boulder Denny used for sitting. The rock, because of its roundness and the uneven sloping ground around it, was somewhat unstable.

As Ben's foot landed, it rolled in the direction he was running. He pitched backwards, and overbalancing, fell forward. He landed in front of the rock, which rolled up his leg and continued toward the pond, coming to rest at the edge. The snap of bone was almost as loud as Ben's scream.

When Denny reached him, he could see the tear in Ben's leg, blood seeping out around the tip of the open fracture. Ben's eyes were huge, his chest heaved, and his color had turned an off-shade of gray, with red splotches.

"My leg! Get Mom!"

"Nice goin' jerk! Now I'm in even *more* trouble."

"*Please*, Denny, get help." Ben's round, cherubic face was now a twisted mass of pain.

"I'm goin'." Denny squatted and jabbed a finger at him. "But you owe me *big time* for this one, Benny boy."

Denny, to his surprise, found himself hurrying home. He had planned to walk, to teach that spying little squealer a lesson he'd never forget. As he emerged from the woods his heart sank. His father's car was in the driveway, and his father was just getting out.

The young boy in him was scared. The intelligent schemer in him realized that once his father knew Ben was hurt, his wrongdoing would be overlooked in the urgency of the moment.

"Dad, you'd better . . ."

"What are you doing out of the yard?"

Denny was caught off guard by the question, and momentarily lost his composure. "It's Ben."

"Don't start blaming your brother for *this*. I gave you a list of chores to be done, and you were not to have left the yard."

Denny felt awake in a nightmare. His father was on him like some homing device. How could his news about Ben possibly work? He couldn't even *say* it. "But Dad, . . ."

"You listen! I'm adding on another week to your punishment for sneaking off, and if I hear another word, you're going to get every thrashing you ever deserved."

Denny glared. *Fine, Dad.* he thought. *Not another word.*

"I want you down in that cellar working on that mess in the corner. Now!"

Denny stomped into the house, turned on the cellar light, and went downstairs. As he worked, he could hear his father upstairs bellowing to his mother, but couldn't make out the words. "Maybe next time you'll listen to me," he muttered.

He heard the phone ring a few minutes later, heard his mother's voice rise as the conversation continued. Before his brain could decode what he was seeing, he heard the phone slammed down, the upstairs cellar door open, and saw his father literally *run* down the stairs. He stood over Denny, his eyes wide with fury, breathing hard.

"That was Mrs. Hubbard on the phone. She said Craig Taylor and a couple of his friends found Ben down by the frog pond with a broken leg. Ben told them you went for help. Why didn't you *tell* me? *What* is *wrong* with you?"

"I *tried* to," came the arrogant reply. "All you cared about was the stupid . . ."

Carl Watson's right hand whizzed through the small space between them, all four fingers catching Denny flush on the cheek, snapping his head back. He grabbed Denny's right arm and hauled him up the stairs. "Your mother and I are going to the hospital. We'll leave you at Aunt Karen's on the way. You'd better pray nothing happens to your brother."

Denny knew better than to say anything aloud. *Sure, Dad, get out the rosary beads,* he thought. *I'll pray, all right. And Ben better pray they keep him in that hospital for about ten years!*

The day after the accident, Carl and Marjorie dropped Denny off at Karen and Gus's house on their way to the hospital. It had been a nasty break, but hade been set properly, with no initial signs of infection. The doctor *had* mentioned that Ben was in the early stages of shock when he was brought in. He asked for details of the accident. Neither Carl or Marjorie bothered to hide the fact that the boy's brother had failed to inform them, because of a scolding he had received.

In private, the Watsons spoke about getting professional help for Denny. The Timekeeper book and the incident at the pond were proof that Denny was "fishing in muddy waters," as Carl put it. "I still think you should have let me burn that damn book in front of him, instead of tearing out the pages," Carl said.

. . .

Ben Watson sat up in the bed of his semi-private room. This really wasn't so bad. He was in some pain, and his parents had brought his school books, but Ben was taking the larger view. He had his baseball cards, portable video game, TV, was out of school, and was free of his brother for a while. He had also made friends with his roommate, a nine-year-old named Jimmy Dablain, who had just had his appendix removed.

Jimmy was holding a large red notebook Ben's parents had brought him, and laughed as he tossed it back to him. "Your brother sounds like a big, mean jerk."

Ben opened to the first page of the former Timekeeper Book. There in his best penmanship, it said, *May 18th— Wouldn't share soda with me, teased me. May 23rd—Made me break my leg, could have died. Didn't tell that I was hurt. May 24th—Refused to come visit me in the hospital.*

Ben's "Torture Book" contained several pages of entries, a smorgasbord of cruelties endured by him over the years. "That's right, Jimmy. He *is* a big, mean jerk. He was right about one thing, though." Ben smiled broadly. "I owe him *big time!*"

"PURPLE HEART"

Most of the cast has changed, but we still play out the same scene in our family when we get together at Christmas, Fourth of July, or any of those other occasions when the calendar has done one of its little tricks.

After the meal has been eaten and the tables cleared, someone starts up with a reminiscence. Someone else keeps it going, and before you know, the Pintalo clan is off on another of their storytelling festivals. These days it's my cousins and I who hold sway, but back in the golden age of storytelling in our family, it was my father Dominic, and his three brothers, my uncles Sal, Charlie, and Leo.

They were all average, hard-working middle class men with traditional values who had dropped out of high school to help support their family. They all went off to war in the early 1940's, and lived to tell about it, over and over. Looking back, it amazes me that the same ten or twelve stories were able to captivate us during our formative years, but they did.

My father and uncle Sal were the headliners, with good reason. Dad was in the Battle of the Bulge, Hitler's last offensive in Europe, and was wounded in the leg early in the battle. He received the Purple Heart in recognition. Uncle Sal was a Marine rifleman, and had been in the invasion of Iwo Jima.

Uncle Charlie was Air Force, and didn't see any combat, but always managed to mention that on Okinawa, the Japanese had overrun positions around him, and all he had was a daggar.

My cousin Mike, Uncle Sal's older son, loved teasing him about that. "Uncle Charlie, it took two atomic bombs to get the Japanese to surrender. What the heck did you think you were going to do with a *daggar?"* Mike's other target was Uncle Leo, the youngest, who had been stationed in Alaska. Mike would ask him, "Did anyone actually think the Japanese would attack *Alaska?"*

The best versions of the stories usually occurred on Christmas Eve, when the entire clan would gather in Uncle Sal's basement for the traditional dinner. The combination of homemade wine and holiday good cheer gave the stories a heightened sense of nostalgia. For my father, it was the day after the anniversary of his being wounded, and he always seemed especially grateful that he had made it through another year. "That Mauser slug could have caught me in the chest or head," he often said. "I've been playing with house money ever since."

After dinner, desserts were placed on a table at one end of the basement, and the many presents opened. While the last of the wrapping paper was being gathered and thrown out, the four veterans would assemble at one end of the table, while an anxious audience jockeyed for positions nearby.

Usually Dad would start off. "My unit, the 106th," he added proudly, "shipped out in October and landed in Le Havre." My cousins and I were usually overflowing with anticipation, and one of us would call out, "The Battle of the Bulge story!" Everyone kept hushing each other, and eventually elbows found their way into neighboring ribs. A 'Knock it off!' from one of the four brought things to closure.

When everyone had quieted, Dad began his Battle of the Bulge story. The first few lines were always the same, as though he read from a script. "Five-thirty in the morning, December 16th, the first enemy artillery started coming in. It got heavier and heavier, until the Germans lit these huge spotlights. They pointed them towards the clouds to reflect down and see our positions. Then we heard the rumble of their tanks in the forest. We knew we were in for it then."

At that point, with the Americans retreating, Dad described the 106's withdrawal to St. Vith, sabotaging our own anti-tank guns to prevent their capture and use by the enemy. That entire first week the Americans fought desperate holding actions until reinforcements could be brought up.

We waited, squirming in our folding chairs, for the climax. Dad always delivered it in style. "On the morning of the 23rd, at about five, we were just coming off patrol looking for infiltrators. Everyone in the unit was armed, even cooks and clerks. We had just come out of the woods when the Germans opened fire. We hadn't seen them."

A dozen pair of eyes widened. You would have thought we had never heard this story before. Even Mike was frozen.

"There must have been a rifle squad at the edge of the woods, " Dad continued. "You could hear bullets whizzing past us. I felt one hit me in the leg. It was like someone holding a hot metal rod against it. Then the cold hit it. It was about forty below that morning, with the wind chill. The medics didn't get to me until almost nine. In the ambulance, the driver said it was gonna be a bumpy ride. We had to fight our way out of town to our next fortifications. I honestly thought I was gonna die there in Belgium that morning."

He paused. No one spoke. "Four hours lying there in the snow, waiting to get captured or bleed to death. The cold saved me, though. It kept the bleeding down. By January, my unit had taken eleven thousand casualties, the most of any unit in the battle." There was always the paradoxical pride and sadness in his voice when he mentioned that.

"I wouldn't want to go through that again for a million dollars, but it was *worth* a million to have survived it."

That usually signaled the end of the Battle of the Bulge story. My cousins often looked at me enviously, or slapped me on the back. *My* father had the best war story.

Dad was a tough act to follow, but Uncle Sal could hold his own. He didn't have an actual *wound*, but he *had* hit the beach at Iwo Jima. Things usually loosened up by the time Uncle Charlie jumped in. "Oh no!" Mike would shout in mock terror. "The daggar that captured Okinawa!" Poor Uncle Leo. All he had were stories of freezing while driving an ammunition truck in Alaska. "What did you use for ammo up there, Uncle Leo," Mike would ask, "snowballs?"

That's how it went for quite a few years. Even through eighth grade, I was still very proud of my father and uncles. When we were covering Iwo Jima and the Battle of the Bulge in school, I could barely stay in my seat, I had so much bragging to do.

Somewhere in there, things changed. They always do in families because the people *in* the family change. My cousins and I eventually outgrew the war stories. Our perception of war had changed through the years. With the tenuous mess Korea had left, and this new conflict starting to get out of control in Vietnam, we no longer viewed war as a glorious preservation of freedom, but a politically-motivated power play, both sides equally at fault. We didn't think it was worth dying for. My father and uncles, with different experiences, did.

For a few years, there was a lot of tension in the family. Conflicts had emerged in each household, and often gained momentum at family gatherings. You never knew which adult and which teenager would end up at each other's throats. What a mess.

My cousin Mike had quit college and was bumming around the country, much to the dismay of his draft board. His brother

Leon and Uncle Charlie's son Jimmy had failed their army physicals, under suspicious circumstances.

I hadn't come through all that well, either. I was in college, and my father and I were basically enemies who resided at the same address. During one bitter exchange, I said, "Dad, I bet you have more respect for those Nazi goons than you do for your own son."

He looked me in the eye. "At least *they* weren't cowards."

The whole thing was hanging by a thread, despite Mom's best efforts as peacemaker. With no brothers or sisters to absorb any of this, Dad's entire anger and frustration at my generation was directed at me. It all came to a head one day quite unexpectedly.

One of his buddies from the rod and gun club was at the house, buying a shotgun from him for his son. There was the usual gun and ammo talk.

"I don't know, Domenic," the man said, "I think the nine millimeter is an overrated bullet."

"Overrated, Paul? I took one of those in the leg in the Second World War. If it hadn't been so cold out, I would have bled to death."

I overheard all of this from the upstairs hallway, and while I honestly didn't care at that point *what* he got shot with, or *where,* I knew something didn't jive. There was no way Dad could have confused the Mauser bullet, a 7.62 millimeter, with the nine millimeter.

I waited a few minutes until his friend had left, and went downstairs. I guess there was still a tiny spark of interest left concerning the Battle of the Bulge story, and these days there was always a tremendous interest on my part in showing up my father.

"So Dad, I heard you tell that guy you got hit with a nine millimeter. You always said it was a Mauser bullet. What gives?" I knew I had something on him the moment he stopped giving me that disgusted look he wore in my presence. He sat down, his head bowed, showing his thinning crop of hair instead of the square jaw and deep-set brown eyes. He exhaled deeply.

"I got hit with a nine millimeter bullet that morning."

"What's the difference what caliber it was? You got hit by enemy fire. I don't get it." He was still looking down at the floor. There was something he wasn't telling, and these days neither one of us cut the other any slack, so I pressed it. It felt good for once to be on the offensive.

"What happened, Dad? What's the big secret?" He looked up at me, and I braced myself for one of his usual long-haired, bearded, college punk insults.

"Randy, we aren't that close any more, but this has always bothered me, so I'm gonna tell you what really happened that morning."

I pounced. "You mean you been *lying* all these years about getting wounded in the Battle of the Bulge?"

"Watch your mouth! I *was* wounded in the battle, but not the way I've always told it."

"Dad, you sound like the government, now. First lies, then doubletalk."

"Randy, I'm trying to come clean on this." He took a deep breath. "We just come off patrol that morning, looking for infiltrators, and when we were walking back to our perimeter, one of the guys with us sees somethin' in the snow and picks it up. He was a clerk, so he didn't know any better. Turns out it's a Luger pistol, probably lost by some German officer. Who knows how long it had been there or how many trucks ran over it. Anyways, this guy picks up the Luger and it goes off, and the bullet catches me square in the leg."

"That's *it?*" I asked. "You got a Purple Heart for *that?*"

"Wait, Randy. There's more."

"*Spare* me, Dad. I've heard enough. All those years I thought you were a hero, and it turns out you were playing 'Abbott and Costello Join the Army'. I can't believe you had the nerve to put in for a Purple Heart on top of everything!"

"That's *not* the whole story."

"You're right Dad, it's not. The rest is that you were too ashamed to admit what actually happened, but you just *had* to have the best combat story, so 'presto' German rifle squad! And you call *me* a coward?"

"Let me tell you something, you college punk. There *was* a German squad out there, and you'll never be *half* the man as any of *them.*"

One hard word led to another, and by the end of the day I was packed and out of there, for good. In my youthful foolishness, I considered it my finest hour. I suppose we could have patched it up after a while, especially after I learned that he *was* entitled to the Purple Heart, under the category of "friendly fire," or "misadventure". I guess it was a combination of going our own ways for so long, and neither one of us wanting to swallow our pride.

A couple hundred calendar pages have been torn off since. The Pintalo family was always a resilient bunch, and gradually lots of reconciliations were made, but not by my father and me. We were back on speaking terms, and my wife and I attended most of the family get-togethers, but that solid wall that solidifies a father-son relationship had been breached.

I didn't do anything real nasty, like keep him away from our three kids. He got to be the grandfather figure he'd always wanted. I insisted, however, that he not tell our children any war stories. I checked up on it with them, too.

Those calendar pages, though. They always have the last word. Father Time gradually accomplished what the Germans and Japanese couldn't. Uncle Sal and Uncle Leo are gone now, and my father had a series of strokes that left him unable to walk or talk. Mom eventually had to place him in a nursing home. I felt badly about it, too. I was quits with the guy, so to speak, but I didn't want him to suffer. Mom prodded me to visit him regularly, which for me was once a month.

On one occasion, his doctor was there and mentioned some contradictory findings on Dad's test results. He looked at me oddly when he said, "I believe your father *can* talk, I just don't think he *wants* to."

Dad's condition deteriorated a little at a time, until one day Mom had me come over for a briefing on his estate. We sat down at the kitchen table and were going over some routine matters. I kept waiting for her to make the last big pitch for me to patch things up with him before it was too late. The way I saw it, if he *could* talk, and chose not to like the doctor said, then what was the use?

After a few minutes Mom asked me to go into her bedroom and get her some lip balm from the top drawer of her bureau. She had taken over my old room a few years earlier when my father's back condition had made it impossible to share a bed. I went down the hallway to my former room and opened the top drawer. Next to the lip balm was Dad's Purple Heart. It wasn't even in its presentation case. She had planted it there.

I held it out to her as I re-entered the kitchen. Trying to look innocent, she asked, "Where's the lip balm?"

"Nice goin', Mom. Where's the first stop on *this* guilt trip?"

She surprised me. Without hesitation, she said, "Belgium, December 23rd, 1944."

"*Please,* Mom. Not *that* again!"

"Randy, this has gone on too long. You never let your father explain that day you left, and now he can't. I *know* the rest of that story, and it's about time you know it. Now you *listen!*"

What the heck, I listened.

"When that gun went off, and your father fell in the snow, the men with him thought he was taking cover, so they all dove for cover, too."

"So what?"

"There *were* Germans at the edge of the woods, and when *they* heard the shot, they opened fire on the Americans! They had taken cover already, so the bullets went *over their heads.* Do you get it now?"

I got it, all right, but all I could manage was a weak nod.

"Randy, there are detailed records of every action from that war. Your uncle Charlie helped me do a little research. There wasn't a German squad in the woods there was an entire *platoon.* Your father not only indirectly saved about ten of his friends, but he caused the Germans to give away their positions when they fired."

Needless to say, I was quite ashamed, but equally confused. "Mom, why didn't Dad simply tell the story the way it happened? It makes him look even better than the way he told it all those years."

"That's right, Randy. But your father was never comfortable with having the best war story, especially when it involved saving men's lives. So he toned it down."

If you could measure shame on a gauge, I think I would have sent the needle off the dial. "What do I do *now*, Mom?"

"You go see him. He's not going to be around forever. Bring him this," she said, handing me the Purple Heart. "He earned it."

I went home that night and thought about all the years that had been lost, mostly because of me. I thought about how he changed the story so it wouldn't appear as though he was bragging. Most of all, I thought about what a prize horse's ass I had been.

The next day I got out of work at five, and drove out to the nursing home. I signed in, got my pass, and went down to his room. His doctor passed me going the other way, and gave me that funny look again.

Dad was in his wheelchair, watching some telethon on TV. I stooped down, showing him the open case containing the Purple Heart. He seemed to recognize it. "This is your Purple Heart, Dad." I could hear my voice shaking, but dignity was no longer the issue. "Mom told me how you saved your buddies. There was a whole *platoon* of Germans out there that morning, Dad. Here, you earned this."

I found I couldn't make eye contact as I spoke, and all I could see were our hands, mine holding the case open, and his in his lap. My heart sank as I saw his hands come up and push the Purple Heart away. I somehow got the nerve to look at his face, and found one of those proud father-son smiles I hadn't seen since I was about fifteen. He continued pushing the case back, and then pointed at me, jabbing his finger for emphasis.

He was *giving* me his Purple Heart.

He fixed his eyes over my shoulder, and I could see him straining in his mind to do or think *something*. I turned my head, assuming his weakened mind had focused on something else. I saw the TV set, but he was looking above it. The only other object was the wall clock, which read five-thirty.

"Five-thirty in the morning," he whispered, "December 16th. The first enemy artillery . . . started coming in."

For me, it was like hearing the Ghost of Christmas Eve Past, and I could feel my neck hair standing on end. I looked at him, and his calm, proud expression was one I had seen on many Christmas Eves at Uncle Sal's.

"It got heavier and heavier," he continued, "until the Germans . . . lit these huge spotlights."

I stepped back out of his line of sight, and he continued the story's beginning lines, word for word, as he had done so many times before. To this day, I'm glad I recognized the moment for what it was.

I sat down and listened to a story of a young American soldier who was wounded on December 23rd, 1944, just outside Bramlauf, Belgium.

It was the last time my father told his Battle of the Bulge story. I listened with childlike wonder and pride, all the while staring down at my Purple Heart.

"HARP AND WINGS"

By way of introduction, my name is, or should I say *was,* John L. Calment. During my lifetime I was an assembly line worker at a GM plant in Wilmington, Delaware. I died recently at the age of seventy-two. It was natural causes, although I might have hurried things along a bit with some bad habits.

The black man standing next to me in this long double line has just introduced himself as Martino Beltrez. He was forty-one at the time of his death. He happened to be in the wrong place at the wrong time while riding the subway in New York. We are standing in line awaiting our entrance into Heaven.

An official-looking angel went down the line, explaining something to each pair of people. When he got to us, he said, "Introduce yourselves, you'll be together for the entire orientation . We use the buddy system here."

He moved along, brushing me with his elegant wings, while Martino and I exchanged brief biographies. I learned that he was a native of the Dominican Republic, living with his brother's family in New York until he could earn enough money to marry his fiancée. He had dark hair with a mustache and the beginnings of a beard, but looked to be about twenty, as opposed to his actual age of forty-one. He remarked that I didn't even look fifty, much less seventy-two.

After checking with others around us, we discovered that everyone looked approximately half their actual age.

As the angel returned down the line, I said, "Excuse me, you said there is a 'buddy system' here. What happens if there is an odd number of people that die on a particular day?"

"We know what we're doing, Mr. Calment," he said, sounding a bit hurried and annoyed. "I assure you, that never happens." I wondered how he knew my name, and our next discovery was that we all wore a picture I. D. affixed to our white robes.

We were divided up and taken to different areas for our orientation. The angels conducting these sessions were called, plainly enough, Orientation Leaders. The first thing they did was explain *where* Heaven is. The simplest explanation is that it is in another plane of existence, another dimension. It's not way above Earth or up in the clouds. A lot of the language here doesn't translate.

We were right about the age thing, as it turned out. You appeared in Heaven as you looked at the midpoint of your life, with two exceptions, infants and unknown soldiers. They had their own sections of Heaven, and appeared as they did on their last day. I raised my hand to ask why. It seemed like a harmless question.

"Mr. Calment, this is the second time, I believe, that you have questioned our operating procedures. I'm going to make note of this, and advise you to listen and observe from now on."

"Jeez, what a grouch," I whispered to Martino.

"I *heard* that, Mr. Calment. I will have no choice but to take this matter to the Monitor of your District Ward."

I didn't know what a Monitor or a District Ward was at that point, but I had the good sense not to ask. The orientation continued, with the distribution of the Heavenly Manuel. They weren't distributed exactly, they just appeared in our hands. The Manuel contained the Heavenly Articles, a Constitution and Handbook of Customs and Procedures. It outlined the requirements for receiving one's Harp and Wings, the types of interventions that we in Heaven may perform, procedures for petitioning St. Peter, and various request forms, such as Earthly Visitations and Regeneration. It's a huge bureaucracy here.

Heaven is *not* a classless society, either. Some of the souls get to wear silver or gold robes, instead of the usual white. The gold robes are worn only by the Apostles, Popes, or religious martyrs. The silver ones are reserved for the general clergy, and those who were devoted to humanitarian causes. The other status symbol here is receiving your Harp and Wings. I checked the Manual to see what that involved. It seemed confusing, so after the orientation I asked Martino.

"What do you make of this Harp and Wings requirement, Martino?"

"John, it seems like there are two ways to get them. One is to achieve some special deed, or high level of leadership. The other way is by Default."

I understood the Default method. It was about the simplest thing we had encountered. When everyone on Earth who was alive at the time of your death was also dead, you automatically got your Harp and Wings. "Jeez, Martino, that could take more than a *hundred years!*"

"Didn't you read the part on Time?" he asked.

"I was still trying to figure out Intervention Guidelines when the Leader went over that," I complained.

"Time passes at a different rate, here."

My buddy Martino seemed to be pretty sharp for someone who had been a common laborer back on Earth, and seemed to be catching on quicker. I made a mental note to stick close by him for the time being. "Okay, then, what about accomplishing some great deed, or achieving a high level of leadership?"

"Maybe becoming a Monitor or Orientation Leader would qualify."

"God, this is so confusing."

"John, you're not supposed to say 'God' unless you're referring to Him or speaking to Him. It says so on page one of the Manual."

Despite my difficulties, it was great being in Heaven. The place is so huge that it is divided into Districts. There are ten Districts, each nominally headed up by one of the Apostles. St. Peter, who *does* check everyone in at the entrance, is the Overseer. I got the impression, from travelling around, that the Districts are roughly the size of Australia.

Each District is divided into Wards, with Monitors and Assistant Monitors for each. Every so often, they appoint new ones, who receive their Harp and Wings in recognition.

I was determined to qualify for my own Harp and Wings before I got them by Default. They seemed so *classy*. The Harps are roughly the equivalent of a mansion and Rolls Royce on Earth. Language cannot describe the magnificence of the Wings. I was hoping that Martino and I could collaborate on a plan to earn them, but he had no interest.

"Sorry John, for a poor Latino like myself to be in Heaven without any more suffering, I'm thrilled just to be here. I couldn't care less about no Harp and Wings."

I pleaded with him, but it was no use. He was content merely to walk around and explore. So we hung out together and travelled around, meeting other souls, sharing in the tranquil feeling you always have.

That's another thing that's hard to explain. You don't miss Earth, or anything you left behind. No one goes around looking for their old friends or relatives, either. You feel a kinship with *everyone.* I came across my mother on one occasion, but we greeted each other and talked as if we were two strangers sharing the bliss of Paradise. I *did* catch her straightening out the folds in my robe, though.

Time passed. I can't say for sure how much. I still haven't got the time conversion down yet, even though Martino has explained it several times. A lot of the Manual still confuses me, and I've had several reprimands from my Assistant Ward Monitor. Anyway, time passed, and we explored all over. Every few hundred miles or so, there would be a large map with an 'X' at a certain point, saying, 'YOU ARE HERE', just like the big shopping malls on Earth.

Eventually, Martino and I worked our way down to St. Paul's District, where two special sections of Heaven are located, the ones reserved for infants and the unknown war dead. We came upon the infants' section first. It was wall-to-wall babies for as far as you could see. I literally waded in among them, leaving Martino a few yards behind.

"Hey, guys!" They appeared startled and confused, but I couldn't contain my enthusiasm. "Goo Goo, Ga Ga!" A couple of them were crying now, but what the heck. Babies cried for no reason sometime, right? I felt a tap on my shoulder, and when I turned, I saw one of the Assistant Ward Monitors for this District writing my name down on a report. Martino was back about twenty yards, giving me a helpless look and a shrug. "What's wrong, sir?" I asked.

"Mr. Calment, the Heavenly Infants cannot talk, and you are not allowed to wander in among them with your idiotic gibberish. They are to be appreciated from a respectful distance. Don't you read your Manual?"

"Yes, sir, but I don't have it with me at the moment."

"Mr. Calment, you *always* have your Manual, if you remember to *think* of it." I looked down, and sure enough, it was in my hand.

When he was out of sight, I went back over to Martino. "Why didn't you warn me? That jerk put me on report."

"I *heard* that, Mr. Calment," echoed a voice off in the distance.

We walked on, and eventually came to the other special section. A sign said, 'KNOWN BUT TO GOD.' It was the gathering place of the Unknown soldiers. I was determined to stay out of trouble, and took no chances. "Martino, are we allowed to go in here?"

"Yes, the Manual says it's okay."

We went in and saw the Unknowns, most of whom appeared to be in their twenties or early thirties. I expected to see the word 'Unknown' on their I. D. badges, but they all wore their names. I could hear Martino behind me, flipping pages in the Manual.

"Don't you fellows ever travel around?" I asked a young dark-haired man whose badge read 'Sgt. Raymond Turner.'

"Hey!" he shouted. "You aren't supposed to address *us!* Don't you read your Manual, pal?" I turned to lead Martino out of there before we had more trouble, only to find him already heading out the gateway. "Civilians!" Turner said with disgust as we left.

More time passed. I half-heartedly skimmed the Manual on occasion, and Martino and I travelled around Heaven. I continued to pick up some violations from the Heavenly Articles, and was written up by a few Ward Monitors in various Districts. I was still happy beyond human comprehension, but there remained a frustration about getting my Harp and

Wings. I had no idea how much longer I would have to wait until I got them by Default. Then Martino came up with a startling discovery.

"John, I found some fine print in the Manual about getting your Harp and Wings by Default." Just what I needed. I wasn't having enough trouble absorbing the regular print. "It says that if you get written up enough times, they can make you go through an entire new cycle of people on Earth before you get them."

I began studying the Manual feverishly, with Martino's help. Next, I devised a plan that I thought would be considered worthy to receive my Harp and Wings. Finally, I petitioned for and was granted an audience with St. Peter.

At the appointed time I appeared at the Gates for my interview. St. Peter had apparently forgotten about me, and was gathering his things at the large desk outside when I arrived.

"Ah, yes, Mr. Calment. You have petitioned to speak with me, I believe."

"Yes, sir, and may I add what an honor it is . . ." He held up one hand.

"Mr. Calment, you have compiled quite a list of violations in your short stay here. Therefore, I am going to determine if you are ready for this audience." He produced a copy of the Manual and proceeded to quiz me. "Mr. Calment, what is God's role here in Heaven, and why haven't souls like yourself ever seen him?"

"Sir, God's role is to maintain the Balance of all Creation, which is so delicate he does not have the time to be personally involved in day-to-day routines."

He looked a bit surprised, then flipped a few more pages. "Briefly explain the three types of Intervention, Mr. Calment."

"Angelic Interventions, if approved, may be used by any soul in Heaven to aid one of the living. Heavenly Interventions may be performed only by those of status for Mankind's greater interests. Divine Intervention is by God Himself, and only when the Balance is in jeopardy."

"Good, Mr. Calment. After twenty-two years, you *are* learning."

"Twenty-two years?" I had no idea it had been that long.

"Yes, Mr. Calment. Twenty-two years. You *do* know how we convert time, don't you?"

"Of course, sir. I thought it was twenty-*one* years. Must have forgotten to carry something over." He looked at me suspiciously, but I could see a faint smile.

"All right, Mr. Calment. What do you want?"

"Sir, I understand from the Manual that if I were to achieve a great deed of some kind, I would qualify for my Harp and Wings."

"That is correct. Did you have something in mind?"

"Yes. My proposal is to get a message to the people of Earth explaining that there *is* a Heaven, and to tell them what it is like." He started to laugh, then caught himself.

"My, we haven't had one of *those* for a long time. It must be all the near-death experiences people have now." He finished gathering his things and prepared to leave. "Your proposal is worthy of Harp and Wings, Mr. Calment. Make another appointment when you have the details worked out. I have a meeting of the Apostles's Forum. Good day."

. . .

At least I had come up with an idea, but I didn't know I had to work out all the particulars, too. Martino was happy for me, but he didn't want to get involved in the planning of it. He and I spent a lot less time together these days. Now I had to come up with an acceptable method of getting the message of Heaven to everyone on Earth.

I played around with lots of possible variations, came up with a couple of backup ideas, and made another appointment. One thing I had learned from the Manual was that St. Peter allowed you to come to these meetings and pitch ideas, like a Hollywood TV writer proposing a series.

I showed up for my next appointment, ready to run my ideas by him. He was sitting at his desk outside the Gates, looking weary. "I hope you have your ideas thought through, Mr. Calment. We had a very long registration process today, almost twice as many souls as usual."

"Another war, sir?"

"Yes, another war. What else?"

He obviously wasn't in the best mood for this, but I had no choice but to plunge ahead. "Okay, how's this? I write everything up, make a quick visit to my gravesite, and leave it there. When my son or grandchildren or someone else comes along, they'll find it."

He looked completely disgusted. "No one would *ever* believe such a document, and even though you *may* transport Heavenly Stationery, being an Angel, you wouldn't be capable of placing anything on the pages to keep them from blowing away. In addition, we do not cater to self-serving visitations to personal gravesites."

"Okay, how's this? I take that same document, and mail it to the President of the United States."

He stared at me sternly, but said nothing.

"Right. Too political. The Secretary General of the United Nations."

His stare grew fiercer.

"Right, right. Still too political. I know. The Pope!"

He slammed a fist on the desk and stood, gathering his paperwork. "Mr. Calment, although your intentions are of the best, you are obviously a soul without much imagination. Good day." He walked through the Gates back inside.

"No imagination?" I muttered under my breath. "You're the one with no imagination, Pete."

"I *heard* that, Mr. Calment!"

. . .

"Forget about it, John, you gave it your best shot," said Martino, after I told him of the disastrous idea-pitching session I had with St. Peter.

"That's just it, Martino, I *didn't.* I've got to go through the Manual from cover to cover. I've got a feeling there's something I'm missing, some technicality or loophole. Care to help?"

He considered a moment, then said, "Nah. John, I didn't have such a great time on Earth. I'm just as glad to be done with it."

My third request for an audience with St. Peter was approved. "But with some reservations," said the stern Assistant Monitor who handed me the official reply. "I hope you know what you're doing," he continued. "This is putting me in a very bad light. I've got my eye on a Monitor's position in St. Michael's District, and I can't afford bad publicity among my superiors from your shenanigans."

"Relax, Mr. Jefferson," I said. "If this works out the way I planned, you could get elected President all over again."

. . .

He was waiting for me at his desk, a very foreboding look on his face. "Make this fast, Mr. Calment, and make it good. I still haven't forgotten that last little remark of yours."

"Sorry about that, sir. Okay, how's this? I go back to Earth as a ghost, and appear to Bernard Westmeyer, the Nobel Prize physicist. He's the most respected scientific humanitarian on Earth. I tell *him,* and *he* tells the world!"

St. Peter closed his eyes and shook his head. "Much more imaginative, Mr. Calment, but it can't be done. A ghost, by definition, is a tortured spirit, which for some reason has never left Earth. You aren't a ghost, you're a *soul.* You can't appear to Bernard Westmeyer. If you could, you would be incapable of communicating with him."

This was becoming frustrating. "How about if I go down there and bump his soul out? I could . . ."

"Stop this nonsense at once!"

I was desperate. "I'll trade places with one of the Unknowns, then they can go back and have a regular . . ."

"Silence!" While he glared at me and stood up to leave, my mind was still churning, trying to find that loophole I was sure existed. I was determined to keep pitching.

"How about if I offer myself for Regeneration, and go back to Earth in a brand new person?" He continued glaring at me, and to my astonishment, grabbed me by the folds of my robe and pulled me close.

"Mr. Calment, why does it always take you so long to get things *right?* "

"Is that a 'yes'?" I gasped. He released his grip.

"We are *always* looking for souls willing to go back and be reborn. Regeneration, or 'reincarnation' as they call it on Earth, is always acceptable. It's in the Manual, Mr. Calment."

"It is? Where?"

"Way in back."

There was still one hitch in my plan, as St. Peter pointed out. As a brand new child on Earth with a regenerated soul, part of me would have knowledge of my previous life as John Calment and the Heavenly Kingdom. The problem would be getting people on Earth to believe that I was the genuine article, and not someone with a vivid imagination, or religious fanatic, or mental case. I told St. Peter that I would know all about John Calment, which would be my proof.

"Not good enough any more, I'm afraid," he said. "Anyone can dig up some records in a city hall and find out about John Calment."

"A publicity-seeker wouldn't go to all that trouble over one auto assembly-line worker," I countered. "Wouldn't *that* be enough to convince people?"

"Trust me, Mr. Calment. It wouldn't. We've had a few of them here. You're going to have your hands full being taken seriously, but that's your problem now. You have agreed to Regeneration, and we need souls on Earth. Say your goodbyes and make your final preparations."

I hadn't come this far to be thwarted by the possibility that no one on Earth would believe me. I had a plan. I spent the next few weeks, or months, or whatever (I *still* don't get this time conversion) at the Hall of Records. Much to my delight, my friend and buddy Martino accompanied me on many of these occasions. I told him of everything that had transpired.

Every so often he would shake his head and laugh. "I still can't believe you're going through with this, John. You got it made here. Why do you want to go back? I'll never understand white people."

. . .

My preparations were complete. I was ready to return to Earth in the body of a newborn infant. I said goodbye to Martino, and told him I'd be seeing him, hopefully in another seventy-five or so years.

"Actually, John, it wouldn't be seventy-five years, because we have a different method ...."

"Will you never mind the time thing, Martino!" We laughed and shook hands.

I presented myself at the Gates to St. Peter after the day's registration was completed.

"I see you're ready, Mr. Calment. Good luck in delivering your message to mankind. I'm sure you'll need it."

"Where exactly will I be going, sir?"

"That, Mr. Calment, is completely random. You could be reborn in one of the media centers of the world, or in some hut deep in the Amazon jungle. Once again, Mr. Calment, good luck."

"Wait!" I screamed. "I *need* to be in a *civilized, modern* place! I *have* to, or this won't work!" Panic overwhelmed me.

"Mr. Calment, you end up where you end up. Happy landing." He spread his hands in front of him, in a gesture that reminded me of a wizard about to cast a spell. There was a humming sound, then a blinding light and a whooshing sensation. Then there was darkness.

. . .

I'm back! Although my *brain* is that of an infant, my *soul* has retained its previous knowledge and communication skills. By listening and observing carefully, I soon determined that I had been born to middle-class parents in Topeka, Kansas, U. S. A. Not exactly one of the media centers of the world, but a *lot* better than a hut in the Amazon jungle. I am in the nursery now, and have just noticed that I am the only black baby here.

A nurse has just brought in yet another white child, and placed him in the receptacle next to me. He looked at me and cried for a while. When he stopped, he was still staring at me, intently. Curiously enough, I found myself fixated on *him*. Then he smiled.

"John! John Calment!" He was communicating with me telepathically, and calling me by my name from my previous life.

I continued staring at him, puzzled.

"It's *me*, John. Martino Beltrez!" I was so shocked, I nearly soiled my diaper.

"What are *you* doing back on Earth?"

"I thought I'd give it one more try. St. Peter needed more souls, and he talked me into going back."

"Martino, did you happen to notice that this time *you're* white, and *I'm* black?"

"Yeah, John. Lucky for you I'm not prejudiced." We had a good telepathic laugh over that one.

Then I started thinking about all the babies born in one day, and had to question the odds of Martino being reborn in the same place and at the same time I was. Throw in the fact that it was *Kansas*, and my suspicions were off and running. Sure, St. Peter needed more souls, but he just happened to *recruit* a regular guy like Martino, of all the souls in Heaven? Since when did he recruit *anyone?* This was *life,* not the Notre Dame football program.

"Martino, this doesn't seem right. It's too coincidental. How did you get St. Peter to do the paperwork so quickly?"

His hesitation convinced me that this was a con. "I guess that I . . . caught him at a good time. There had just been an earthquake in Peru and a tidal wave in Japan. You should have seen the long lines at the Gates! He signed the papers just to get rid of me, I think."

"C'mon, Martino, you can't expect me to believe that! Nothing happens that quickly in Heaven unless St. Peter *wants* it to."

He laughed, and hung his head a bit. "Okay, John, you got us. The Apostle's Forum, with God's approval, decided that the human race needed a morale booster, something uplifting to believe in. They authorized St. Peter to come up with something."

"You mean St. Peter performed a Heavenly Intervention so that you and I would be born at the same time in the same hospital?" I was astounded.

"Yeah. He liked your idea a lot more than he let on. He wanted you to know from the day you were reborn that you would have help. I'm not sure if that part is legal, but he did it. Anyway, after your Regeneration had been approved, he called me in and told me to find out what you were up to, and make sure that I could help."

Noticing my blank, confused expression, he added, "That's why I went to the Hall of Records with you those times." There seemed to be a hole in St. Peter's plan, but I couldn't put my finger on it. Then it hit me.

"How could you possibly help, Martino? You were just sitting there while I was memorizing all those records." That was it, then. I was alone in my knowledge, probably doomed to go through life being laughed at as the "Black Prophet of Heaven."

"John, use your imagination a little," Martino said. "When you thought I was out sightseeing, I went back and memorized the same records. When you're ready someday to tell your story, you'll have somebody to back it up." He winked. "A *white* somebody."

I should have been reassured, but another hole presented itself. "How will we find each other when it's time? We could grow up miles apart?"

Martino widened his eyes in frustration. "Just check the birth records for today's date. Do a little investigating. You'll find me, or I'll find *you.* "

I started to breathe a sigh of relief, when my little heart nearly stopped at my next discovery. We had no idea *who we were!* "What's your new name?" I asked, panic again flooding my thoughts.

He wrinkled his tiny forehead. "Uh, I don't know yet. What's yours?"

"I don't know either!" I telepathically screamed. "We're doomed! We won't be able to find each other when the time comes, because we won't know *who* we're *looking* for!"

A nurse came to take me back to my mother a few minutes later, while Martino and I shared a sinking feeling of futility.

. . .

St. Peter, as it turned out, had one last trick up his gold-robed sleeve. Our mothers were in the same room. They jokingly mentioned that we might grow up to be friends, sharing birthday parties and such.

Have we got a surprise for them. Charles Hanson, my "soul brother," and I , Roland Blake, will be sharing a lot more than birthday parties.

When the time is right, we'll be sharing a complete history of every person who entered Heaven the day we did. We memorized every imaginable fact about all 9,548 of them. We'll need a three-foot high stack of computer disks to store it.

Two prophets of Heaven, one black, one white. It might help improve things here on Earth. They'll take us seriously, all right.

Oh yes, one last thing. Martino—I mean Charles and I compared notes on all the intervening St. Peter did. It turned out he *did* overstep his authority.

It's ironic, really. For all the trouble I had with that Manual, I *do* remember a little-known regulation that would allow *me* to write up *St. Peter*, and send the report directly to You-Know-Who.

I think I'll casually mention it to him when I stand at that desk next time, and watch him go running inside the Gates to get my Harp and Wings.

"THE TEN OF SPADES"

"Dad, this isn't the way, where are we going?" asked ten-year-old Paul Virras, leaning over the front seat of his father's 1940 Chevy. His father, Russell, exchanged a knowing smile with his wife Nancy, sitting beside him on the bench seat of the six-year-old sedan.

"Where do you think we're going?" he said.

"I thought we were going to see the bomber factory at Willow Run."

"There's nothing to see there any more since the war ended, Paul."

"I give up, then," Paul said good-naturedly. His father usually took him to fun or exciting places on Sunday afternoons when they headed out of the city. The Detroit area was full of great things to see, especially if you loved airplanes as Paul did.

In reality, he *liked* airplanes, he *loved* bombers. They had a vitality you didn't find in any other airplane. With the colorful names and designs, it seemed to Paul they had a life of their own.

It was obvious that neither of his parents were going to reveal the surprise destination. He decided to take another guess. "Dad, isn't this the way you go to work?"

"There's no one out there today, Paul. It's Sunday."

"Well, how much longer . . ." Paul stopped in midsentence and struggled to comprehend what his eyes were registering. Rounding a turn, they were passing a large open field used for carnivals, an occasional circus, and other such events. The field itself could hardly be seen. From end to end were the olive-drab and silver bodies of dozens of airplanes—bombers.

"Dad, look! Stop the car!" Paul was surprised and frantic. His parents smiled as his father pulled into the entryway of the field.

"Good surprise, huh Paul?" asked his mother. "Your father found out at work that there would be bombers here for a while, so we kept the newspapers from you and told your aunt and uncle not to mention it."

"Were these the extra ones they made?" asked Paul, as his father guided the car into the makeshift parking lot by some small wooden buildings at the front of the field.

"No, Paul," replied Russell. "Every one of these birds was in combat. I was told they still have all their guns on board, too."

"Can we go right up to them?"

"Better than that. You can go inside."

"This is the greatest! I'm heading for the top turret of one of these babies."

Paul zigged and zagged his way among the many B—17's and B—24's lined up on the dusty surface of the old fairgrounds, as his parents tried to keep up. The day was hot, approaching ninety, and the sky cloudless. Russell and Nancy's futile efforts at staying with their son were matched by his frustration. Every plane had several kids *and* adults entrenched in the pilot's seat or the gun turrets. When Paul eventually found them, much of the luster of the surprise had been dimmed.

"Dad, can we come back another day? There's too many people around."

"Paul, Sunday is my only day off since we got so busy at work." Russell, an executive with Wayne County Contractors, was overburdened with the post-war housing boom.

Walking back toward the buildings and parking lot, Paul noticed another plane parked off to the side, its silver finish reflecting the bright summer sun. He correctly identified it as a B—17G. He had overlooked it in his initial enthusiasm. Apparently, so had everyone else. It seemed to be deserted, except for one of the maintenance crew that were stationed among the planes. Paul could not believe his good luck, and sprinted ahead of his parents and up to the man.

"Can people go inside this one, too?" he asked.

"It's all yours." Even in his hurry, Paul couldn't help taking a closer look at the man. He was young, about twenty, Paul supposed. His face was an explosion of freckles surrounding bright blue eyes. Paul could see a trace of red hair beneath the cap. It was as though Huck Finn had joined the Air Force.

"How come this plane is way over here?" Paul asked.

"It was the last plane in, and there wasn't any room left on the field, so we had to put it here."

Paul noticed the stripes on the plane's nose that identified it as a squadron commander's aircraft. It was named the "Ten of Spades," and had a large playing card of the same name on the side, under the pilot's compartment.

While his parents remained outside to let him fully enjoy the experience, Paul had the entire bomber to himself. He made a beeline for his favorite spot, the top turret, just behind the pilot. Paul squeezed into the gunner's seat, and was overwhelmed not only by what he saw and felt, but what he could *smell*. Plexiglass, gun oil, rubber, and plastic combined with the heat to create one magical smell that Paul knew was ordinarily reserved for the men who manned these guns.

He squinted through the gunsights, found the manual traverse lever, and revolved around, sweeping the blue skies clean of imaginary enemy planes. Paul felt that no other moment in his life could ever be as special and magical as this.

From the moment they got in the car to drive the thirty-one miles back to Detroit, Paul was begging his parents to return the following Sunday. By Tuesday, he had gotten a 'we'll see,' which usually meant yes. By Thursday, it *was* a yes, depending on the weather. Paul prayed for clear skies.

Sunday arrived, and while it wasn't as hot, it was partially cloudy, the air thick and heavy. In church, Paul's mother complained of feeling ill. When they arrived home, she went into the bedroom to lie down while Paul helped his father with a makeshift Sunday dinner.

After eating, Paul knocked on the bedroom door and asked her if they were still going.

"You and Dad can go if you want. I'll be all right, I just need to rest. I couldn't take riding in the car the way I feel." After being reassured by his wife, Russell and Paul got in the Chevy and headed west, toward Ypsilanti, and the old fairgrounds.

Paul's restlessness and squirming indicated to Russell more than anticipation. "Paul, two things. Hit the restrooms when we get there, and don't be disappointed this time if there are other kids in all the airplanes. That's what they're there for."

"Dad, it's not the same," Paul insisted. "You can't pretend what you want when people you don't know are around."

When they arrived, they discovered that the cloudy, humid weather had held down the crowd somewhat. After parking the car, Paul and Russell went inside and used the bathroom.

They found an information counter there, with bulletin board displays of some of the exact planes on the grounds, group photos of their crews, and other memorabilia.

"Paul, a lot of the planes look empty. You can take your pick."

Paul shook his head. "I'm going straight for *my* plane, the Ten of Spades."

Russell thought this a bit odd, but assumed it might make perfect sense to a ten-year-old with a vivid imagination. Perhaps Paul didn't want to "transfer" to a new crew after flying several missions with his imaginary comrades on the Ten of Spades. He decided to indulge the boy and wander around for a while.

Paul dashed over to the Ten of Spades. He was surprised to find the same maintenance man. "Anybody in there?" he asked.

The young man smiled. "Nope, all yours again."

Paul climbed inside and took his position in the top turret. Moments later, as he was pretending to enter German air space, he sensed movement in his peripherals. Looking down, he found the young man who had been standing by the plane. His coveralls were gone, replaced by an Eighth Air Force bomber crew uniform, designating the 303rd Bomber Group, 359th Bomber Squadron. Paul stared at him in surprise.

"Mind if I join you in my old spot?" he asked.

"*You* were the top turret gunner on this plane?" Paul gasped.

"That's right. Seventeen missions."

Paul continued to stare in admiration and astonishment.

"Lane Thomas, United States Air Force," said the man, as he pointed to a name patch over one breast pocket.

"You get to travel around with your old plane?"

"For now, I do. So you like being a turret gunner, huh? You stay there, I'll squeeze in up here." Somehow, he settled into a position next to Paul. "What's your name, son?"

"Paul Virras. Did you shoot down any Germans?"

"I guess so."

"That's *neat*. How many?"

"I don't know. It's not important, now."

"*That* must have been neat, seeing those Kraut planes dropping out of the sky."

"Paul," Thomas interrupted, "they were Germans, not Krauts, and they were just like me, young and scared. There wasn't anything neat about it." His bright smile had disappeared.

Paul was embarrassed, but regained his composure and continued his conversation with Airman Thomas. He found out that Thomas was twenty-two, from Billings, Montana, and had gotten engaged before the war. Paul already knew he was touchy about things Paul considered fun and exciting. Other than that, he seemed open and friendly. It was almost like having an older brother.

Thomas delighted in telling Paul stories about England, where he had been stationed, and some of the men he served with. Paul's favorite was how many bomber crews took containers of ice cream up with them, because the vibrations and freezing at high altitude made it taste so good.

Paul happened to look out the turret and saw his father waiting for him. "That's my father standing there, Mr. Thomas." Paul waved, and felt the Airman lean over and wave, also. Russell returned the wave, then pointed to his watch. "I guess we gotta go now," Paul said, disappointment filling his voice. "How much longer will these planes be here?"

"I think another week should do it," replied Thomas.

"Do what, Mr. Thomas?"

"It's just an old Air Force saying, Paul."

Before they had reached the car, Paul was campaigning for a third excursion to the fairgrounds. "Dad, you know that man we saw by the plane last week? He was the top turret gunner on the Ten of Spades. He came inside in uniform and told me about the plane and their missions and stuff."

Russell looked at his son with puzzlement. "What man by the plane, Paul?"

"The one in the turret with me." Paul was equally puzzled.

Russell stopped walking and looked at his son closely. "Paul, your mother and I didn't see anyone by that plane last week, and there wasn't anyone in the turret with you just now. You were alone." There was a hint of concern in his voice.

"Dad, the young guy with the red hair and freckles. Lane Thomas. He came *in* the plane. You *waved* at us, Dad."

"Paul, I waved at *you.*" His voice and expression had gone from concerned to stern, approaching a warning. "You've had a lot of excitement today, and I think you're letting your imagination get the better of you." He softened his expression. "I'm glad you had fun today, Paul, but you're old enough to know when to pull back on the old throttle."

"But Dad, he was *there!*"

"That's *enough,* Paul. I don't want to hear any more about some man with red hair in the turret with you. Let's go home."

. . .

"Is Paul still in his room, Nan?"

"Yes, he is. What *happened* out there? I haven't seen him this upset in ages."

"He spent the entire time in that one plane he went in last week. Everything seemed fine. On the way back to the car he comes out with a story about some young man with red hair and freckles standing by that airplane last week."

Nancy searched her memory of that moment. "There wasn't *anyone* by that plane, Russell. That's what was so odd. It was deserted."

"Wait, there's more. He tells me the same man came in the plane later, introduced himself as the top turret gunner, and told him all about his experiences in the war. He capped it off by having the man wave to me from the gun turret."

Nancy exhaled in disgust. "Is *that* what this is about? Russell, you know Paul was just pretending. You're the one that's always encouraging him to use his imagination."

"Nan, you don't understand. He can pretend *Hitler* was in the turret with him for all I care, but he should know where this stuff is supposed to stop. He was acting like he believed his own story. You can't encourage *that* in a ten-year-old."

Nancy was still not convinced this was serious. "What are you going to do, Russell, punish him for pretending?"

"No, Nancy. Paul has to learn to take responsibility for what he says. On my way home from work tomorrow, I'm going to check out his story."

Twelve miles from Wayne County Contractors, Russell Viras took a left into the parking lot of the old fairgrounds. A handful of people were browsing among the planes. As he headed for the information building, Russell took a quick glance over toward the Ten of Spades. There was no one near it.

He went to the information counter, laid his briefcase down, and waited until a heavyset man with dark, slicked-back hair and a small moustache came over to him. The name badge on his blazer said 'Ginsberg'.

"May I help you, sir?"

"I was wondering if any of the crew members from those planes accompanied them here."

"None that I know of. There are a few Air Force ground crew, though."

"Would one of them be a young red-haired man named Lane Thomas?"

"I'll check. I have a list right here." He looked up and down one of the papers in a nearby pile. "There's nothing even close to that name, sir. Sorry."

"That's okay, I didn't think so. Thanks anyway." Ginsberg gave him a puzzled look and went back to his paperwork.

Russell walked aimlessly towards the display boards on his way out. Paul had just made him up, but why? He glanced at the photos of the bomber crews and started reading about the Ten of Spades. The crew, it said, had selected the name because there were ten of them, and they wanted to pay Hitler back "in spades." Although the autographed photo of the crew was in black and white, it was obvious the man on the far right had red hair and freckles. His signature read *Lane W. Thomas.* Russell checked the caption. For a brief moment, he thought he owed Paul an apology. Near the bottom of the printing it said "Far right, Lane Thomas, Top Turret Gunner." Anger and disappointment returned as he read the last line. In parenthesis were the words, *"Killed in Action, 1945."*

. . .

It was the longest thirty-one miles Russell had ever driven. He concluded that Paul had gone back inside on that second visit and seen the photos. That explained how he knew the man's name and appearance. Why had he used a man whose death could so easily be checked? Paul could be as naïve as any ten-year-old, but he wasn't stupid. He did have a tendency to fantasize. Maybe, he couldn't bear the thought of his favorite bomber's top turret gunner being dead. Maybe Paul wanted the man alive so badly that he *made* him alive, and got carried away. Russell wanted to give his son the benefit of every doubt, but there was no excuse for this, and it was up to him to correct it.

After dinner, Paul's parents sat him down in the living room. He sensed that this was serious, they looked grim. Russell explained about his side trip to the fairgrounds, and his discovery about turret gunner Lane Thomas.

Paul was overwhelmed with grief and confusion. His father was trying to remain calm, but there was an undercurrent of punishment or consequence in his manner. Paul sensed that to deny he made this up would only make things worse. He wanted one more visit to the fairgrounds, as this coming weekend would be the last time the planes would be on display. He hung his head, and nodded in all the right places during his father's speech about fantasizing, respect for war dead, and truthfulness. His father did not rule out a last visit, but made it clear that it would be under "controlled conditions."

In the solitude of his room later, Paul tried to put the pieces together. He *knew* he had seen Lane Thomas. Why wouldn't his father believe him? What was this really about?

. . .

On the way to the fairgrounds, Russell put these conditions on the visit. First, Paul must read the photo caption that documented the death of Airman Thomas. Second, Russell would accompany him inside the Ten of Spades. Third, this would be the last visit, even though the planes were going to be held over for an extra week. Paul agreed, and resolved that he would tell his father whatever he wanted to hear.

When they arrived, they went inside to the display boards. Paul read the short bio on the Ten of Spades, and looked at the photo and caption. He knew his father had not been *lying,* but *he* hadn't been lying either. He could not understand this, but kept quiet as his father took him to the counter where Mr. Ginsberg stood.

"Mr. Ginsberg," Russell asked, "would there happen to be a young red-haired man here as a ground crew or flight crew member?"

Ginsberg recognized the man *and* the question from a few days back. With raised eyebrows, he answered, "No sir, there is *no* one here by that description."

"Thank you very much."

It had been a long three weeks for Arnold Ginsberg, kids running and yelling all around the usually quiet fairgrounds. He had answered the same silly questions over and over.

"You see, Paul," said Russell, as they walked out toward the Ten of Spades, "the man is dead, no one even resembling him has been here."

"Okay, Dad."

Paul climbed aboard the Ten of Spades, and instinctively got into the turret gunner's seat, his father still beside him.

"Paul, I didn't see anyone standing outside this plane, did you?"

"No."

"Is there anyone else inside with us now?"

"No Dad, there isn't." This was the price, then, Paul thought. His father, the man he most admired, would not believe him, and didn't trust him not to start "telling stories" the minute they got here. He knew a lecture was coming, one that was supposed to make him feel ashamed.

"Paul, a lot of good men like Lane Thomas died so that we could be free. I don't think that's something we should make a game of, do you?"

"No, Dad." There would probably be a pause while his father thought of something else to add. Paul waited, his expression a blend of sadness and hurt.

Russell sensed how diminished Paul's spirit was. He loved his son's curiosity and exuberance. He did not wish to press the matter further. "If I walk around for a while, will you be all right by yourself?"

Paul recognized the peace offering from his father, and managed a smile. "I'll be fine, Dad."

Within two minutes Paul sat looking at the other planes and people, including his father, about thirty yards away. There was no joy left in pretending to be a turret gunner. He sat and thought about Lane Thomas, a man whom one reality claimed was dead, while some other reality insisted was still alive.

"Glad you made it back, Paul." The boy jumped involuntarily. Lane Thomas was crouched beside him, in uniform. There was a sense of relief, but Paul was confused. There were questions here. Paul was sure this was his last opportunity for answers.

He returned the wave of his father, who now left his spot to walk around, as promised. "My dad can't see you, can he?"

"He's not part of this, Paul."

"What are you, Mr. Thomas?"

"I'm a soldier, Paul. I'm a turret gunner. Isn't it *neat* being a turret gunner, Paul?" The voice was heavy, had lost all of its former sparkle and flow.

Paul felt a sudden hitch in his chest, his eyes started to well up. He was sure Airman Thomas was here for him alone, that there was some message for him in all this. "Am I the only one that sees you?"

"That's the plan, Paul."

"What plan?"

"Some of us got sent back. This is my last mission, my most important one. I have to convince someone like you that we can't have this stuff any more." He swept out an arm, indicating the planes.

"No more *airplanes?*"

"Lots of airplanes, Paul, but none with bombs on them, or turret gunners."

Paul could feel his chest getting tight, his breathing labored.

"When you're convinced, Paul, I want you to pass it on to another young person like yourself, one that thinks all this is *neat.* Ask them to do the same. Maybe someday we can put an end to all this."

For the first time, Paul felt an eerie sense of discomfort in the turret gunner seat. It occurred to him that Lane Thomas probably died there. "I don't think I'll be coming back here again," Paul whispered.

Lane Thomas smiled, the freckles, red hair, and blue eyes combining in an unforgettable look. "I don't think I will either. It's about time I moved on."

"Mr. Thomas, can I ever get my father to believe I didn't make this up?"

"People have to have faith and trust, Paul. That's what it's all about." He winked. "But I'll see what I can do." Thomas climbed down. Paul did the same and extended his hand to the

Airman. Thomas shook his head. "Sorry, Paul, can't do that." He straightened and saluted.

Paul tried to speak, but found his throat closing on him. He returned the salute, looking down to make sure his body was militarily correct. When he looked up he was alone. He held the salute for half a minute before leaving.

Paul was quiet and reflective on the trip home, and Russell wanted to break the tension. He felt the boy had learned an important lesson, and wished to compliment him. "Paul, I know I was tough on you today, but you took it like a man. They're going to have the planes here an extra week, you know. We can come back again next Sunday."

"No thanks, Dad. I've seen enough."

Russell was surprised, and felt guilty, thinking he had ruined the boy's love of planes by rubbing his nose in reality that afternoon. They rode in silence for a while.

"Dad, do you have faith in me?" Paul asked, without warning.

Russell was caught off guard by the question. "Of course, Paul, why wouldn't I?"

"Do you trust me, Dad?"

"I certainly do. You've always been very honest about—" He stopped, and looked over at Paul, staring out the window. Russell scolded himself. Paul had not mentioned the bomber or Lane Thomas. He was just now making the connection between his son's questions and the fantasizing problem. "Why do you ask, Paul?"

"Just wanted to know."

They didn't speak for the rest of the drive, but Russell could not help feeling that he'd been suckered by a ten-year-old.

Russell Viras had no intention of stopping by the fairgrounds the next day on his way home from work, but here he was again. Furthermore, he had no idea *why* but he felt that Faith and Trust were involved somehow.

He found himself at the display boards, and wandered over to the information counter, where one Arnold Ginsberg stood, feeling as though he had been trapped in a bad play rehearsal. They had done this scene twice, and apparently were going to have to do it until they got it right.

"Please, mister, there's *no* young man here with red hair."

"I know, it's okay," said Russell. "I'm here for my son." Ginsberg was looking on either side of Russell, attempting to find the son he was here for. Russell identified the man's confusion. "He's not here now, I . . . never mind." Ginsberg put his hand on his forehead and looked down. "Mind if I leave my briefcase on the counter? I want to take a quick look by the window"

"That's fine, sir. I'll be in back if you need me." Ginsberg walked off, looking at the ceiling.

Russell drifted over to the large plate glass, staring at the Ten of Spades. "Faith and Trust," he murmured, "are you on board somewhere?" He fixated on the top turret, almost willing himself to see someone. His heart leaped momentarily. Someone *was* in the turret. He moved slightly, then realized that the late afternoon sun, the window, and turret bubble had combined to create an illusion. He shrugged and walked back to the counter to retrieve his briefcase, which was not supposed to be left unattended.

He was about to lift it when an alarm went off in his head. The two metal buckles had been undone. Russell *never* left it like that. Someone opened it while he was at the window. He could feel himself breaking into a sweat. Inside were contracts, bids on prospective jobs, and other confidential papers. He did a quick inventory, found all the folders there, and opened each one to check their individual contents. Nothing was missing. As he was reminding himself to be more careful, he noticed, under the bottom folder, a small rectangular object. It was a card, bearing the Eighth Air Force insignia. He turned it over, and two more discoveries had him perspiring again. It was a playing card, the *ten of spades.* In the right-hand margin, was the signature, *"Lane W. Thomas."*

It could not have been there before he got to the fairgrounds. The briefcase had been with him the entire time. He latched it and picked it up. Holding the card in his other hand, he walked over to the crew photo of the Ten of Spades. He stared at the boyish, freckled face of Lane Thomas, whose signature exactly matched the one on the playing card. The smiling face seemed to be mocking him.

"Why?" he whispered. "Why Paul?"

On the drive home, Russell realized that Messrs. Faith and Trust *had* been out at the fairgrounds, and had left their calling card as a reminder of how he had unintentionally wronged his son.

He was a man who dealt with real things in a real world, but in his shirt pocket was evidence of something *un*real. He pulled the card from his pocket, looked again at the signature. It was real.

He debated with himself during the entire drive home. Should he matter-of-factly tell Paul he now believed him and leave it at that, or would a wounded ten-year-old need something more concrete, more *real?*

Pulling into his driveway, he was still undecided. Paul was in the yard, and came trotting over, his rich smile giving no indication of the breach of trust he had been forced to endure this past week. Russell had half-expected him to shy away, retreat into the house.

He got out of the car and watched him, the most valuable commodity in his life, simple ten-year-old adoration on his face. "Carry your briefcase, Dad?" he asked.

Russell handed him the briefcase with his left hand, while with his right hand, which had begun to tremble, he reached into his shirt pocket.

"E-6"

Go figure. I was just startin' to get things worked out in my mind, about bein' black in D. C., and where I want to go to college next year, and if I can even afford it. Now it looks like we go back to square one and start sortin' through the whole thing again.

It started when I signed up for Contemporary Problems in Society, a senior elective, 'cause Mrs. Adams the teacher. All the kids like and respect her. She can help you raise your consciousness, give you pride in the race. That's what I was lookin' for.

Early in the year she gives us this research project, says it gonna involve "field work."

"Hey, Mrs. Adams," yells out Leon Briggs, "ain't our people done *enough* field work already?" The class was laughin' big time, and Leon was takin' his bows, but Mrs. Adams can handle stuff like that.

"Very clever, Leon, but I think you know that I'm referring to research done in the community."

"What we gotta research *this* time?" he moaned.

"I've assigned all of you, alone or in pairs, to senior citizen's homes in the area. We compiled a list of very interesting people for you to get to know in the next few weeks. At the end of that time, I want you to write a four-to-six page report that is both factual and contains a human interest angle." She looked at the class and saw confused and questioning looks.

"I think you'll get a different perspective on your own lives."

There was the usual moanin' and groanin', and good old Leon couldn't resist bendin' over in his chair, one hand on his back, and the other on some imaginary cane.

Mrs. Adams smiled. "Leon, I sincerely hope you don't picture all older people that way. You might find this a valuable learning experience."

I got the impression she meant that for all of us, though.

. . .

The Capital District Home for the Aged was about a twenty minute bike ride from my house. I didn't mind that Mrs. Adams hadn't paired me with anyone, but on the ride over I was startin' to get uneasy about being *assigned* a person to interview. I was hopin' to sort through a bunch of them, and then pick an old brother who could really show how our people have suffered. Mrs. Adams put the nix on that. She said this wasn't no *menu*. We had already been assigned people to interview.

My assignment card said to ask for Lucille Hernandez, who would introduce me to my "subject," a Mr. Lowens. I stopped at the reception desk and identified myself. "I'm Robbie Barnes. I'm supposed to meet Lucille Hernandez here."

"I'm Lucille," said the attractive dark-haired Latino woman, pointing to her I. D. badge. She appeared to be in her mid-thirties, and had a pleasant smile. She came out from the enclosure and gave me a visitor's badge to clip on my shirt, and had me sign the guest book.

I'm sayin' to myself, 'What they think I'm gonna do, *steal* one of 'um?'

My face must of give me away, 'cause Lucille says, "There are a *few* regulations I have to enforce, Robbie, but I try to be non-threatening about them."

Last time I heard anybody call himself that, it was a D. C. police officer givin' a talk at school.

"I think you'll find Mr. Lowens a very interesting man," she said, as we walked down the main corridor. I gave her my 'prove it' look.

"He was a major league baseball player in the 1920's and played in two World Series'. There was an article on him in the *Post* a few weeks back that you might enjoy reading. We have a copy on the main bulletin board."

"Mrs. Adams know about this article?"

"Yes."

"I'll read it."

Here's the thing. I get mostly A's in school. I seen enough flunkies on the streets to know what I *don't* want to do in life. I gotta get the grades, then hope I can quality for some student loan or one of those grants they give to minority students. I already know my parents can't help much on what they earn. So I was determined to get an 'A' on this project, even if it meant readin' some boring article off their bulletin board.

We turned down another corridor, and Lucille asked, "Are you interested in sports, Robbie?"

"Mostly football and basketball."

"What about baseball? Mr. Lowens would love to talk about that with you."

"I guess I can make do."

She stopped and put her hands on her hips. The eyes had turned to flamethrowers. "Look, Robbie, this man is ninety years old, and has no family left. He may be just an assignment to you, but he's still a human being. Can you make do with *that?*"

"Sure," I said uneasily. "I'll be nice." Number one, I need an 'A' on this, remember? Number two, I *don't* need old Lucille bad-mouthin' me to Mrs. Adams. Number three, this lady was *scary* when she got mad.

We came to a large sitting area, or lounge, and I could hear a voice in my head saying, 'What's wrong with this picture?' Except for one lady, everybody was in wheelchairs or had those metal walkers. That wasn't it, though. Every single one of them was *white*. So much for a valuable learning experience. Thank you, Mrs. Adams. I wondered if this is what she meant by getting a "different perspective."

Lucille brought me over to where Mr. Lowens was sitting. He was one of the wheelchair dudes. She introduced us, and I extended my hand down to him, but from behind his chair she was shaking her head.

"I can still manage a handshake, Lucille," the old man says, like he's got eyes in the back of his head. "She fusses over me too much, you know," he continued, looking at me with a smile.

He was an odd-looking guy, even for ninety. He had a small body, but his head and face didn't seem to match up with it. His skinny neck looked like it had a hard time supportin' his head, with its large hooked nose and those ears that stuck out some. His eyes were a bright hazel, but were way back there, almost inside his skull, it seemed.

He spoke clearly, though and in a deep voice. That didn't match his body *or* face.

Next thing I knew, Lucille was gone, and I was on my own. I didn't know where to start, but the old guy seemed to know that he was unique. Without any formalities, he started talkin', and I started takin' notes.

"I was in the Majors from 1922 to 1928, all with the Washington Senators. We won the World Series in 1924, beat the Giants in seven games. I recorded the final out of the Series," he added proudly.

"What position did you play?" I figured I should at least *act* interested.

"Shortstop. I was pretty good, too. Started from '23 through '27. Not much money in it in those days, but Mr. Griffith was committed to winning."

"Who?"

"Clark Griffith. He owned the team. Leastways we let him think he did. The game belongs to the players. Always will."

There was somethin' about that last thing he said that kind of got my attention. I still wasn't interested in old-time baseball stories, but the old man seemed to have a little bit of *soul* if you get my drift.

For the next twenty minutes or so, he told me enough facts about being a major-leaguer in those days to fill up that part of my report. When he got around to telling me the names of his teammates, I almost laughed in his face. Can you feature guys named Goose Goslin, Muddy Ruel, and Bucky Harris? Lowens had a nickname, too. It was *Binky.* Sounds like some rich, white girl, if you ask me.

"Why they call you 'Binky'?"

"'Cause I was short."

"Why didn't they just call you 'Shorty'?" I demanded.

"We already had a guy named Shorty."

I couldn't tell by looking if he was serious, or pullin' my leg. About this time Lucille comes back and tells me it's time for his nap. Lowens gets this disgusted look on his face.

"I ain't even *tired,* Lucille. She fusses over me too much, you know," he said, turning to look back at me as she wheeled him back to his room.

I waited for Lucille at the front desk to make out a schedule of visits, and read that article she had mentioned earlier. Most of it was the same stuff he had just told me, with some other facts about how he got to the Majors from a semi-pro team in Maryland, where he was from, and how he was the last living member of the 1924 championship team. It still didn't do anything for me, but I figured I'd put in my time, write the report, and be done with it. But I still had to come up with a human interest angle.

I went back twice more in the next week, and Mr. Lowens looked pretty happy to see me. Lucille seemed to sense I was bein' nice, as I promised, and she was back to bein' friendly. 'Binky', as he insisted I call him, filled me up with more details of the 1924 championship season.

Finally, I asked him why he didn't talk about any other part of his baseball career.

"Young man, there's nothin' in this world like winnin' the Series. That whole season had a special magic to it." He looked off into space and squinted. "Takin' that throw from Bucky Harris and steppin' on second for the final out was the greatest moment of my life."

"Didn't you play in the Series the next year, too?" I asked, remembering the article I'd read.

"Wasn't the same no more after we won. We lost the '25 Series in seven games to the Pirates, and that felt worse than the years we finished last. Nope, nothin' can ever match that day we won it." He paused a second and frowned, still squinting off into space. "Too bad we won it in New York, and not Washington. When I took the throw at second, we all screamed for joy and ran off the field as fast as we could before any of those New York fans could get to us. You see, the Giants had the tying run on third at the time." His eyes got wide, as though his own recollection had taken him by surprise. "That whole stadium just went silent. All you could hear was us screamin' and the guy I forced at second screamin', too."

I found myself drawn into this story. It had a more human interest side than all the facts and stats he'd been giving me. "Why was *he* screamin'?" I asked.

"Him? He was screamin' at the umpire for callin' him out. The guy was yellin' so loud and so fast I couldn't hardly make out what he was sayin'. I think I remember him yelling' at me to get back out there."

I admit it. He had me hooked now. "What did you do?"

"Couldn't do nothin' but keep runnin' off the field. The ump called him out, so that was the game. Besides, Joe Judge, our first baseman, had me in a headlock and was sprintin' to the dugout, and Bucky Harris had jumped on my back." He gave an exaggerated smile. "Worst beatin' I ever took in my life, from my own teammates."

I burst out laughin', don't ask me why.

He looked away and squinted again. "What a great bunch of guys. They've all answered the clarion's call. I'm the last one."

He threw his hands out in front of him, like it was no big deal, but it wasn't very convincing. Funny, I had *read* how he was the last living member of that team, and it hadn't meant a thing to me. Now, hearin' it, I felt like somebody had kicked me in the chest.

When I got home, I began thinking about a human interest angle for my assignment. It struck me that Binky could focus on one moment in his long life as being his greatest. When I thought about it more, it was simple to figure. The *team* won the Series, but only *he* got the out at second. That moment belonged only to him, in a way. So that became by human interest angle. I began piecing the report together, and went back for a final interview a few days later.

Lucille wasn't at the desk, so a took a visitor's I. D. and signed in. I could hear what was going on in the main lounge long before I could see it. There were several voices shouting. I thought one of them was Lucille's. When I got there, I saw this real old guy in a wheelchair yelling and pointing at Binky, while Lucille and another staff worker tried to calm him down.

"E-6! E-6!" he screamed, as he jabbed his finger at Binky.

"Yer full of it, Blythe," Binky kept shouting back, but he seemed to have himself under better control. Lucille and the other woman kept trying to get Blythe to calm down, but he ignored them and kept screaming 'E-6' over and over. He finally tried to take a backhand swat at Binky, and that was when the other staff member turned his chair around and wheeled him out toward one of the residents' wings.

I had to laugh thinkin' about two old-timers like that havin' a go at each other. I didn't think either of them could crack an egg. Then I started tryin' to figure out what they could have been fightin' about. What was E-6? I looked around for a jukebox. That's all I could think of.

I started over towards Binky, but Lucille intercepted me. "Robbie, I think you'd better come back another time. We just had an incident." She hustled me out of there before Binky could catch sight of me.

"Lucille, what the heck was that about?"

"Mr. Blythe transferred here from another home that went bankrupt. We thought it would be a great reunion, the two of them. They actually played against each other in the World Series."

"Why was he so mad at Binky? What's E-6?"

"It's baseball talk for error by the shortstop. Mr. Lowens got Mr. Blythe out at second to win the Series in 1924. I'm sure he told you that story already."

"You mean *that's* the guy that was screamin' at the ump that he was safe?"

"That's him."

"Man, he ain't changed a *bit.* "

"It's more serious than that," Lucille said, shaking her head. "Mr. Blythe is ninety-five years old and could easily suffer a stroke losing his temper like that."

"So what's all this 'E-6' stuff? The *ump* called him out. What's he got against Binky?"

Lucille arched her eyebrows. "He claims Mr. Lowens dropped the ball, then picked it up before the dust settled to make it *look* like he caught it."

I don't mind tellin' you I chewed that one over a few times on the way home. Go figure. A man's greatest moment in ninety years of livin', and there's *still* somebody left sayin' it was a fraud. It got me wonderin', too. Binky seemed like a guy that knew what sports was supposed to be all about. How far would he have gone to win the Series when it looked like victory was slippin' away?

. . .

"Sometimes it's just like dealing with a couple of kids," Lucille explained to me a day later, as we walked down to the lounge. "You set some ground rules and let them take it from there." She was giving me the latest on the Blythe-Lowens feud. They were trying to patch it up, but things had gotten worse first.

The second time the two met, Blythe kept his voice under control, but started bumping Binky's wheelchair with the footrest of his own chair. Binky retaliated, and it kept escalating until it looked like some geriatric demolition derby. The Assistant Supervisor suggested keeping them apart, but Lucille had disagreed.

"They're such an important link to each other's past, it would be a shame not to allow them to see each other," she told me. "We finally got them both to agree that World Series talk was off limits."

There I was, in the visitor's lounge, with the man who recorded the final out of the 1924 World Series, and the man who would refute it, Harold Blythe. I had been plannin' to work up the nerve to come right out and ask Binky if he really caught the ball or not, but with Blythe sittin' ten feet away, it was no go.

With Binky's special moment off limits, I went back to general questions on playing conditions back then. I could sense Mr. Blythe sizin' me up from where he was sittin.' It was obvious he was just itchin' to get in on the conversation, but I didn't want to slight Binky, so I tried not to make eye contact with him.

As Binky and I were about to call it a wrap, he jumped in. "Speaking of playing conditions, back in our day there weren't any colored guys in the Majors."

Colored? I hadn't heard black people referred to as 'colored' since I was about six, but I didn't want to call Blythe on it and take the chance of trouble startin'.

"That's the truth, too," he continued. "Even Lowens here could tell you there wasn't a single colored ballplayer in the big leagues till after World War II."

"I know," I replied. "Jackie Robinson."

"Nope, nope." He shook his head and waggled a finger at me. "That would be Jackie Robinson."

"He *said* Jackie Robinson, Blythe!" Binky shouted angrily. "Are you *deaf* as well as stupid?"

That was all it took.

"I ain't deaf, Lowens. I can still hear as well as I did that day I heard the ball hit the ground on that play at second." He didn't say it *loud,* he just said it *nasty.*

"What you heard, Blythe, was your sorry ass draggin' in that dustbowl you called an infield."

"Yeah? How's *your* hearing, Lowens. E-6! E-6! Did you hear *that* okay?"

I was hopin' this would die out on its own, but when Blythe mentioned 'E-6', I figured the floodgates were gonna open. Did they ever. They both lit into each other, yellin' insults and all kinds of accusations. Lots of people and places and things before my time were mentioned, along with each man's ancestry, and the marital status of their respective parents at the time they were born. I rushed off to get Lucille, and as I turned the first corner, saw her hustlin' down the corridor toward me. She heard them all the way from her station. I started to explain, but she just waved at me and kept trottin' down there.

I went back to the reception desk and waited for things to get settled, but after about fifteen minutes I got restless, and had stuff to do at home, so I took off.

I had all my facts, and my human interest angle, one man's special moment, so after school the next day I went home and started in on it. I figured I'd stay clear of the home for awhile. For all I knew I might be getting blamed for what happened between Lowens and Blythe. I got a couple hours work done, and then my mother called me to the phone.

"Robbie, this is Lucille from Capital District Home."

She didn't sound quite right. "Am I in trouble for what happened yesterday? I waited as long as I could."

"No Robbie, what happened was unfortunate, but it wasn't your fault. There *is* something you should know, though."

"What's that?"

"Mr. Blythe had a massive stroke a few hours after you left, and died at about two this morning."

I was sorry the guy died, but I was worried for myself, too. "That last argument, Lucille?"

"It's impossible to say for sure. I don't think it helped any, but he could have gone at any time."

Another worry jumped out before I could even identify it. "How's Binky takin' all this?"

"Kind of hard. He feels partially responsible. He told me you were finished with your interviewing, but he could use someone to reassure him that it wasn't his fault. He's taken quite a liking to you."

I went out there the next day to try and cheer him up, and while he seemed to stop blaming himself, he was still pretty subdued.

He squinted and looked off into the distance like I'd seen him do so many times. "Young man, Hal Blythe has answered the clarion's call. If he'd only let it go, he might still be here."

"You mean—"

"I mean when a thing's done, it's *done,*" he said forcefully. "All those years he must've let it eat away at him." He paused, and shook his head. I was surprised to see a trace of a smile. "Anyway, I bet I know the first thing he'll do when he gets to Heaven."

"What's that?"

"Run around lookin' for Melvin Symington."

"Who's he?"

"The ump that made that call at second base." He chuckled softly, his shoulders vibrating slightly.

I'm not sure why, maybe a sense of familiarity, but I asked, "What's the first thing *you'd* do in Heaven?"

He turned serious, looking almost irritated. "Find that fat, arrogant windbag Babe Ruth and beat the pants off him in a home run contest!"

I couldn't believe what I was hearin'. Babe Ruth had been the greatest home run hitter of all time, that is, until Hank Aaron. Even *I* knew what Babe Ruth had done. "Binky, Babe Ruth hit 714 home runs. How many you hit?"

His face didn't change expression. "The same." My jaw must have dropped, 'cause Binky broke into a huge grin. "Minus the 700." He'd put one over on me, but I guess I didn't mind.

"Don't get me wrong, young man, he was a great ballplayer, but I'll be darned if he wasn't so full of himself." He looked off again, and squinted. "I can dream, can't I? What else is left for a guy who's outlived his own time period?"

That was kind of depressing, so I mumbled something about how I was hopin' this report would help me get into college, provided I could come up with the money to go. "Thanks for your time and everything," I said. "I'll stop by someday and say hello."

He smiled, but it was that smile he had when he talked about bein' the last member of the 1924 Senators. He extended his hand. "My pleasure, young man. In case you get busy and can't make it, it was nice knowin' you. Good luck getting' into college."

I was real uncomfortable with this whole goodbye scene, especially the way he almost made it sound like I wouldn't be back now that I had what I needed. I was still dyin' to know what actually happened on that play at second, but decided to let it go. After all, it *was* his special moment. I got up and walked down the corridor. I looked back once to find him watching me. He gave a slight wave.

"Come back and visit us sometime, Robbie," Lucille said, as I walked past her station.

"I will, Lucille."

. . .

I only got an A- on the report. Go figure. Mrs. Adams said the facts and human interest parts were good, but I was too wordy and jumped around too much. Plus there were some grammar mistakes.

I wasn't sure if I'd learned anything, either, except that two old white guys could still hate each other over somethin' that happened nearly seventy years ago.

It was the first week in November now, and there were basketball tryouts, college brochures to look at, and girls to impress. I was still hustlin' for ways to put together some cash for college.

Next thing I know, we were back from Christmas vacation before I realized I hadn't even thought to send Binky a card, let alone go out to visit. So much was happenin' though, so fast. I felt like my entire future was at stake.

Toward the end of January, I was accepted at Towson State. Now I really had to scramble. Last time I looked, there wasn't no money tree growin' in my backyard.

By February, I was workin' in a supermarket six days a week. I would come home from school on Wednesdays, my only day off, and collapse on my bed. The last thing I needed, one Wednesday in March, was my mother tellin' me that Lucille Hernandez had left a message to call her at the home.

I was sure old Binky had put her up to it. I had sort of enjoyed listenin' to him, but I didn't have time for any more strolls down memory lane. I made the phone call, rehearsin' in my mind how I would tell Lucille 'no can do'.

"Robbie, this is concerning Mr. Lowens, the man you interviewed last October."

I jumped right in before she could get up a head of steam. "Yeah, Lucille, tell him I says 'hi', but I'm workin' now, and I don't think I can—"

"Robbie," she interrupted, "Mr. Lowens died peacefully in his sleep last night."

While part of me was bein' mature and grownup and sayin', "I'm very sorry," to Lucille, another part of me felt sort of ashamed of myself.

"He left a shoebox with some baseball stuff he wanted you to have," she said, her voice weakening with each word, "and a letter he wrote you last week."

That's all I needed to hear. Why couldn't the old guy just have forgotten about it? *I'd* done a pretty good job of it. I knew goin' back there would be the mother of all guilt trips. "Could you mail those things to me, Lucille?"

"I can't, Robbie. It's against regulations. I'm not even allowed to take them out of his room, and there *is* a waiting list to get in here. Please come today or tomorrow, if at all possible."

Half an hour later, Lucille and I were standing in Binky's room. "He was a resident here nine years," she said, with a touch of fondness.

I looked around. This is what it had come down to for Binky. It was a pleasant enough environment, but I couldn't escape the feeling that the man had been under house arrest for the crime of living too long. One thing caught my eye, though, a five-by-seven framed picture on the dresser of the 1924 Senators.

It reminded me that there were times when I fancied that Binky and I were playin' at fiction; him tellin' it, and me writin' it. It seemed unreal even now, seein' that picture. Lucille handed me the letter.

"He wanted you to read it here."

My face must of give me away again. "It's okay," she said, "I already know what's in it. I had to write it for him. His arthritis was so bad of late, he couldn't even hold a fork or spoon. He told me last week that he thought his time might be coming to answer . . ." She struggled for his exact words.

"Answer the clarion's call?"

"That's it. He said he wasn't in any pain, he just felt like he was . . .fading away."

I opened the letter and started reading, while Lucille, who had produced a shoebox from one of the dresser drawers, sat quietly on the bed.

Dear Robbie:

I'm sorry we didn't get to see each other again. I thought of a few more stories you might have found interesting. By the way, Lucille is writing this for me 'cause of my arthritis. I don't want you thinking I have girly handwriting.

By the time you read this, I'll have answered the clarion's call. Don't feel bad. How many guys can say they were on a World Series winner? Right now, I'm probably beating the pants off you-know-who in a home run contest. Stop reading now, and look in the box.

I looked up, and Lucille handed me the box, right on cue. Inside were a couple dozen old photographs and one decrepit baseball. The photos were of old-time ballplayers and stadiums. They had that brownish-red tint, and were in pretty bad shape. A few of them cracked when I uncurled them, and what writing had been on the backs was impossible to read.

There was a larger photo beneath the others. It looked professionally done, and had been well-preserved in a clear plastic sleeve. It was Babe Ruth, in his Yankee uniform, holding a bat on his shoulder. What was *this* doin' in here, I asked myself. Binky *despised* the man. I turned it over. A date on the bottom read, "Sept. 11, 1924." I remembered from Binky's stories that was when the Senators and Yankees were fightin' it out for the pennant.

Even more surprising was what had been written above the date: "To Binky, best wishes—in second place. Babe Ruth." I still didn't get it. Why would Binky accept *any* autographed picture from Babe Ruth, let alone one with an insult on it?

I stuck it back at the bottom and picked up the ball. It was in the same sad shape as the snapshots. It was fading, and the stitching starting to come undone in places. There was writing across the side facing me, and although it had faded, I could still read the indentations on the horsehide cover. It said, "7th game, 1924 World Series, last out."

"Oh my God," I said aloud. "It's the same ball. . . " I looked over at Lucille. She nodded and wore a tender smile, but the tears in her eyes were demandin' equal time. She pointed at the letter, indicating it was all right to read again. I picked it up and continued.

Not bad huh? I never cared at all for Babe Ruth, but I always figured an autographed picture of him would be worth something someday, so I got him to give me one on that last trip to New York in 1924. He never missed a chance to take a dig at me and the Senators, arrogant windbag that he was. I never got around to sellin' it, but if you take it to one of them card shows, you might be surprised how much it's worth these days. It could help you get a good start on your college fund. The other photos in there are ones I took. They probably aren't worth anything, though. Speaking of pictures, you can have the Senators team picture on my dresser. I'm third from the left, top row.

I took a quick peek. It was the same odd-looking face, with those deep-set eyes, hook nose, and ears that stuck out a bit. Like somebody had let life's film run backward for seventy years. I had that funny tightness in my chest again, but I found my place and kept reading.

The ball is the one Bucky Harris threw to me for the final out of the World Series. For the record, I did drop the damn thing, like Hal Blythe said. Harris threw it as he was fallin', and it dipped as I caught it, just as Blythe and his dust storm arrived. It squirted out, but somehow bounced right back to me. I'm almost sure Blythe himself kicked it back into my glove with the bottom of his shoe without ever knowing. No matter. Mel Symington yelled 'out' and we won.

Remember what I said, young man, when a thing's done, it's done. It wouldn't have served any purpose to tell what really happened. Blythe would have felt even worse, and I had nothing against him, at least not back then. Mel Symington would have been finished as an umpire. So I kept my mouth shut, and I kept my special moment that was all mine.

I've rambled on long enough. Lucille probably has more important things to do, like fussin' over guys like me. Have a good life, young man, and good luck. In the meantime, I hope Hal Blythe doesn't find me and go yellin' 'E—6!' at the top of his lungs.

Best Always,
Richard "Binky" Lowens

What can I tell you? I felt like I was gonna melt right there. I had been turnin' away from Lucille a bit as I read so's she couldn't see me startin' to lose it, which I was well on my way to doin'. I heard snifflin', though, so I didn't feel so self-conscious. She came up behind me and patted me on the back.

"We better go now," she said.

As we walked down the corridor, I had a lot to think about. Mrs. Adams had been right. I *did* have a different perspective on my own life now, and I *had* learned something valuable. The hard way, of course. The old guy had been thinkin' about me ever since I left. He'd done the best he could for me. I was wishin' I could say the same for myself.

Lucille held out the Senators team picture when we got back to her station. "You forgot this."

I winked. "You fuss over me too much, you know." She laughed, but I could tell she was still a bit weepy.

I opened the shoebox to stick the team picture in, and noticed that the ball had rolled around to its other side. There was new writing on it. In shaky, tortured-looking wobbly letters, it said, "To Robbie, from your friend Binky Lowens." Below that, in parenthesis, it said "E—6." His hands had hurt so badly he couldn't even hold a fork or spoon, but he had somehow managed to write his own goodbye on the World Series ball.

The photos and the ball were just objects, things anyone could own. The writing was a little piece of himself he gave just to me. The dam broke about then, and I waved over my shoulder at Lucille and ran out of there as fast as I could.

. . .

All that was a couple of weeks ago. I made a special scrapbook of the photos, even the damaged ones. My father put out some feelers on the Babe Ruth photo. He knows a lot of people who know a lot of people. A collector in Bethesda offered a thousand dollars, but he's up to eighteen hundred now. Dad found out that Ruth's autograph was worth about a thousand *at most,* but the *personalized* message to *another player* makes it worth a lot more to collectors.

"Sometimes," Dad said, "I think your friend Mr. Lowens knew a lot more than he let on."

I just smiled. "Dad, you'd be surprised."

The Senators team photo and World Series ball are on my dresser, the ball in a special round plastic case I got from a sports catalogue. I even called Lucille to explain why I ran out of there so fast that day. We agreed not to tell Binky's secret. When a thing's done, it's done, you know?

In my spare time I been lookin' up baseball info from the 1920's. I brought home a two volume set titled Baseball From 1890-1940. I was thumbin' through Vol. II today, and a picture on one of the pages made my hair stand on end. On one page heading, I read, 'Senators Win First Series.' Right beneath it, in the middle of the page, was that moment, frozen in time for anyone to see.

Hal Blythe is sliding into second, and above the huge dust cloud is my man Binky, waiting for the throw. The ball, the same ball on my dresser, is in mid-air. The caption beneath the picture says, "Binky Lowens takes throw from Stan Harris for final out of 1924 Series."

I must have stared at that frozen moment for hours. Not once did I ever let the play "finish." I prefer to leave them like that, with the ball in mid-air, all the bad feelings and second guessing gone. No E—6. Just a frozen moment that belongs to me, now.

It's almost funny. I went out to that home hopin' to connect more with my own people, and what did I get? An old *white* guy who'd outlived his own time period. And what's *he* do?

Trades his past for my future. Go figure.

"ALAMO ROSE"

One-hundred-eighty-eight men stood in three ragged lines, staring at the young Lt. Colonel, sword in hand, fifteen feet away. Behind them, in the dirt-packed courtyard, stood the unfinished chapel façade of the Spanish mission, San Antonio de Valero. The dress and weaponry of the garrison suggested a largely volunteer makeup, with perhaps thirty regular army troopers.

One man lay in a makeshift cot, coughing sporadically in the chill March air, his broken ribs taped with a crude bandage. The men were subdued, sensing the news would not be good.

"Men," said the officer, "the latest couriers from Goliad bring bad news. There will be no further reinforcements. My orders remain to hold this position for as long as possible." He paused and looked up and down the lines. "I estimate the enemy's strength at nearly four-thousand. I intend to fulfill my sworn duty as an officer, but any of you volunteers who wish to, may leave."

William Travis walked to one end of the assemblage, all eyes upon him. Sticking the tip of his sword in the sand, he walked to the far end of the garrison, the blade he dragged behind him creating a line in the dirt outside the chapel.

"Any man who wishes to leave may do so. If you choose to stay and fight, then cross this line and stand with me." He raised the sword skyward. "For God and Texas, gentlemen!"

The line bubbled in several places. The bubbles became a trickle, then a stream, and finally a river of humanity crossing the fifteen feet of open ground. In less than thirty seconds the garrison stood on the other side of the line.

One figure remained, stationary, as though he had been a boulder in the stream. He stood with his rifle butt on the ground, perhaps a touch of apology in his eyes.

At one end of the garrison stood the men of the First Tennessee Volunteers. As Travis walked over to the lone figure to confer, one of the Tennesseans, a tall, bony man in his late forties, tapped his lifelong friend and said, "What do you make of *that*, Davey?"

"Jacob, I always said everyone has to follow his own conscience. I think we're goin' down to the last man here, myself. Leastways now they'll be someone to bear witness to this, so's someday people can read about it, maybe learn from it."

"But Davey, *I* want to be around to read about it," said Jacob, a sense of urgency in his voice.

An unexpected smile broke on Davey's face, and he slapped his friend on the shoulder. "Jacob, you know you can't *read!*"

As darkness fell several hours later, Col. Travis stood at the north wall. Beside him stood Moses Rose, a Frenchman who had decided that this was not his time or place to die.

"You know where the Mexican patrols are likely to be," said Travis. "After that, just keep headin' northeast. You should make it."

"Sorry, Colonel," said Rose.

Travis took a long look at him, then turned and walked away.

"Moses Rose," came a voice from the shadows. A small, dark-skinned, intense man stepped into the moonlight, a few feet away.

Rose recognized the man's face, knew he was one of several Louisiana Cajuns who had ridden in with Jim Bowie.

They were a strange lot, thought Rose. Perhaps the man had come to help him scale the wall, although a tall red-haired Tennessee man had said he would meet Rose here to assist.

"You don't be goin' nowhere, Rose, till I tell you dis. My name Andre De La Croix." He moved closer and shook a finger in Rose's face. "Da spirits, dey gonna fix dis but good. I make sure of dat, you bet."

At first Rose had no idea what this odd half-Frenchman meant, then realized that the Cajun took offense to his leaving.

"What you doin', your people gonna pay. Der gonna be a kinsman of you gonna die in every war till dis is paid off. You hear?"

Rose stared at him, his eyes wide with surprise and fear. He had heard stories of Cajun spirits and curses through the years. He thought it best to say nothing to this strange, seething dark man.

"Only da spirits decide when it's paid, Rose. Until den, your kin's gonna pay!" At the sound of approaching footsteps, De La Croix allowed the shadows to swallow him again.

A tall red-haired man ambled to the wall. "Here," he said, "I brought you some extra clothes," and handed Rose a grimy bundle. In an instant, he had squatted and cupped his hands. As Rose inserted one foot into the fleshy receptacle, he was catapulted into the air, where he grabbed hold of and straddled the low wall. He looked down at the ruddy, thoughtful face.

"Good luck, Mr. Rose. No hard feelings," he called up.

"Thanks, Meester . . ."

"Crockett," said the man. Rose slipped over the wall as his ally shook his head. "Poor fool's likely to get hisself killed tryin' this." He trudged off toward the Long Barracks.

Moonlight once again sliced across the face of Andre De La Croix. He rushed to the wall, knowing Rose was still within earshot. "One in every war, Rose, you hear me, till it's paid." His face brightened with a new possibility. "Hey Rose, maybe it *never* gets paid!"

New Braunfels, Texas, 1964

George Hiram Rose, having worked up his courage, sat nervously in his mother's Boston rocker, looking across the small living room at her and his uncle Elvin.

"I made up my mind to enlist come graduation." He closely monitored their reaction. His mother was startled, her face assuming that sorrowful, pleading look she had perfected. Uncle Elvin looked grim, yet proud, too. George knew his uncle cherished the memory of his older brother Ralph, killed in action in WWII while his mother was pregnant with George.

"Please, George, don't do this," his mother began. She began all her pleadings with him the same way. Whether it involved staying out an extra hour, or joining the army. Same reaction.

"Beatrice, I think it's time to tell him," said his uncle.

"Tell me what?" asked George, suspecting some standard adult response that parents and their conspirators kept ready.

"George, you know your mother don't want you in the army, 'specially now that all these troops are getting' shipped over to that Vietnam place."

"Uncle El, I—"

"Just hear me out, George. You know I always treated you like my own son."

"Uncle El, I ain't lookin' to die like my father did. I wanna get an education after high school, maybe go to college someday. Nobody in this family has ever done that."

"George," his mother interrupted, "can't you just—"

"No, Mom. I can't just go to college the way things are. We been over this. My grades aren't good enough. I want to be a *soldier* like my father was, and get an education, which he didn't get to do. I'm eighteen now, so I can do it on my own if I have to. All I ever heard, growin' up, was that a Rose fought in every war, a Rose never backed down from a fight."

"George, what your mom and I told you all these years was so's you'd be proud of your daddy and what he done. I guess maybe we should've told you the whole story." He looked over at his sister-in-law, his eyes seeming to ask her permission. In a gesture resembling resignation, she extended her hand toward him, palm up. Elvin looked at George and inhaled deeply.

"Back in 1836, one of your great-great-great grandfathers, Moses Rose, was part of the garrison at the Alamo."

George's eyes lit up. "One of *my* ancestors fought at the *Alamo?*"

"No, he didn't *fight.*" Uncle Elvin had gone back to looking grim. "When the men there were given the choice to stay or leave, he chose to leave. He was the only one who did."

George looked embarrassed and slightly annoyed. "What's that got to do with—"

"I'm getting' to that part, George. Just give a good listen. When Moses was leavin', some Indian or Cajun or somethin' put a curse on his kin. Said a Rose would die in every war from then on 'cause of what *he* was doin'."

"This can't be true, Uncle El," said George cautiously. He had heard stories of Cajun spirits and curses through the years.

Elvin held up one finger. "Count with me, George. Moses's younger brother Luke was killed in the Mexican War in

1848." A second finger uncurled. "Moses's son Jedadiah fell at Gettysburg in 1863." Elvin raised three fingers now, looking like the world's oldest boy scout. "Samuel Rose died at San Juan Hill in 1898." All four fingers went up. "Your grandfather's brother Charles was killed at Belleau Wood with the Marines in World War I." The hand was open now. "Your father died in the Battle of the Bulge, 1944." The index finger of his other hand joined the open hand. "And when you were young, maybe you remember, my cousin Joey died in Korea."

He paused, and moved the extended fingers closer to his nephew. "Six wars, George, and six dead from our family. We're cursed, George, that's all there is to it."

Beatrice held one hand over her mouth, quivering. With each name in the litany, she had lost more of her composure, until the mention of her husband had broken her. She sobbed quietly.

Elvin stood, moved closer to George. "Do you really want to fly in the face of this thing, George? You still want to enlist?"

George now stood, and looked his uncle in the eye. "My father didn't back down, and I won't either." He struggled with the wording of an important thought, and held up his own index finger. *"One* Moses in the family is enough."

. . .

George Rose unpacked an old suitcase containing a week's worth of clean clothes and stuffed them into various drawers in his single room at the Independence Motel, across the street and a hundred yards south of the Alamo.

It had taken several heated discussions, but he finally convinced his mother to let him go, and his uncle to let him go alone. He had a credit card and enough money he'd saved to last a week, provided he didn't squander it. All bases were covered, he thought. School was off for winter break, this third week of February, and his '59 Chevy was dependable transportation for the forty-five minute drive.

If he persisted, he could usually get his mother to go along with any grownup adventure he proposed. After all, he *was* the man of the family.

He had told her and his uncle he wanted to get away by himself and think, and visit the Alamo, where his ancestor Moses Rose had made a different sort of stand. He didn't think his mother knew why he was really here, but there was a look in Uncle Elvin's eyes that led him to believe that *he* did.

After checking in and unpacking, George had spent over two hours in and around the Alamo shrine, requesting information on legends or curses associated with the landmark. The friendly women inside the chapel had no such knowledge, but referred him to a separate library facility nearby. George was not the library or research type, and held off on that strategy as a last resort.

Instead, he took to asking people in the vicinity, as long as they seemed to be natives, rather than tourists. Most were friendly, but one or two walked away quickly. He bought a noon snack from a street vendor, and asked the short, rotund man for information.

"What you wanna know?" he asked.

"Would you know any legends or curses having to do with the Alamo?" George asked hopefully.

The vendor thought a moment, seeming to search through files of street information. "There was an old Mexican man called El Viejo. I haven't seen him for over a year now, but he would know about that kind of thing. He lived over on Mesa Verde."

"El Viejo?" George took out a pen and notepad he carried on this quest and wrote down the name and street.

"You write ghost stories or somethin'?"

"No, it's . . . for school."

The vendor displayed a calculating smile. "The Alamo's haunted, you know."

"What?"

"That's right. People seen a lot of strange things through the years. So I heard, anyways. You figure, all those guys that died the way they did. The Mexicans were brutal. You die like that, your ghost maybe don't rest so easy. A lot of other stuff, too."

"Like what?" asked George, hoping to open some avenue of discovery.

"People hear things there late at night." He laughed. "Am I scarin' you, kid. You don't look so good."

"No," replied George. "I just have to find out stuff about curses . . . for school."

"I don't know nothin' firsthand, but I remember El Viejo used to tell a story to all the little Mexican kids about a man called El Cobarde."

"Who's El Cobarde?" asked George, scribbling the name on his notepad.

"The one who ran away. Maybe El Viejo can conjure up his spirit for you. He used to claim he could do that stuff. You probably don't know this, but there was one guy at the Alamo who escaped before the actual—Hey! Where you goin'?"

George had heard enough. He sprinted up the street to the motel garage where his car was parked.

The vendor watched him running away, looking like a one-man urban track meet. He smiled, secretly pleased at the reaction. "I guess I *did* scare him."

. . .

George turned his Chevy right onto Mesa Verde. He was appalled. House after house was in disrepair, with paint peeling, and yards overgrown with weeds, rusted cars, and broken toys. Here and there Mexican children yelled and chased each other. Old tires, beer bottles, food wrappers and dog crap were scattered over the remains of what had once been sidewalks.

George drove the entire length of the street and doubled back before realizing he had no idea who he was looking for. There would be no mailbox with the name 'El Viejo' neatly lettered on it. He saw three young men standing in a yard, talking. They appeared to be slightly older than he. One wore black leather, the other two had tee shirts with the sleeves cut off, despite the weather. It had been so cold out this winter that much of the year-round flora had long since died.

George cut the engine, got out, and walked over to them. He took out his pad and pen, hoping to look like he was on official business. He approached tentatively, and couldn't help but notice the mistrust and contempt on the three faces. They all seemed to gradually assume a semi-crouching position, as it poised to spring on him.

"What you want, Anglo?" said the man in leather. "This ain't your turf." He moved a half-stride closer.

George measured each word, trying to sound official, yet non-threatening. "I was looking for a man known as El Viejo. I was told he lived on this street."

The two wearing tee shirts laughed, but the man in black leather squinted even more dislike from his eyes. "That's my grandfather, Anglo. What you want with him? He's an old man. He's sick."

"It's about a curse. There was a man called . . ." George looked down at his notepad to get the Spanish name correct. A hand shot into his vision and slapped it to the ground. The man in leather was now standing next to him. George was several inches taller, and twenty pounds heavier, but a genuine fear arose in him. The two men in tee shirts no longer appeared to be enjoying this, either.

"Where you getting' all this stuff, Anglo? You don't come around here askin' questions like that."

George fumbled for an answer, found none, and was planning to start over when he noticed one of the other men pacing by the side of his car.

"Hey Carlos, check out these wheels," he said.

The man in the leather jacket looked at the car, smiled, and then winked at his companions. "Tell you what," he said to George, "the going rate for an Anglo to see my grandfather is twenty dollars. But for you, I'll make it forty." Three sets of laughter followed.

George, dismayed but determined, reached into his pocket, pulling out the cash he had thought to carry with him, grateful now he had left most of it at the motel. He counted out forty dollars, and handed it over. As he stared mournfully at the five-dollar-bill that remained, a hand once again shot into his vision and snatched it away.

George looked up to see Carlos holding the bill in two fingers, his eyebrows dancing up and down for the amusement of his companions, who had apparently regained their sense of humor.

"You said *forty,*" George stated, with more indignation than he realized.

Carlos smiled. "It's customary around here to give a tip, for . . . services rendered." There was more laughter. "You guys wait here and keep an eye on Anglo's car." The eyebrows danced again. "I hear this is a bad neighborhood." Still more laughter.

Carlos pointed to the adjacent house. "Right over here." He reached down and picked up George's notepad. "Hey Anglo, you don't want to forget this."

George made an angry grab for it, but Carlos quickly put it behind his back, then offered it to George again, a warning look on his face. George reached for it calmly this time, Carlos handing it to him with exaggerated courtesy.

They crossed the yard to the house next door and entered. The smell inside was a new one to George, but he sensed what it was. Beneath the household odors of stale air, moldy furnishings, and Spanish cooking, was the unmistakable smell of squalor.

Carlos shooed away a little boy and girl who were staring at George as they entered the kitchen. They ran into another room, talking excitedly in Spanish. George distinctly heard the word 'Anglo' in their babbling.

Carlos knocked on the door of a room off to one side of the kitchen and entered, motioning George to follow. The room was dark, and offered George a new smell that he subconsciously identified. It was the smell of sickness. Carlos's grandfather lay propped on a small bed. A candle on a nearby bureau was the only light. George could hardly see him, and could tell only that he was very old, and wrinkled beyond what one would believe a human face could endure, and still *be* a face.

Carlos spoke very softly to him in Spanish, George noticing that all the young man's bravado and toughness had evaporated.

"What you want me to ask him? He doesn't speak no English," Carlos whispered.

"Ask him about the curse on the man who left the Alamo. Is there any way to get rid of it?"

Carlos leaned to his grandfather's ear and whispered. George watched closely, but could see no reaction on the man's face. He answered Carlos in a high, shaking voice. The only word George recognized was 'El Cobarde'. The old man continued talking for a full minute before drawing several deep breaths. The speech seemed to have exhausted him.

Carlos turned to George. "When my grandfather was a little boy," he began, *his* grandfather told him of an old Caddo Indian he knew when *he* was little. He spoke of a curse on El Cobarde, the one who ran away. The curse would last until many of the coward's family had paid with their lives."

George inwardly bristled at the word 'coward', and wondered if six could be considered 'many'.

"Can it be lifted?" he whispered.

"He said it could, but the spirits would have to be summoned to give a sign. It would be dangerous for him. The Evil Ones are strong, and he is weak."

"Ask him if he'll do it."

Once again a hand shot out. Carlos grabbed George by his shirt collar and pushed him out into the kitchen. It was the fiercest look George could remember ever having seen. "Who the hell you think you are, asking an *old man* to mess with the spirits?"

"Carlito!" came a weak cry from the next room.

Carlos thrust George aside and hurried back into the bedroom. What George heard this time sounded more like an argument.

"*No,* mi abuelo," shouted Carlos. The old man talked for a half minute, but George couldn't make out any words.

Carlos returned to the kitchen, and glared at George with an intensity that made the previous glares seem like warm-up exercises. "He said he doesn't have long. He wants to do one more good deed for God to see. He thinks you are a distant son of El Cobarde."

"I am," replied George.

"He needs time to make himself worthy and pray to his protector spirits. He says you are to leave now. I will come get you when it is time. Where can I find you?"

"The Independence Motel." As George turned to leave, Carlos grabbed his arm, stopping him. With his other hand he reached into his pocket and waved the money at George.

"This is to buy him medicine. You understand?"

George looked down, embarrassed, and nodded.

Carlos sneered. "You don't understand *nothin'*, Anglo."

George lay on the bed in his motel room that evening, and thought about the six men named Rose who had died on battlefields in six countries and six wars. Would he be the unlucky seventh? If his grandfather had done what *he* was doing now, would his father have been alive today?

He was tempted to call his mom or uncle Elvin to tell them about these strange happenings, but resisted the urge. He had never had any opportunities to make his father proud of him, but he sensed that this could well cover all of it. Dad had faced the German panzers like a man. He was not about to call Mommy over being roughed up and shaken down by some Mexican tough guy.

He flipped on the TV and watched, waiting for something to happen, all the while thinking of the six men who had died because of the curse. By eleven P. M. he was asleep. His dreams were punctuated by battle scenes, from musket fire in Mexico City, to machine gun bursts across the frozen wastes of Korea. At intervals in the dream he could see a lone soldier standing in front of him, ragged and bleeding. One of them, a WWII G. I., spoke. "Put paid to it, George." He awakened at that point, uneasy. The clock read 4:19 A. M. Carlos had not come.

He spent the entire day in the room, a virtual prisoner. How long could it take El Viejo to prepare himself for the confrontation with the evil spirits? Or had Carlos taken it upon himself not to show up? No, he reassured himself, Carlos would do whatever the old man asked.

From lack of sleep and rest he drifted off during the late afternoon. The tumultuous battle scenes raged again, and a Civil War soldier who looked like his father appeared to him. "Put paid to it, George," he said.

By dinnertime, George felt like an addict quitting cold turkey. He paced, he counted his money, he looked for Roses in the San Antonio phone book. There were none. Shortly after eight, the phone rang.

"Mr. Rose, this is the front desk. There is a man named Carlos Gonzalez to see you."

George hopped the elevator down to the lobby, and found Carlos sitting in a large chair in the corner, looking restless and out of his element. George sat next to him.

"He's ready, Anglo. You drive out to the house at midnight."

"Why so late?"

"The spirits are not active until the Hour of the Dead. Midnight to one." He leaned close. The voice took on the familiar threatening tone. "This is serious business, Anglo, and dangerous. The price is one-hundred dollars. For services rendered."

George nearly gasped. He didn't think he had that much left. He reached into his pocket, removing all his remaining cash, as well as his charge card.

"We don't accept credit cards, Anglo," Carlos said with a mischievous grin. George gave a polite laugh, then swallowed it.

He counted out the money. It came to eighty dollars. Carlos looked at it, appeared to be in deep thought. He smiled a false smile and put one hand on George's shoulder, the other hand possessing the cash.

"No problem, Anglo. You can owe me."

George, grateful for the credit, said, "Need a ride back?"

Carlos looked at him with contempt and pity. "It's early, Anglo. You think I wanna' be seen in public with *you?*"

. . .

George pulled the massive Chevy to the curb of 127 Mesa Verde. This day seemed so unreal to him. Twenty minutes earlier, he had packed his things and used the credit card to pay his motel bill. But his "day" so to speak, was just beginning.

A miniature reddish-orange beacon marked the porch where Carlos sat waiting, smoking.

"Inside, Anglo, hurry up," said Carlos nervously, tossing the cigarette away. "I have sent my mother and the little ones to a friend's tonight." When they were in the kitchen, he waved a menacing finger in George's face. "Nothin' better happen to him. Get in there."

George entered the sickroom. It was ablaze with the light of dozens of candles, arranged in various patterns and groups ranging from three to nearly a dozen.

Carlos leaned over and exchanged words with the old man, helping him to sit upright in bed. George could see the face better, now. There seemed to be a thousand creases in it. El Viejo had the look of a proud, but nervous combatant.

"Take his hand, Anglo," Carlos said to him. George moved forward and took the old man's right hand in his own. The creases George could feel were in harmony with the ones on the face. There was another sensation, an odd, seemingly *electric* one. The old man released his grip and nodded to Carlos.

"Okay, Anglo, we have to wait outside, now." They left the room and sat at the kitchen table. George was too nervous to attempt conversation. Carlos sat facing away from him, looking at the closed bedroom door.

From the bedroom, they could hear the old man's voice. It sounded strong, a warrior's voice. It had the rhythm and tempo of an incantation. Within minutes, though, the words came in sporadic gasps, the force gone. Carlos sat upright, his eyes wide.

"What's going on?" George asked.

"The Evil Ones have answered him."

"What did they say?"

"Only *he* can hear them. Shut your face!"

The voice from the bedroom now rose. There was pain and pleading in it now. Carlos shot from the chair, hands clenched at his sides. The pleading turned to sobs, followed by a long, agonizing scream.

Carlos reached for the door, motioning George to follow. Inside they found the old man lying on his back. His breathing was uneven. Most of the candles were out. Carlos took both his hands and murmured to him in soft tones, but there was a hint of panic in his voice. After nearly five minutes, the old man somehow found the strength to speak a few short, gasping sentences to his grandson.

Carlos looked back at George. "It is done, he says. Go to the place before the Hour of the Dead is past. You will find a sign that the curse has been lifted." He smiled slightly. *"If* the spirits have decided to keep their word."

George panicked. "What do you mean *'if'*?"

"Hey Anglo, what can I tell you? They're evil."

A hand floated out of the darkness and pulled Carlos nearly onto the bed. El Viejo's eyes were open wide in terror, he gasped acutely for breath, pulling Carlos down next to him, whispering to him in what seemed pure desperation.

"No, abuelo!" Carlos shouted.

"Si`, tiene que`" came the forceful reply. Then, as though reacting to an electric shock, he jolted himself upright in the bed, looking at the far wall. His face showed both fear and defiance. "Me buscan, y si me hallan, me moton!" he shrieked. He still held Carlos in a death grip.

Suddenly, he sagged and dropped back onto the bed, as though whatever energy source he possessed had been unplugged. The hand fell away, the entire wasted body relaxed.

George moved closer, and saw his first real glimpse of death. El Viejo's eyes were open, as was his mouth, a look of unbelieving terror showing. He touched Carlos's arm gently. "I'm sorry, Carlos. Is there anything—"

The quick hand again. This time it had the front of his jacket, and forced him down. "I should kill you right now, Anglo. Only one thing is stopping me."

George attempted to ask 'what', but found himself unable to manage even that one syllable.

"He said I was to make sure you came to no harm." Both honor and hatred shared equal space in Carlos's expression. "I will drive you to the Alamo now."

Again, George tried to utter a one-syllable word, 'why', but could not get it to surface. Carlos seemed to have read his thought, however.

"Why? Because, Anglo, *you* don't have a car anymore. I told you, nothing better happen to him." His voice shook with anger and sorrow. "I lose a grandfather, Anglo, you lose a car."

Under any other conditions, barring gunpoint, George told himself, he would never agree to something as outrageous as this. But in the wake of what he had just witnessed, all bets were off. He looked down at the old man's lifeless body. "What about—"

"What do you care, Anglo?" came the hate-filled reply. "You got what you wanted."

As Carlos drove the Chevy down Mesa Verde, George took out his notepad, and as Carlos had demanded, wrote, "Paid to Carlos Gonzalez, one green 1959 Chevrolet, for services rendered." He handed him the paper, and as quickly as it was taken from his hand, his watch slid off his wrist and into the pocket of Carlos's jacket.

Carlos turned to his open-mouthed, stunned passenger. "Remember, Anglo, the hundred-dollar fee? You came up a little short."

At 12:45 they pulled up in front of the brightly-lit Alamo chapel. Carlos turned to George, his new-found wealth having done nothing to soften him. "Get out, now. If I ever see your Anglo face again, I will forget my promise to my grandfather." George opened the door, letting in a draft of the bitter cold February air.

"Vaya con Dios," Carlos said mechanically. George recognized the words as a Spanish blessing, and looked back, hoping to see in Carlos a last minute change of heart. The face showed all of its original contempt.

"*That* was from my grandfather. You're getting' my car cold. Shut the door, Anglo."

George closed the door, and the green Chevy with its new owner slid off into the night. He stood mesmerized, watching the large fin-shaped taillights fade away, suddenly remembering his suitcase still in the trunk. No matter now. He snapped back to the reality, or unreality, of why he was here. His sole purpose now was to find the sign that the curse had been lifted . . .*if* the Evil Ones had kept their word.

He paced every inch of the front courtyard and Long Barracks and found nothing. One look at the barred windows on both floors of the chapel told George that the building had a state-of-the-art security system. He didn't think the sign would be inside, at any rate. That left the courtyard behind the chapel.

He followed the sidewalk, and went around back. The larger courtyard was also brightly lit with floodlights, adding to the surrealistic atmosphere.

As George was telling himself that this was probably his last chance, he realized that he was looking at an Indian, standing just off the sidewalk by some shrubbery, about seventy-five feet away. He appeared to be middle-aged, wearing a blue denim shirt and matching pants, and a small, round, brown hat. He stood facing George, motionless.

His pulse skyrocketed. There could be only one reason an Indian was waiting behind the Alamo at this hour. As George walked nervously toward him, he sensed something wrong with his vision. The Indian seemed to be less defined, while everything else remained clear.

"I don't like this," he said aloud, and walked faster. The Indian remained motionless and expressionless, and faded a bit more as George approached. "God, no, this *can't* be happening." George could hear his voice echoing. The Indian was semi-transparent now, and George's panic was evident by his double-time pace. As he closed to within twenty feet, he could barely see the figure's outline, but *could* see bushes *behind* the Indian that should have been blocked from his view.

"No! Wait!" George screamed. He sprinted the remaining distance, his arms instinctively reaching out. The Indian evaporated, like some cinema special effect. George's momentum carried him to where he had been standing, pawing the air in desperation.

He wanted to scream in rage and frustration, but held back, a tiny measure of self-control remaining. Frantically, he looked around, above his head, and at the back of the chapel for any possible sign. There was nothing. An agony of sobs heaving in his chest, he fell to his knees on the grass and pounded the cold earth.

It was from that position that he saw it. A thing he had seen a thousand times before in other places. A thing which had no earthly business here now, not during the coldest winter on record in years.

It was a small bush. Growing from it were six of the most exquisite roses he had ever seen, of the brightest blood-red imaginable.

With unbelieving eyes, every pore tingling, he crawled forward to smell and feel their substance. He grabbed the bush and put his face to the nearest flower. There was a sharp, stinging sensation in his right index finger as a thorn pierced him. Pulling his hand back, he watched the blood well up and drip down his finger. A malevolent, teasing laugh sounded above and behind him.

He spun around and jumped to his feet, expecting to find a security guard or police officer. There was no one. The laughter pealed again, an hysterical, malicious tone to it. There was a faint echo in the sound quality. Evil spirits, he thought, suddenly remembering the street vendor's claim that people heard things here late at night.

What were they laughing at, he wondered. His bloody finger? The price they had extracted from El Viejo? Or had they decided to play another trick on the living, fooling him into thinking the curse was broken? Only his enlistment in the army would be the true test.

He knelt and looked again at the bush. Six roses. One for each of his family who had paid for the flight of his great-great-great grandfather, Moses Rose, "El Cobarde." He took a last look at the red monuments, deciding it was only right to leave them here. His blood was on the thorn as well, and now began to trickle down the stem.

"Paid, Dad," he whispered. "It's all paid, now."

. . .

The streets of San Antonio are still. In the chill winter evening, a young man steals away from the back of the Alamo, heading northeast on his flight to safety, much like another on a winter night one-hundred-twenty-eight years earlier.

Those who know of such things say that the Alamo is a place of restless spirit activity, rife with the constant motion of those who died before their time. On this night, however, the ghostly garrison stands at ease.

"BELOVED DAUGHTER"

A cemetery is a history of people—a perpetual record of yesterday and a sanctuary of peace and quiet today. A cemetery exists because every life is worth loving and remembering.

I've read those words every day for the past forty-one years, since I was twenty. They hang over my desk here at Three Maples Cemetery, where I've been head caretaker for thirty of those years. I'm retiring in a few days.

We've always been a cemetery family. My father, Carl Goddard Sr., was head man here before me, and I came to work for him fresh out of the army. My wife Doreen is secretary here, and my son Blaine the senior member of my three man crew. He's out on the grounds now with Lenny and Tim, making my final days here easier.

I have some time now to reflect on what has happened the past eight months. I ask myself if I would have done anything differently during that time, and was I true to myself. One thought keeps coming back to me: 'An eye for an eye.'

. . .

Last year, around Labor Day, I was in the office, going over billing invoices, when a beat-up, red Honda Civic pulled into the small parking area by the gates. An odd-looking man entered the office. He was in his late forties, it seemed, with shaggy, thinning hair, and unkempt clothes. His eyes had a quiet fury in them.

"Could you help me sir?" he said softly. "I was looking for Joyce Beaudoin's grave."

He couldn't have shocked me more if he'd stripped down to his underwear. But you acquire control when you've been witness to as many funerals as I have. "Bear right at the flagpole, take a left, then a quick right. It's there on that small connecting road, next to the big marker that says 'Stanton Pyne'." He thanked me, and left.

I shot a quick look at my wife to see if she had noticed my reaction. She had her back to me, typing grave registration forms. I tried to sound casual. "That's the only person I remember ever looking for the Beaudoin girl's grave."

Doreen turned from the typewriter. "Beaudoin, that sounds familiar. Wasn't she the one that was kidnapped and murdered years ago?"

"Twenty-one years ago," I said, worried that I had answered too quickly and precisely. Doreen shrugged and went back to her typing.

On February 8, 1972, after leaving friends at a pizza place around 8:00 P. M., Joyce Beaudoin cut across a parking lot on her way home. She never made it. They found her half-frozen body on a doorstep twenty-five miles away the next morning. She had been stabbed and sexually assaulted.

A few days later, police arrested George Pascale, a local hard-core mental misfit and drug user, and charged him in the killing of the fifteen-year-old. The evidence against him mounted, and finally he admitted snatching her, but didn't remember anything else. He said he was sorry. He got twenty-five to life. Case closed.

The Beaudoin family was a fragile unit, and fell apart after that. Mr. Beaudoin had run off years before, and Joyce's older sister stuck around just long enough to graduate and join the army. Nancy Beaudoin, the girl's mother, stayed for a while, then moved away.

We were well-acquainted, Nancy and I. How well? Joyce was *my* daughter, not Vincent Beaudoin's, that's how well.

I met Nancy Terreau when we attended high school here. We were young and passionate, as they say. By Christmas of our senior year we were engaged, and by graduation night she was three months pregnant.

I did the honorable thing and married her the next week. Both families were outraged and ashamed, said it couldn't possibly last. It didn't. By the end of that summer we were divorced, and I headed off for the army to clear my head and get away from everyone and everything. Nancy gave birth to Joyce that December, and lived with her parents. By the time I got out of the army and started working for my dad at Three Maples, Nancy had married Vincent Beaudoin, who adopted Joyce.

I don't know if they ever told her anything about me, but I sincerely doubt it. It had not been a pleasant parting between us.

I eventually met Doreen and fell in love again. Real love this time. Dad, recognizing this, hired her as secretary at Three Maples. We were married shortly after.

Things didn't work out so well for Nancy, I heard. Vincent walked out on her a few times, then left for good when Joyce was four, leaving Nancy with her and his daughter from a previous marriage. Our disastrous union was a dark family secret that I chose never to share with Doreen.

It wasn't easy for me, knowing I had a daughter in whose life I would have no part, but I couldn't risk losing what I had. Can you possibly imagine the grief I had to suppress when I read of her horrible death; the effort it took to supervise the digging of her grave, and watch the funeral from a distance on that bitter February day, trying to keep control in front of my crew, and my wife? No, I don't think you can.

I had to bury my grief with her. It poisoned me, I'm sure now. Over the years I found myself vowing revenge on the monster that did this.

On many occasions, when no one was around, I would walk or ride out to that grave, so small and insignificant next to the huge marker for Stanton Pyne, who had been football coach here for forty-five years. All that marked Joyce's very existence in this life was a small, pathetic stone which read, "Beloved Daughter." And beneath that: "Joyce Beaudoin, 1957-1972."

Then came the day that man asked directions to her gravesite. I was sure it was George Pascale, that after twenty-one years the state of Massachusetts had decided he had paid his debt to society. As far as I was concerned, though, he hadn't paid his debt to Joyce. She was *still* dead. An eye for an eye.

Two agendas began taking shape in my mind. First, I had to verify that it was him. Twenty-one years is a long time. Faces change, and the only pictures I'd seen of him were in newspapers. Second, I had to plan how I would put the matter to rest.

I jumped into one of our turf trucksters; small, three-wheeled vehicles with a flatbed for carrying tools, and designed not to mark up the grass. I headed out to Joyce's grave on a "recon" mission. He was already parked there, kneeling by the stone, mumbling under his breath.

How ironic, really. The only visitor to that forgotten grave in years was the person who had caused her to *be* there, instead of carrying on the life she was entitled to.

I parked across from his red Honda, and the car between us, looked inside. I don't know why. Did I expect to see his name written on the dashboard in bright, bold letters? What I *did* see was his mail, scattered across the passenger seat. There, in plain view, was a typed envelope bearing the address: "George R. Pascale, 75 Barry Road, Pittsfield, Massachusetts." It was from the Department of Corrections. I could have told them to save their postage. *I* would take care of whatever *correcting* needed to be done.

An engine sounded behind me. I whirled around to find my son and Lenny in our two-ton all-purpose truck. Blaine leaned out the passenger side window, wearing his familiar St. Louis Cardinals cap. "Dad, Timmy went home sick. Want to help us trim some bushes up by Section'K'?"

Trying to look nonchalant, I agreed. I hoped they hadn't seen me snooping by Pascale's car. I took a look in his direction. He seemed oblivious to us, still kneeling by the grave, his forehead resting in his hands.

Blaine asked in a low voice, "Who's *he?*"

"I think it's one of Stanton Pyne's ex-players come to pay his respects."

They looked at each other in disbelief, then Lenny burst out laughing. Neither of them mentioned anything else about it, though, so I followed them out to Section 'K'.

Blaine and Lenny pruned away happily, partially because they had a third hand, but mostly because they were rid of Tim, with whom they were feuding. They had passed the arguing stage, and were well into daily practical jokes.

Tim would hide Lenny's car keys, so Blaine would open Tim's locker and put thorn bush debris in his pants pockets. Then Tim would put huge branches on Blaine's car, and Lenny would steal Tim's lunch pail. I stayed out of it. They did their work and didn't cause any real harm. Besides, I had my own little prank I was planning. I was going to take something of George Pascale's, and hide it where he'd never get it back. His *life,* in a five-foot-deep hole.

I never thought I would actually get the opportunity to avenge Joyce's murder. But I had talked it over with myself on many a peaceful day up at Three Maples, as I walked calmly among its 9,300 residents. I had decided that if I ever got the chance, I would kill George Pascale, and if they caught me, so be it. Maybe going to prison would square me with The Man Upstairs for my own wrongdoings.

I was lucky. I wasn't going to have to go after Pascale. He would come to me. In his burnt out, scrambled egg mind, he needed repentance. He visited the grave every Saturday. By the end of September, I had a fix on his habits and patterns.

With a sense of exhilaration, I began to plan how I would do it. Whenever he drove in, I would put on my coveralls and get in one of the turf trucksters. I took my trusty hand clippers, with a hammer or wrench for backup.

Here's where it got tight, though. I didn't want to be seen, so I would abort the plan if there was anyone anywhere nearby. Saturday is a busy visiting day at Three Maples. It could take weeks or months worth of Saturdays before the window of opportunity was not being watched. An additional problem was the crew. They worked half days on Saturdays, and were constantly seeking me out for various reasons. This was *not* going to be easy.

. . .

I watched George Pascale all that autumn. He always came on Saturday mornings and stayed at the grave for half an hour, and then left. I stayed far away from him, but I watched.

November expired, and December arrived. He continued to visit on Saturdays even after snow covered the ground. One large snowfall covered her small, slanting headstone. He still came. I still watched, and waited.

Then, on the Saturday after Christmas, I got a rude awakening to the fact that I was getting careless. Lenny came up to me that morning and asked, "Hey Carl, how come every Saturday you put on your coveralls, but you don't actually *do* anything in them?"

"What?" I asked, stunned.

"Yeah even Blaine and Timmy noticed. You put on your coveralls on Saturdays, but you don't work on the trucks or anything when you're wearin' them."

Think fast, Carl. I handed him some b. s. about the coveralls making me feel more comfortable, as though I could lounge around on a Saturday morning, like other working men.

He shrugged, and went off to steal Tim's lunch pail.

After that, I knew I had to get rid of the crew on Saturdays. A couple days later, I found all three of them in our all-purpose room by the repair bays.

As I entered, Tim yelled, "Who's got my damn wallet?"

"Not me," said Blaine, looking at the ceiling.

"Not me," said Lenny, covering his mouth as he looked at the floor.

I laid out my proposal to them. If they put in an extra four hours during the week, they could *all* have Saturdays off. I would take care of whatever needed to be done. The only exceptions would be Saturday funerals, which I would sneak onto their time cards as overtime. They agreed happily.

"Any questions, guys?"

"Yeah," Tim piped up. "Who's got my damn wallet?"

· · ·

Another complication arose. All through that tense winter of unfulfilled Saturdays, my wife was after me about selling the house and moving to Florida or Arizona when I retired in May. We could sell the house to Blaine, she argued, and we'd have a place to stay if we wanted to come back and visit. He was living home again, and as Doreen pointed out, the payments he made to us, along with my Social Security checks, would make us quite comfortable.

"Why do you want to do this, Doreen? We've lived here all our lives. And we'd have Blaine to look after us."

She frowned, half sad, half angry. "This is *my* retirement too, Carl. I can see where you're heading. Half the time on the golf course, and the other half at the cemetery, helping Blaine!"

"Doreen, you're being—"

"Carl, I want us to be together. We need a *new* life, not pieces of the old one."

"Could we please drop this? I've got plenty of problems to deal with."

"Like what?"

Like planning a murder and getting away with it, I was thinking. "Plenty of serious stuff right now," I said.

"Like what?"

Think fast, Carl. "Well, for one thing . . .Tim's lunch pail keeps disappearing!"

· · ·

It was an unhappy time that followed. Doreen and I snapped at each other often, and the retirement argument came up a few more times. Neither of us gave an inch. Blaine, meanwhile, seemed to be going through a restless phase, carousing with some new friends that struck me as borderline sociopaths.

Saturday after Saturday came and went without anything close to an opportunity to get to George Pascale. Winter melted away toward early spring. The crew and I had to seed the winter graves, take plow attachments off trucks, and a dozen other tasks dictated by earth's annual rebirth.

March blossomed into April. Doreen quietly dropped the topic of selling the house and moving. I concluded she was unhappy with Blaine's new friends, and didn't want our home turned into an orgy hall in our retirement. He continued to keep bad company, although he maintained his sobriety on the cemetery grounds and did everything asked of him otherwise. The Saturdays continued to roll by without the chance to get George Pascale alone. With the spring weather, Three Maples was busier than ever.

Gradually, reluctantly, I abandoned my vow of vengeance, coming to grips with the obvious: there would never be an opportunity to do the deed unseen. I found myself looking forward to retirement, tired of living my life from one Saturday to another.

Saturday April 30th, I sat alone in my office, watching and listening to one of the heaviest spring thunderstorms I could remember. It was like looking through a beaded curtain. I doubted that Pascale would bother showing up. He still came regularly, but no longer had perfect attendance for Saturdays. On two occasions that winter, he had come on Sunday instead. I couldn't picture him driving twenty-five miles in this deluge to stand by a forlorn gravestone for half an hour. He could drown out there. I wouldn't want *that* to happen.

At eleven-thirty, half an hour later than usual, the red Honda sputtered through the gates, past my window, and out to the gravesite. I must have sat at my desk for a full minute before realizing that *he was absolutely, positively, the only person on the grounds. Except for me.*

I rushed into the locker room and threw on my coveralls. From a desk drawer I removed the clippers and a large wrench, then ran through the garage and fired up one of the turf trucksters. I was just pulling out of our back entrance when I heard another car coming through the gates. As it passed by the office and into view, I couldn't believe what I was seeing. It was Blaine's black Chevy Corsica. Although I couldn't see the driver or read the license plate, I recognized the loud muffler, and saw the bright red St. Louis Cardinals cap through the driver side window.

Expecting him to drive around to where I was, I tried to think of an excuse to why I was heading out in this downpour. He kept going up the main road, though, out toward the middle of the cemetery, hidden from view by trees and hills. He occasionally took a spin around the place when he was bored.

"You're ruining everything, damn it!" I shouted. Just when I *needed* him to be with those loser friends of his. Had they *all* found jobs on the same day?

I put the truckster back and sat in the locker room, dripping all over the floor, holding the clippers and wrench. Lost in thought, another engine sound roused me. I looked up to see the Chevy roar out through the gate.

There was *still* a chance. I got back in the truckster and headed out to my daughter's grave. The red Honda screened me from Pascale himself, so I stopped short of the intersection and climbed out. The tremendous downpour must have covered any engine noise from the truckster. I had been *driving* it and couldn't hear anything but the rain and distant thunder. I crept around the Honda, staying low, holding the clippers.

I knew Pascale was a head case, but he was carrying it to a new level. He was hunched down by the grave on his knees and elbows, like some Muslim at worship, tilted slightly to one side.

I came up on him, careful not to splash water, walking on my toes to avoid any squeaks from my workboots. The clippers I held over my head, while its partner in crime, the wrench, waited in my back pocket. I closed the distance until all my field of vision included were my boots and him.

"An eye for an eye, you son-of-a-bitch," I whispered, reaching back with the clippers.

Pascale didn't react, didn't move a muscle. It was then that I noticed all the puddles near him were a deep crimson.

Three holes the size of quarters had been punched into his head. Happiness over his death and revulsion over the sight of blood, brain, and skull had a brief tug-of-war. Then I realized that *Blaine* had driven out this way a short while ago. *He* had killed George Pascale.

I sped back to the office. Once inside, I put the tools back in their rightful place and hung up the coveralls. Then I sat down to think. Blaine had no knowledge of who Pascale was. Why had he killed him, then? Robbery? Was he on drugs he'd gotten from his new friends? After half an hour, my thought process was breaking down.

The rain was letting up as I pulled into our driveway behind Blaine's car. I rushed into our living room to find Doreen reading a magazine.

"Where's Blaine?"

"He went out with his friends."

"I just missed him?"

"No, he's been gone over two hours. They were going to a beer fest in Rivington."

"Yeah, well I got news for you. I just saw him drive through the cemetery."

Doreen shrugged. Blaine driving around the cemetery was not cause for alarm. "Maybe he changed his mind," she said.

I walked over to her and put my hands on her shoulders as she closed the magazine, inserting a finger in her place. "Doreen, this is serious. There's a dead body in the cemetery."

Her mouth curled at the corners, and I felt her shake with the beginnings of a girlish giggle. Then it dawned on me. A *dead body* in the *cemetery.* "You don't understand. There's been a *murder* up there, and I think Blaine's involved. I think he's the one who *did* it."

"That's ridiculous, Carl."

I stared at her in disbelief. Where was the shouting, the crying? Why wasn't she insisting I call the police? She was amazingly calm for a woman who has been told her son may have committed a murder. As much as I didn't want to believe it, part of me concluded that she *already knew* what he'd done. She was covering for him.

"Don't do this, Doreen. You want the police to gun him down like some animal? This is our *son!"*

"Carl, I'm sure you're mistaken."

Again, she was too calm, too composed. What would he have to do to upset her, overthrow the government? I happened to glance over at a small end table next to the couch, and saw Blaine's Cardinal's cap, a darker red now, soaking wet. Doreen noticed me looking at it.

"Oh, that," she said.

Yeah, *that*. I was still looking at it in disbelief when she opened the magazine to the page she'd kept.

"I think you'll like Arizona, Carl."

"What?"

"You've only got two weeks left. I found some nice property in Scottsdale. I really *will* have to get far away from here, don't you think?"

I had to force the words out. Even knowing they were true, they still seemed incomprehensible. "*You* did it. *You* killed Pascale. Are you *insane*, Doreen?"

She gave me a hard stare. "Are *you*, Carl?"

"What's that supposed to mean?"

"You were planning to kill him for months. I know."

"How did you know?" I said, without thinking to deny it.

"Let's sit down, Carl. We've got a lot to talk about. A lot of *catching up* to do."

. . .

We hadn't gotten far when the police were at our door. A visitor to the cemetery after the rain stopped couldn't help but notice that one of our dead was still *above* ground.

I went over to my office with them, and told them as much of the truth as I dared. I'd seen him drive in during the rainstorm, around eleven-thirty. No, I didn't know the man, but I had seen him there for some months. Was he alone? Yes. Had he ever been there with anyone? No. Did I see anyone on the grounds other than him? No. And so on.

They spent parts of the next three days there, but as one detective told me, the rain that afternoon made the crime scene an investigator's nightmare. They had Pascale's shoeprints and those of the guy that found him, and not much else.

They even made a routine search of our garage and facilities. Behind some spare parts in our utility shed, they found Tim's lunchpail.

The newspapers had a field day with the irony of it: a murderer found murdered at the grave of the person *he* had murdered.

. . .

Doreen knew everything, *had* known everything, all along. Although not from these parts, in our first year together Doreen made friends with someone who knew Nancy Beaudoin. Women talk. It's not bad enough they're smarter than we are, they can be more patient, too.

She went on to say that she noticed a change in me since that day back in September when Pascale first showed up. There was a silent, brooding fury showing that escaped even myself. She put two and two together, did a little research into back issues of the city newspaper, and concluded that the Saturday visitor was George Pascale. And from her desk in the office, *she* tracked his visiting patterns, too.

But the big question, why? Why would a woman who cried over dead animals in our yard, who couldn't bring herself to kill the occasional crawling thing in the garage, brutally kill another person?

It was simple, she told me. She felt that Pascale being alive and in close proximity would destroy me, in time. She *needed* for my retirement to be a new chapter in our lives, far away from Three Maples.

I tried telling her that I had pretty much made my peace with George Pascale, but she chose to ignore it. Blaine had an alibi, she said. I was innocent, technically, and *she* would not even be suspected.

She was right. As my retirement date drew closer, little or nothing was in the newspapers, and although I assumed an investigation was ongoing, less and less of it was crime scene investigation. That last week you would never have known anything had happened, except that now, in another of life's ironies, Joyce Beaudoin's grave attracted visitors, most likely people who wanted to see where a paroled murderer got wasted.

It was strange how things fell into place. Doreen and I closed a deal on our new home in Scottsdale, Arizona. I recommended Blaine, senior crew member, to the Board of Directors to be my successor. They followed my recommendation, and when informed of his new responsibilities, he abandoned his new-found friends as quickly as he had fallen in with them.

Doreen and the crew wanted to throw me a party in the office that last Friday, but I declined. I wanted a quiet, reflective final two days. I sent everyone home early and told them to have a nice weekend. I came in Saturday and cleaned out my locker and other belongings.

On Sunday, May 15th, I took my final inspection walk around the grounds of Three Maples Cemetery, stopping briefly at the grave of Joyce Beaudoin to say goodbye to the daughter I never really knew. At sundown, as I had done for the past thirty years, I took down the flag and locked the gates for the last time.

. . .

It is September now. Doreen and I are ready for our new life. Blaine has agreed to pack some additional things for us when he gets the chance. He is busy training the new crew member, Allan, who spends lunch hours trying to find his thermos, which has been disappearing lately.

I packed light. Some summer clothes, my new golf clubs, and all my tools, of course. All except my favorite Craftsman hammer, which I can't find anywhere, and know enough not to bother looking for. Doreen assures me they have hardware stores in Arizona.

I asked her once, and once only, how she kept quiet some thirty-six years about all that she knew. Her answer terrified me more than the brutal act she committed.

She smiled and said, "You had *your* secret, I had *mine*. A secret for a secret, an eye for an eye."

"THE MAGIC PEN"

Etruscan Publishing's newest author waggled the knot of his blue and brown striped tie and checked himself in the mirror again. It was his first appearance and lecture at a public school, and he wanted to look the part, wanted to look *authorly.*

He couldn't let Mathias Tucker down. The Chairman of the English Department at Worton High School had extended him this invitation. He and Mathias went all the way back to Worton High School, class of '66.

In college, both had majored in journalism. They were going to break stories for the *New York Times* or write bestselling novels. Or both. Mathias fell by the wayside, though, changing his major to Education. *Just as well,* thought Robert S. Banks, picking up a glossy paperback with his picture on the back cover. Mathias wasn't a *writer,* he was a *plodder.* Let him teach *Ivanhoe* or dangling modifiers to bored, underachieving, oversexed high school kids.

Leave the serious writing to people like himself, people prepared to expose their inner selves as they told the BIG TRUTH about life.

He had been willing to sacrifice to find the BIG TRUTH, had worked for paltry wages paid by his cousin's husband and let his wife Michelle work full time in a clothing store while he sought not only the BIG TRUTH, but a publisher for it.

After more than twenty years of frustration and rejection, the floodgates of success opened. Every query brought an eager reply from a trade-mag editor or literary journal. Articles, interviews, and short stories were sent out and never came back. They were published. And then, in a literary coup,

Etruscan had picked up his short story collection and his historical novel, *The Glimmer,* set in 17th century Italy. That was when he *knew* he could do no wrong. Generet Literary Review read his collection and called him "the second coming of Raymond Carver." Yes, after years of sweating in the hot sun operating cousin-in-law Mike's roto-tilling equipment, he could stay home and write down all the BIG TRUTHS.

Michelle would still have to work full time, at least until they had become more solvent, but she shouldn't mind. Not when her husband was the second coming of Raymond Carver.

The pen was lying on the bed by his valise. Ah yes, the lucky pen. The rational part of his mind insisted that his sudden glut of successes had been the result of years of hard work, natural talent, and tempering his style to fit an ever-changing market.

Another part of him claimed that he only succeeded when he did notes, outlines, or rough drafts using the lucky pen. He tested the theory. After selling two historical non-fiction pieces on French General Rochambeau, and three short stories using the lucky pen, he approached the same editors with pieces done using a different pen. They were flatly rejected. Then came the *real* test. He rewrote them, changing language and point-of-view, but kept the same *topics.* The reworked articles, sent back to the same editors, all sold. One even sent him a gushing letter stating, "You have breathed badly-needed vitality into an otherwise overdone theme."

He had done no such thing, he reminded himself. He had *purposely* made the numerous changes superficial ones, but he had done them with the lucky pen.

He picked it up from the bed and admired it. Its hefty bottom half was a smooth, metallic jade green, with a gold top half. The nose was gold, the top ending in a rounded, jade green bullet shape. A .38 caliber pen.

There were probably thousands like it, but it was classy-looking. *Authorly*. He had picked it up at a nearby pharmacy on one of his supply-buying expeditions, the ones Michelle used to roll her eyes at while grudgingly opening her purse and handing him a ten when he was between roto-tilling jobs.

Looking at it with affection, he frowned at where Michelle's nail file, left on his dresser, had taken a fleck of the green color away, leaving a flat, silver dot. He inserted it in his front jacket pocket, and looked in the mirror again. The gold top went well with his brown suit. It looked *authorly*.

He would do this favor for Mathias, would give all the proper answers to the students. They would want to know where he got his ideas, and he would tell them about writing the BIG TRUTH. Then, he laughed, they would all run home and try to be authors for a day or two before returning to cheat sheets, love notes, and bathroom graffiti.

Would he tell them about the lucky pen? Not a chance. Not even Michelle knew about that. It just wouldn't be *authorly*.

. . .

Shawn Cavell pushed a red curl away from his eyes and smiled. He had it figured out now. The pen only worked in English, where you made up stuff or told actual experiences on compositions, or in history, when you did an essay explaining why something was important, or why it happened in the first place.

It was no good in math, where you had to use pencil, or in science, where everything happened for a definite reason.

This was the third day of using the pen he had taken from that author guy that had given the talk on Monday. What was his name again? Banks? It was no big deal, Shawn told himself. The guy was a famous author, he could buy a hundred more just like it. Banks had put the pen down after signing some autographs, and Shawn picked it up and took it back to his seat, sort of as a souvenir. Looking at it again to make sure, he recognized a common brand name. It was an ordinary five-dollar pen. No big deal, he told himself again.

Freshman year had been a struggle for Shawn. His report card, through three quarters, showed a procession of C's and D's, with an occasional 'F'. Here was the chance to bring up his grade in two of his subjects. He wasn't cheating, either. When he used this green and gold pen, ideas seemed to *jump into his head and onto the paper.* No doubt about it, it was a magic pen.

. . .

Robert S. Banks, in cutoff jeans and white tee shirt, sifted through his converted attic workspace for the fifth time in three days, going through envelopes, stacks of manuscripts, index cards, books and markers in search of his lucky pen. In addition, he had turned the master bedroom and the downstairs of the house into a disaster area during the same time frame.

As frustrated as he was, his most prevalent emotion was anger for not remembering where he put the lucky pen when he returned from his talk at the high school Monday. Following close behind, but not allowed to creep to the surface, was panic.

Banks, at an utter loss now, sat down amid the clutter. "*Damn* it, where would I have *put* the darn thing?" He called down to his wife, who had just arrived home after another long day at the clothing store. "Michelle! I still can't find the green pen. Look in the drawers by the nightstand again, will you?"

"Rob, I just got home. Could I at least get changed first?" The voice had a familiar, impatient tone. "How long do we have to look for a freaking *pen?*"

He hated when she used that word. "Until we *find* the freaking pen, *okay?*" He tried to calm himself. It wasn't her fault. She didn't know their future hung on whether he could find the lucky pen. Maybe he should tell her now, so she could appreciate what was at stake. Provided he could get her to *believe* that his recent success was due to a *pen*.

He was more convinced than ever that this was true. Yesterday he tried to make some progress on several short works, and do character charts on his second novel, but it was no good. It read as though it had been written by an average creative writing student. This was not writer's block. This was a career-ending problem he was facing, and the answer lay down the barrel of a common green and gold ballpoint pen. *The kind you can buy anywhere, idiot.*

Trying to trick himself like that didn't work for long. There was only one lucky pen, and he had somehow misplaced it when he got home from school. He once again tried to visualize himself taking the pen from his jacket pocket, where he had placed it for effect.

Now *where was he* then? Dining room? Bedroom? His car? *You were in school, idiot. You had to be the big shot and sign autographs, remember? And you couldn't lower yourself to use some crappy pen a kid handed you, so you took out the lucky pen. Remember now, idiot?*

That annoying inner voice again. It *had* made him stop and consider something for the first time. Perhaps the reason he couldn't find the pen anywhere in the house was because it never got home with him. What if he *had* lost it at the school? Any one of twelve-hundred kids could have it. Or worse, it could have been swept up and thrown away at the end of the school day.

Sweat broke out on his forehead. He was ruined unless he found the lucky pen, of that much he was positive. Forcing his mind to do a "videotape replay", he was able to remember a brown-haired girl with glasses and bandanna asking for his autograph, and how *famous* he felt at the moment. The tape wound forward, slowly. As if a dam had broken, kids clustered around him, all of them wanting autographs. Okay, this was the most important part. *Show me what I did with the pen when I was finished.*

The tape moved again. Not used to carrying a pen in his jacket pocket, (it was just for effect, remember?) he *placed it on the teacher's desk where he was leaning!*

Good! Then what happened? Mathias was standing next to him now, thanking him for coming. Students were going back to their seats or lining up at the doorway, waiting for the bell to ring. The tape moved forward ever so slightly, and . . .wait!

There's a *hand* reaching in and taking the lucky pen! Banks requested a wide-angle shot with freeze frame. His mind complied.

He sees the culprit, a gangly, unpretentious-looking boy with dark red, curly hair. Preoccupied with Mathias and making a positive parting impression, he did not *realize* that the boy, in his peripheral vision, had picked up the pen. It is unmistakable in his mind now, that he *did.*

Banks now focused on anything in his memory circuits that might help him. Surprisingly, he found previous images of the boy stored there. As he was being introduced, he observed a sea of eager, interested faces, and one mildly disinterested one. He remembered looking at the disarray of red curls and unassuming face. *Huck Finn is alive and well and living in*

Worton, Maryland, he remembered thinking. During *his* question and answer session, he recalled the boy asking *Mathias* if he could use the bathroom.

"Not *now,* Shawn," came Tucker's exasperated reply.

Banks now smiled with some relief. He had a description of the thief, and knew his first name. It shouldn't be a big deal to go back, pop in on the class, and have Mathias tell the boy to return the pen. "Thank God," whispered Robert S. Banks.

. . .

Shawn Cavell sat under his favorite oak tree in the woods. "Darn teachers," he muttered. He had not foreseen the effect of turning in crisp, intelligent writing in history and English after nearly seven-and-a-half months of muddled, superficial blurs. Mr. Tucker and Mrs. Browning did not believe it was his work!

First, they checked the papers of those around him. Nothing matched. Being teachers, Shawn concluded, they would never admit to being wrong, so they proceeded to accuse him of getting help at home. Just his luck to have a smart sister attending college. But he got them on that one, too. Linda was in college, all right . . .in *Rhode Island.* He even told them they could call his house to check. They said that wouldn't be necessary, but *still* refused to believe that the work was his.

Today, both teachers had gotten together and made him stay after to rewrite his latest English and history papers. Shawn figured this would show them once and for all. But with *both* of them pacing near him and *staring* at him, he couldn't concentrate. Even with the magic pen, *nothing* came out. What he ended up writing was far worse than his usual pathetic ramblings. Both teachers nodded to each other, and gave him a zero.

"I don't know what you did, or how you did it, Shawn," Tucker had said, "but don't try it again."

He left without saying anything. Why bother to tell them they made him nervous standing over him? Teachers never believed you unless you were one of the "good kids." There was no way he would tell them about the pen. That would probably just make them *mad.* Teachers could make your life miserable enough when they *weren't* mad at you.

And what if they *did* believe him about the pen? What if, somehow, he could *prove* that it was a magic pen? Even worse, he thought. They would probably figure out some way of taking the pen away, maybe even search the student handbook until they found some *regulation* against having a magic pen.

He was on their turf. Teachers thought they could get away with anything when they were in school. He would just have to find a way to use the magic pen without arousing suspicion. Or a way of concentrating when he was asked to rewrite something.

. . .

It was a bold decision by Robert S. Banks, and he followed through on it. He had softened it a bit, though, watered it down. He told Michelle that he misplaced the green pen at school, and had a mental block about working without it. She had taken it well he thought ... for her.

"Jeez, Louise, Rob! It's a damn *pen,* for cripe sakes! Just buy another one like it. We still have a ton of unpaid bills from before your *big break.* When the hell do you run out of excuses?"

Yes, Banks thought, she had taken it better than anticipated. "Michelle, not being a writer, I wouldn't expect you to understand this, but a state of mind is vital in the creative process. I simply *depend* on that pen in the early stages of my work."

She clenched her fists, exasperated. "Rob, I don't give a rat's rear end about the *creative process,* except that you had better *create* some income. I'm tired of supporting you. Go get the damn pen if that's what you have to do. Just *do* it, and start pulling your weight around here!" She stormed out of the room.

On the drive over, he began to have second thoughts about how this might be perceived by Mathias. His old friend had seemed just a bit resentful of his success, especially when he had nearly laughed at the mound of papers on his desk.

"Do you actually *read* all of that drivel, Mathias?" he had asked.

Mathias had looked peeved, almost insulted. "Yes, Robert, I do. That's my *job.* Do you actually *write* all the words in your books?"

Banks thought some more about it. Would Mathias think he was nuts, wanting a simple pen back, or some spoiled prima dona, whose recent success had gone to his head?

He parked in the visitor's parking lot, went to the office, and asked one of the secretaries where Mr. Tucker was. He was directed to a classroom on the second floor. Mathias was teaching expository writing to a class of juniors. He knocked on the open classroom door. Mathias looked surprised to see him, and walked out into the hallway.

"Robert, can I help you with something?"

"I hope so. When I was here Monday, I believe one of your students picked up a ballpoint pen of mine." He saw concern on Mathias's face, and tried to allay it somewhat. From the goings-on in the classroom, his old friend had enough problems right now. "It's no big deal, Mathias, it's not a *valuable* pen or anything. I just wanted it back if at all possible."

Tucker's face turned from concern to disgust. It had been a long, hard year; behavior problems, budget cuts, and a school reorganization in which he stood to lose his department chairmanship.

"Let me get this straight. You interrupt my worst class *ever* to ask for the return of a common, ordinary pen?"

In the classroom behind him, shouts and laughter could be heard, along with the unmistakable sounds of people dashing around. Tucker leaned into the room. "Knock it off!" He turned back to Banks, his face showing a rise in tension and blood pressure.

"Mathias, it's not so much that it's an—"

"You should try *working* for a living, Banks, and you wouldn't worry about a stupid *pen!*"

"Really, Mathias, there's no need to get—"

"I would feel like an utter fool going into one of my classes and asking if one of these kids has your precious pen! Take some of your book royalties and buy a few! Better yet, *here!*" He reached into his shirt pocket and handed Banks a clear ballpoint pen. Banks took it without thinking.

"You'll have to excuse me now, Robert." He indicated his classroom, which had once again disrupted into a lunacy festival. "My *public* awaits me." He turned and went back into his classroom, slamming the door behind him.

Robert S. Banks remained in the hallway, embarrassed and angry. So, Mathias *did* resent him, and in a big way. Well, that was just too bad. He'd earned everything he achieved, and he wasn't going to see it all go down the drain because of one man's jealousy. He would do this without Mathias's help. A plan was already forming.

He went back to the main office. A different secretary asked if she could help him.

"Yes, my name is Mr. Banks. I was here Monday to talk to Mr. Tucker's classes. A boy names Shawn in his lunch period class asked me to take a look at his writing, and I said I'd come back for it. I wonder if you know where he would be right now."

The secretary went to a file cabinet, and retrieved a folder with Mathias Tucker's name at the top. "Let's see, lunch period, that's period four. There's only one Shawn in that class, Shawn Cavell."

"I believe that was his last name," said Banks, feeling like a government agent in a story.

"He'll be in science in a couple of minutes, if you care to wait for the bell."

"Certainly, what room would that be?"

"Room 102, Mr. Shultz. It's right by the teacher's lounge."

The passing bell rang within thirty seconds, and Banks waited until the halls cleared, then went down the corridor to Room 102. He found Mr. Shultz standing by the door. He was a slight man, early thirties, with large brown glasses.

Science nerd in high school, Banks thought. He told the man his cover story about wanting to read Shawn's "work," and Schultz called him out into the hallway, then went inside, closing the door.

There was a surprised look on the boy's face. *He's not just surprised,* thought Banks, *he's flustered. He knows what this is about. Didn't think I'd catch up to you, did you, Huck?*

"Shawn, you remember me from Monday, don't you?"

The boy's eyes widened. "Yeah, you're that writer."

"I believe you have something of mine."

"I don't have anything of yours," Shawn said innocently. It didn't convince Banks, though. Too much eye movement. The face seemed too innocent.

"Yes, you do, Shawn. You took a very special green and gold pen of mine. I had just put it down on Mr. Tucker's desk."

"I didn't take it, " Shawn pleaded, but he looked as though he had been caught in a lie.

"I *saw* you take it, Shawn. I need it back. I really do." The boy seemed to sag when told he had been observed. *There you go, Huck,* Banks said to himself, *float THAT down the old Mississippi.*

"Please, Mr. . . ."

"Banks."

"I always been stupid in school. But with that pen, I write *good.* It's like it's *magic* or somethin'."

Banks's eyebrows lifted. *You too?* he thought. *It wasn't my imagination. Hey Huck, how about coming home with me. There's a lady I'd like you to tell this to. Then we'll go get Tom Sawyer and build a raft.*

"Please, Mr. Banks. A guy like you that's a writer, you must be smart *all* the time. I'm only smart when I use that pen."

Me too, thought Banks.

"Are you gonna be like the teachers, now, and think you can do anything just because you're an adult and I'm a kid?"

Before Banks could answer, the door to the adjacent teacher's room swung open, and out walked Mathias Tucker. He stopped dead when he saw Banks and Shawn Cavell. His face set in a prepare-for-battle pose. It was about time, he thought, people like Robert S. Banks learned that their status didn't have to be catered to.

"Get back in class, Shawn. Mr. Banks and I have something to discuss."

"I'm going, Mr. Tucker," said Shawn, grateful that he had been ordered away. He scuttled back into the classroom, closing the door behind him.

"Just couldn't leave it alone, could you Robert?" asked Tucker.

"Now, Mathias, you're not being completely fair about this."

"Robert, I think you'd better realize something here. This may be fun to you, watching the little people scramble around because you lost a five-dollar pen, but there's something else involved. School security. It's a very black and white issue these days, and you just turned up on the wrong end of it."

Banks stiffened with outrage. Was Mathias accusing him of being a child molester? Words flew out. "Why, you pompous . . . *municipal employee,* you."

Mr. Banks," said Tucker, straining for self-control, "leave this school right now, before I swear out a complaint against you."

Banks turned and walked away, sure that Mathias was watching. He had nothing left to lose, and one salvo left in his cannon, so he turned and fired. "You always were a no-talent *plodder!"*

Mathias had one round remaining, too. "Don't come back, Banks, unless you're invited! And the chances of that are about the same as *me* becoming a famous author!"

For the first and only time in his school career, Shawn Cavell was the only one in class who had the answer. The question was, what was all that shouting in the hallway? Shawn knew it had to do with him and the magic pen. The adults were at it again, trying to get the better of a kid. They were smart, but mostly they took you by surprise. He was determined not to let that happen this time. He had to plan ahead to protect the magic pen. Sitting at his desk, he tried to come up with such a plan, oblivious to Mr. Schultz and the science lesson going on around him.

. . .

Robert S. Banks had walked dejectedly back to his car, parked at the edge of the visitors parking lot, by the bus exit lane. He sat behind the wheel glumly, still holding his keys. Why bother hurrying home? He wouldn't be able to work. Let's see, what else could go wrong? Michelle was pissed, the kid had promoted the pen from *lucky* to *magic,* for God's sake, and Mathias had all but banned him from the school.

Banks refused to start the car. *Damn it, I'm supposed to be the creative one here. There's got to be another way.* He was pleasantly surprised to find that a couple of alternatives surfaced. He could call the kid's house, talk to his parents, maybe tell them that the pen had sentimental value. He could offer fifty dollars to get it back. He was sure they'd be reasonable about *that.* Let Huck try telling *them* it was a magic pen. As doofy as this kid seemed, Banks was positive he would not want to appear childish in front of his parents.

That should work, and if it didn't, he remembered Michelle telling of a co-worker whose son Ralph was a troublemaker at the school, a sophomore whose disciplinary record resembled a felon's rap sheet. Yes, it the money offer didn't work with the Huck family, he was sure it would with old Ralphie boy. Desperate times, desperate measures.

He had become so absorbed in his scheming that he failed to notice the arrival of several school buses. The sound of the dismissal bell inside the building brought him back to reality, and he started the car. Then he noticed that there were more buses than room in front of the school. The backed-up vehicles blocked him in. He would have to wait now until the first few were loaded and went around the exit lane past him, leaving room for the others to pull up.

"That's okay, I've got a plan now," he mumbled.

Shawn Cavell sat quietly by himself in bus 341, the third in line, as others climbed aboard and rushed for their favorite seats. Shawn was still worried about the magic pen, but he had a plan now. He gazed vacant-eyed out the window at the crowd leaving school.

Trouble climbed the steps of the bus, stopped, and surveyed the assembled riders. Trouble was Kevin Arnone, a tall brown-haired junior. He was ADS, Attention Deficit Syndrome. He was LD, Learning Disabled. He was mostly PITA, Pain-In-The-Ass. Kevin was in a *mood* today.

He walked slowly down the aisle, hitting people on the shoulder, knocking hats off, turning up the volume on Walkmans, laughing as their owners nearly lifted off their seats, holding their ears and clawing for the volume control. He grabbed an apple from one girl's hand, took a bite, and gave it back to her. Like a human tornado, he was rending everything in his path. He came to an empty seat, and having grown tired of his destructive spree, prepared to sit. The boy behind him was staring absent-mindedly out the window. One last number for the fans. His eyes fell on a green and gold pen in the boy's pocket. He reached over the seat.

It wasn't only the feeling of something touching his shirt pocket that catapulted Shawn Cavell back to reality, it was the slithering sensation as the magic pen seemed to be escaping. He slapped his hand over the now-empty pocket, and looked up to see Kevin Arnone, kneeling on the seat in front of him, waving the pen in a teasing manner.

"Hey! Give that back. That's my magic pen!" The bus erupted into laughter at the words, accompanied by the sight of Shawn leaning over, reaching for the pen that Kevin Arnone now held out the window as further torture.

Shawn did not allow the torture to affect him for long. As soon as the bus driver yelled for everyone to shut up and sit down, or they would be here all afternoon, he calmly resumed sitting, his expression one of calm neutrality. This was a new reaction for Kevin Arnone. He was accustomed to pushing people's buttons, getting their goat. As the bus began to move out, he pulled his hand inside.

What was this doofus trying to pull on him, going ballistic one second, and acting as though he didn't care the next? Then it came to him. It was that reverse psychology crap his teachers and guidance counselor used on him. They reacted the *opposite* way, so he would tire of whatever he was doing and behave. Well, it was one thing when they did it, but he couldn't let some dip freshman get away with it. He had to make sure, though.

"Whatsa matter, curly? Don't want your *magic pen* anymore?"

Shawn looked straight ahead. "Nope."

"You sure?"

"Yep."

"Okay, then." Kevin held the pen out the window and checked the kid's reaction again. Nothing. It was that reverse psychology, all right.

"Hey!" yelled the bus driver. "Get your arm inside the bus right now!"

As the bus pulled around the circle, Kevin tossed the pen from his dangling hand, checked the kid's face again. Shawn glared momentarily, then looked down at the floor.

Robert S. Banks had calculated that he would have to wait for nine buses to leave before he could pull out behind them. As he counted a third bus, something clinked off the rim of his open window, and fell to the floor, disappearing under the seat. He reached down, feeling around until his fingers felt something metallic. He pulled it up, looked at it, and nearly forgot to breathe. It couldn't be. It just *couldn't* be. Nobody was *this* lucky.

It looked like his lucky pen. He examined it further. On the green barrel was a tiny spot of silver showing, courtesy of Michelle's nail file. It was, indeed, his lucky pen. He was back in business.

What just happened here? he asked himself, as the seventh bus passed him. Did Huck feel guilty, see him in the car, and toss it back to him? He doubted that. Did he accidently drop it? Fat chance. Somehow, though, the lucky pen had come home to Papa. Banks laughed out loud as a ninth bus passed. Maybe it *was* a magic pen. He pulled out of the parking lot, a happy man.

. . .

Shawn Cavell rushed upstairs to his bedroom, locked the door, and from the front pocket of his jeans removed a small shank of metal, tipped in blue plastic at one end, a small rolling ball at the other. It was the ink cartridge from the magic pen. Good thing, he told himself, he had planned ahead.

"A pen is just a pen," he said aloud, as if for reassurance. "It's the *ink supply* that's magic." He could buy another pen and insert this inside. If he planned carefully, it could last him well into his junior year. By then, his grades might be good enough, at least in English and history, to get into a two-year college.

He wouldn't have to be the family dummy anymore.

. . .

Robert S. Banks stood by his bedroom mirror, wearing a calm, content face. He held his lucky pen. He twisted the top to get the tip to descend. Nothing happened. Pulling the top half free, he found the inside empty.

He smiled a pitying smile. "Nice try, Huck," he said. Banks *knew* that *eventually* the ink supply would run out. He would merely buy a refill. It was the *pen* that was special. He thought again of the remarkable upswing in his writing, how the kid had claimed he wrote '*good*' with it, and how against almost unbelievable odds, it had practically fallen back into his lap.

"You were right, Huck. It *is* a magic pen." He headed upstairs, pen in hand, ideas for short stories, articles, and novels now crashing against the sides of his brain.

He could write successfully till the end of his days, now. The magic pen was his.

"PERFECT FOR PACKING"

It was Saturday, December 21st, the first day of Christmas vacation, and the snow pouring down from the northern Michigan sky was perfect for packing.

Maybe you've heard of me. I was mentioned in the book *Gruesome Coverups of Ordinary Crimes*. They won't let me have a copy here. That's okay for now. I'm a patient person if I have to be. The past thirteen years is proof of that.

On that Saturday morning in question, my older brother Alan and I were walking home from the YMCA. I'd been taking swim lessons, he was hanging out with some friends. I was eight years old, Alan was fourteen.

We cut across Holdridge Park as a shortcut, although we probably lost time wading through the fourteen inches of wet, heavy snow that had fallen in the last three hours. We get some blockbuster snowfalls here in the Upper Peninsula.

We had nearly crossed the park to Gates Avenue, when we came upon a weird-looking snowman. It had a cylinder shape, but the walls seemed to have been pushed in all around. It was shaped more like a tree trunk. It reminded me of the snow castles we would build around kids, in a tower shape. This snowman looked something like one of the snow towers, but much thicker. The top was decorated with rocks for eyes, nose, and mouth. It was a sort of hybrid snow tower-snowman.

Alan was a few feet in front of me, trying to climb over the huge snowbank to the street. I could hear his grunts, along with the sounds of snowplows in the distance, and the warning beeps of sand trucks backing up. There was one other, nearly inaudible sound from just behind me, a muffled, half groan, half cry. I turned. The odd-looking snowman was all I saw.

There was a grunt and thud from behind me. I snapped around to see Alan's head rise from the other side of the snowbank. He cursed and brushed snow from him.

"Let's *go,* Christopher!" he shouted.

As his words died away I was almost positive I heard yet another sound behind me, more like loud exhaling. I looked back again, positive the sound came from the snowman. I scrambled over the bank, landing on my hands and knees, looking up at Alan. "The snowman! It made sounds!"

Before I knew it, he had grabbed the end of my long maroon scarf and was running up Gates Avenue, dragging me on all fours like a stubborn dog, stopping only after I fell onto my stomach. I got up and held my sore neck. "You idiot! That *hurt!*"

"Too bad! We still got a half mile to go in this stuff. We gotta *move!*"

"Alan, I told you, I heard—"

"I don't have time for your make-believe crap. Now *move,* or I'll drag you the rest of the way."

I didn't say anything else on the way home. Every so often, though, Alan would look sideways at me and mutter, "Stupid jerk."

We were half frozen by the time we reached home. I was terrified by what I thought I heard, but I kept quiet because of Alan. When Dad's office let him out early, we helped clear our sidewalk and driveway. The temperature was down to zero by then, and the chunks of snow we dredged up felt like concrete.

Dinner was the usual affair, pleasant, but subdued. Dad liked it that way. Alan excused himself when he was finished, whistling "Frosty the Snowman" under his breath. I shuddered. Mom and Dad smiled in appreciation of what they thought was his pleasant Christmas spirit.

That was the first of many tortures he inflicted on me that Christmas.

I was too uncomfortable and afraid to talk about the snowman to my parents, but I wanted to avoid Alan, so I hung out in the living room with them and watched TV all night. At eleven, when the local news came on, I was on my way to bed, but the lead story caught me halfway out of my chair.

Two boys, Brady Matthews, age 8, and Lewis Tranker, age 9, were reported missing. They had been on their way to a friend's house that afternoon, but never showed. The police had no reason to believe they were runaways. They were exploring the possibility of kidnapping or other foul play.

Dad shook his head slowly, Mom covered her mouth. The TV screen flashed their pictures, side by side. I didn't recognize Lewis Tranker, although he went to my school. Brady Matthews I did know, just by sight.

It was scary to think that something like that could happen to kids I went to school with, which made me think of the sounds I was sure I'd heard from the snowman. The two fears kind of ran together, and before I knew it, my mind was conjuring up images of one of those kids *inside* the snowman, calling for help.

Then it occurred to me. What if one of them *was* trapped inside, and by saying nothing all these hours I had helped kill him? Wouldn't that make me a murderer? I nervously excused myself and went to my room.

As I crashed down on my bed, it made the usual thump on the wall between my room and Alan's. I heard him moving around, then the slapping sound of a record being dropped onto his stereo turntable. There was a scratching sound as he lifted the needle. Then came the unmistakable musical intro to "Frosty the Snowman," from the Beach Boys Christmas album. I buried my head under the pillow and quietly cried myself into a restless sleep.

The next three days seemed like a blur to me. Temperatures hovered between minus ten and zero, I was confined to the yard because of the missing boys, and Alan hounded me with the humming, whistling, and singing of "Frosty the Snowman."

On Tuesday afternoon, while rummaging around under my bed for a game I could play solitaire, I heard sounds outside my window. Pulling up the shade, I found a proud Alan putting the finishing touches on a snowman, just two feet from the window. He had gone to great lengths to dig out chunks of the frozen snow, and had spray-painted eyes, nose, and a gruesome scowl. Seeing me at the window, he gave the neighborhood his loudest rendition of "Frosty the Snowman," laughing and pointing at me as he sang.

I pulled the shade and jumped onto my bed, more haunted than ever by the snowman in Holdridge Park, and the pictures of Lewis Tranker and Brady Matthews on the TV screen.

On Christmas Day, the cold abated long enough for eight more inches of snow off Lake Superior, followed by more sub-zero cold. The two boys were still missing, and Alan continued his covert torture of me. Both awake and asleep, I was beset by haunting images of snowmen. In my dreams they groaned, growled, lunged at me. By daylight they seemed to me gruesome, grotesque parodies of death.

And by now, of course, I convinced myself I had killed the missing boys by my silence. At some point in that turmoil, Christmas presents were opened. I don't even remember what

I got. I opened box after box, not really seeing what was inside. "Just what I wanted!" I kept yelling.

. . .

Death is a magnet. I had to get to Holdridge Park. I asked Mom if I could go the day after Christmas, assuring her that lots of my friends would be there. It would be safety in numbers. She reluctantly agreed.

The capricious weather had done another turnaround. December 26th was balmy by contrast. The sky was clear, and a warm winter sun drove the temperature to nearly forty by noon, when I set out for the park, carrying my sled as a decoy. The warmth had penetrated the outer crust of snow. You could skim off an inch or two in round, mini-pellet shapes. It was perfect for packing, if that's what you had in mind.

There were a few kids in the park when I got there, and some adults, no doubt still mindful of the missing boys. No one was near the snowman, who had been left undisturbed, covered with a few more inches of snow.

I threw my sled over the bank and climbed into the park. I approached the snowman cautiously, as though expecting it might *know* it was me again. Working up what little courage I possessed, I walked up to it and listened. It was quiet, except for normal background sounds of kids shouting at each other in the distance.

Encouraged, I removed the stones that had served as eyes, nose, and mouth. Faceless now, it didn't seem frightening at all. Further emboldened, I poked my finger where one of the eyes had been, drilling in an inch or so, scolding myself for ever having so much as lost my composure over this preposterous chunk of snow. I became nearly flippant about it. I knocked on the head. "Anybody home? Anyone in there?" I asked jokingly.

I picked up a nearby stick and drilled farther into the hole until it seemed to reach a hollow center, then swished it around several times, making it wider and cleaner. "Peek-a-boo," I said, sticking my eye up to the hole.

There was another eye looking back at me. It was blue, half-closed, and spotted with ice crystals.

Everyone in the park, even those at the far reaches of it, eighty yards away, claimed later their ears were pierced by my scream. They saw a small boy, me, run toward the embankment, trip and fall over something, (my sled) and not so much *climb* the snowbank as *vault* over it.

I never stopped running, even when I reached home. I tore around to the back of the house and threw myself at Alan's hideous snowman, knocking it down and smashing it to powder and crystals. I crept into the house, shaking as I entered the living room, where Mom was tidying up. She looked at me with surprise and concern.

"Christopher, you look terrible. Did you get a chill?"

I nodded.

"Well, take off those wet clothes and hang them over the shower rod in the bathroom."

I nodded again.

"You go lie down after that."

"Okay."

I did as Mom asked, and crumpled down on my bed. I tried feebly to sort through the terror and guilt. Did anyone see me run away? Would I get blamed? Then it all seemed to wash over me in a sea of black and gray.

I slept until 4:30, when Mom awoke me and took my temperature. "One degree high," she said. "Not too bad."

I wish I'd stayed awake those three-and-a-half hours that afternoon. When you're awake you can brace yourself, make a plan. Asleep, your mind seeks its own level, and then *sets.* Maybe for good.

Dinner with my parents was mercifully quiet and uneventful. Alan was at a special all-night Christmas party fundraiser sponsored by the high school, and would not be coming home. I picked at Mom's homemade stew, then asked to be excused. She usually made a fuss when I didn't finish, but perceived me as "coming down with something," and was agreeable to me going back to my room.

I lay there for hours, tortured by thoughts of snowmen, dead bodies, and what might be done to me if—no, *when* my part in the death was discovered. I finally fell asleep at about 8:30.

I dreamt I was on trial for murder. Alan was the judge. Brady Matthews and Lewis Tranker sat at the prosecution table, dripping wet, staring at me with anger and betrayal. The jury was made up of twelve identical snowmen, all clones of Alan's grotesque model.

I was shaken awake at that point, and looked into the concerned face of my father. Mom stood behind him, her eyes red. "Christopher," Dad said, "were you at Holdridge Park this afternoon?"

I nodded sleepily.

He produced my maroon scarf. "Were you wearing this?"

"I guess so." I didn't understand.

"What did you find in the park, Christopher?"

I sat up in bed, petrified. I didn't know what to say.

"Christopher, we were just watching the late news."

I glanced at the clock, which read 11:10.

The lead story had been the discovery of the bodies of Brady Matthews and Lewis Tranker, missing since the 21ˢᵗ. Matthews had been discovered in Holdridge Park by some kids and their parents, who heard a boy scream loudly and then run. He was reportedly wearing a long maroon scarf, and left his sled behind. The adults investigated, and found that the column of snow the boy was near when he fled contained the frozen, suffocated body of Brady Matthews.

Police were called, and searched the nearby area. Under the snowbank bordering Gates Avenue, only twenty feet away, they found Lewis Tranker. He had died of head and internal injuries.

No one knew how the tragedy occurred, but police were going on the theory that Tranker had built a snow tower around Matthews in such a manner that he could not move to free himself. Tranker was subsequently hit by a car or snowplow during the ongoing storm, and was covered up in the snowbank. The additional snow and freezing temperatures concealed his body, while nearby, his friend suffocated and froze.

I had, indeed, heard sounds from the snowman, Brady Matthews's last cries for help. Alan and I had probably climbed right over Lewis Tranker getting to Gates Avenue.

"Christopher," Dad was saying, "that was you those people saw in the park, wasn't it?"

I looked away, shaking, my eyes filling up.

"Why didn't you tell your mother when you got home?" he asked gently.

I threw my arms around his neck, letting the sobs loose. "I couldn't, Dad," I blubbered. "I was so afraid."

"Christopher," Mom said, "don't worry now. It's all over, honey." They consoled me as I cried some more, mostly out of relief that they weren't angry.

Something occurred to me. Neither one of them mentioned anything about my *first* encounter in the park. They obviously had no knowledge of it. That didn't change the fact that I had actually *heard* Brady's cries for help. In my mind I was still to blame for his death.

So, despite my mother's comforting words, it *wasn't* over. I knew I would still be traumatized by the sight of snowmen and Holdridge Park. But my brother Alan was my biggest worry. He might not only continue to spook me, but might let it slip that I had claimed the snowman in Holdridge Park made sounds that day. I wished with all my eight-year-old might that there would be some way that he would remain silent.

That very night, I got my wish. But it didn't come cheap.

Here's what happened. I can't prove it, but I know it's true. My parents and I had gone to bed. Alan had grown tired of the Christmas fundraiser, and had come home at some point. Everyone was asleep. He snuck into my room, apparently feeling the need to deliver one more stunning torture. He crawled under my bed, the bastard, and started whisper-singing "Frosty the Snowman."

In my half-asleep, guilt-filled mind, I was positive Brady Matthews was next to me, to take me to the hereafter with him for failing to save his life. I rushed screaming from the bed and down the hallway to my parents' room, babbling about snowmen, Brady Matthews, and dying. They had been expecting long bouts of nightmares from me, and immediately began to reassure me.

Alan popped in a few minutes later, having taken the time to get into his pajamas and mess his hair. "What's going on?" he asked.

Mom and Dad filled him in on the day's events. He put on his most convincing sympathetic older brother face. "Gee, that's tough, Chris, you findin' that kid. You gonna be all right?"

I was still shaking and sobbing into my mother's shoulder. But I recognized his voice as the one I heard singing. It *hadn't* been a nightmare, or Brady Matthews's ghost. I didn't dare entertain the thought of telling on him. After all, I was terrified still that he would tell on *me*.

How did I know that it was Alan under my bed, and not a nightmare? The next day I looked under there. My games and baseball glove had been pushed over to the opposite side. Two or three game boxes had indentations, as though someone's leg or elbow had come down on them.

I knew he would never admit it, especially not after what that little prank of his caused.

I was one screwed-up kid after that. I had to have all kinds of counseling. Not that it did much good.

I may have been the only eight-year-old in the world who was scared of snowmen. I nearly fainted when I heard "Frosty" played. Yes, I was afraid of snowmen, but I was *more* afraid of what might be *inside*. Someone could be trapped in there, dying. I couldn't let that happen again.

I began to destroy every snowman I saw, whether it was on school grounds, in a neighbor's yard, or on stranger's property in another part of town. I got in quite a bit of trouble for it over the years. My parents had to keep explaining to people what was behind it. Or should I say, what was *inside* it?

From April through October, when there was rarely any snow on the ground, I seemed okay to everyone, but I wasn't. I knew they would be back. The snowmen, that is. They always came back, and I had to knock them down to make sure no one was trapped inside. Regardless of the weather, I couldn't pass by Holdridge Park without flipping out a little.

Alan knew enough not to tease me any more. He played the All-American boy in front of Mom and Dad, but to me he was a vicious, cruel bastard who had driven me insane.

Yes, insane. What else would explain why I'm here at The Northern Michigan Institute for the Criminally Disturbed?

I bided my time with Alan, but one winter night seven years ago, it was just too much for me. Too much snow. Too many snowmen. There was no end to them. The snowmen, that is. Mom and Dad were on vacation in the Bahamas. I was not considered a danger to anyone.

Merry Christmas, Alan! I won't go into the gory details, except to say that I killed him in his bed, as he had killed part of me in my bed that December night six years earlier.

Then, in our spacious, snow-filled back yard, the fun began. I turned on the floodlights so I could see better. That was my big mistake. The neighbors all knew by now that I was pretty whacked. When they heard laughing and shouting late that night, and saw twenty-seven snowman illuminated in our back yard, they called the police.

There was enough blood on the snow for them to conduct an on-the-spot investigation. I didn't help my own cause any, continuing to build snowmen as I answered their questions with whatever came to mind. I couldn't waste the opportunity, though. The snow was perfect for packing. Within minutes they made me stop, and began toppling my snowman society. I offered to help. After all, who was better qualified?

They found Alan in a snowman leaning against the corner formed by our stone wall and stockade fence. All that work for nothing, as it turned out.

. . .

I've spent the last seven years in places like this, playing the game, continuing my education, impressing the psychologists and social workers with my answers to their trick questions.

Recently, they put me in a room alone and played "Frosty the Snowman" repeatedly. Your tax dollars at work! I'm sure there was a two-way mirror or hidden camera somewhere. What did they think I would do, cover my ears and scream 'Stop it!' at the top of my lungs?

I merely suppressed all my rage and fear and sat there, quietly.

Now, the state of Michigan has determined that I, Christopher LeCoutre, am fit to re-enter society.

True, I have been *trained* and *prepared* to live a normal life. But the only definitive experiences I have had outside these walls are with snowmen: making them, knocking them down, discovering dead bodies inside them . . .and *placing* dead bodies inside them.

I'll *try* it their way for a while, but I'm positive that it won't be long before I gravitate back to them. The snowmen, that is.

And whose bright idea was it to release me in the middle of February? There's nearly two feet of snow on the ground. The kind that's *perfect* for packing.

"SACRIFICE FLY"

Sixty-seven pairs of eyes in the bleachers of the Babe Ruth field followed the baseball as it rose in an arc towards the Rocky Hills left-fielder. On third base, a Silverton player rejoiced in the realization that he was about to score the winning run on the sacrifice fly.

One set of eyes, however, jammed inside the eyeholes of a pair of high-powered Taika binoculars, had stopped following the ball's flight. The eyes belonged to Ollie Mendenhall, a thirty-three-year-old industrial arts teacher at Silverton High School. Ollie's passion was looking at faraway things close up. The expensive, imported binoculars were his most prized possession. He had stopped following the most exciting moment of the game because of what he now observed at a distance of one thousand yards.

Beyond left field was the interstate leading to Rocky Hills. Above it, another road led out of Silverton, and set back from it were modest apartments. He had zeroed in on a fifth floor dwelling, where a young woman stood at a window. The powerful field glasses showed him two additional nuances. The woman dangled a child's doll out the window, as though she meant to drop it. And she was crying, brushing tears away with her free hand as her shoulders convulsed.

It was the kind of hidden drama Ollie reveled in. You could see so much from half a mile away. Up close, people hid, showed you only what they wanted you to see. From a thousand yards away, the world was his microscope.

He could watch the baseball game, and no one would think anything of the binoculars. And while he was here *at* the baseball game, he could watch anything else he pleased.

People around him stood and cheered as the Silverton runner crossed home plate, ending the game in a 3-2 Silverton victory.

Ollie was confused by what he had just secretly witnessed. He looked again. The woman was still there, now closing the window. The doll lay on the sidewalk below. There were so many things people did in their private moments that baffled him.

. . .

During the summer, when school was out, Ollie got up at eight o'clock, drove to a nearby convenience store, and bought the local paper. He was now sitting in the downtown shopping center, reading it, another summer routine. He usually read the paper from back to front, but this morning's headline on page one had jumped out at him.

A four-year-old girl, Kristina Deegan, had fallen from her bedroom window to her death, five floors below. The address was the Silverton Hills Apartments, the same complex where Ollie had seen the woman. His mind raced to keep pace with his eyes as he scanned the article for more details. There were no known witnesses. The girl had been discovered by a resident of the apartments returning home. She was lying on a sidewalk, next to a doll. She had been holding it when she fell, police assumed, or had dropped it from her bedroom window, directly above.

That's not right, his mind screamed. *The doll was already there on the sidewalk. The WOMAN dropped it.*

He read on. Kristina Deegan had been pronounced dead at the scene. She was survived by her mother, Catherine Deegan, age 32, two brothers, and a sister, ranging in age from eleven to six. There was no mention of her father. Catherine Deegan was quoted that she had warned her daughter many times about the window, and how she assumed that Kristina had probably dropped her doll and leaned out to look at it.

There it was again, Ollie thought. Up close, it was one thing. A little girl had fallen from her bedroom window. From a thousand yards away, as he had seen it, it was something else. He reread the article, looking for anything else that might add to his strong suspicion that Catherine Deegan was somehow involved in her daughter's death.

The last paragraph mentioned that Ms. Deegan was having financial problems, and some neighbors of the Silverton Hills Apartments were trying to establish a fund to help with funeral expenses.

Ollie tried to recapture *exactly* what he had seen. He specifically recalled seeing the woman holding the doll as though intent on dropping it. And she was crying, he remembered. He looked at the accompanying photo, showing the thin, attractive Catherine Deegan weeping while being consoled by police. "What are *you* crying about, lady?" Ollie said aloud. "Isn't that what you *wanted* to happen?"

. . .

Ollie was nowhere near secure enough in himself to waltz into the police station, or even call anonymously. In truth, he feared being asked what he was doing with binoculars at a baseball game, or worse, what he was doing looking into someone's apartment.

Every day for the next two weeks, however, he combed the local newspaper for any note of the event or its aftermath. There were occasional updates on the burial fund for Kristina Deegan. One neighbor stated that if Ms. Deegan could have afforded safety bars, the tragedy would not have happened. There were further mentions that Catherine Deegan, a single mother, carried no insurance policies of any kind due to financial hardship.

She didn't do it for the money, Ollie thought. *But she DID it.* Of that assertion, he was convinced.

In this morning's paper there was an article, written as a follow-up to the outpouring of sympathy and contributions to the Deegan Fund. They had surpassed what was needed, but continued to pour in. The Deegan Fund, after funeral expenses, stood at nearly four thousand dollars. The story had been picked up by other newspapers throughout Colorado. Money had been sent from as far east as Denver, and as far west as Grand Junction.

Apparently, the article continued, there was something about the plight of Catherine Deegan and her children that brought out the generous side of people. Perhaps she epitomized the struggle single mothers faced. For lack of money to buy safety bars, an innocent child had died needlessly.

Ollie reread the section on the dollar totals. *She IS making money off this,* he mused.

. . .

In the next few days, Ollie went to war against himself over what he had been insinuating about Catherine Deegan. Perhaps he had been jumping to conclusions. Then, an adamant part of him would remind himself that she had dropped the doll, a clearly premeditated act. *And she lied to the police.* It was a shame you couldn't read minds from a thousand yards away.

As much as divergent thinking was not part of Ollie, he began to see an interesting analogy between the Deegan tragedy, and the baseball game. That last batter knew that if he sacrificed, his team would win. Ollie remembered that he had been taking warm-up swings in the on-deck circle, purposely arcing them upwards. That kid knew what everyone there knew: a sacrifice fly would win the game. *He* would be out, but the *team* would benefit.

What had been going through Catherine Deegan's mind as she stood crying at the window? Had she decided to sacrifice the life of *one* for the betterment of the *rest?*

And was there any guarantee that strangers would come to her aid? There had been enough publicized family tragedies, though, over the years to believe that *was* what usually happened. Death always brought out the best in people, Ollie concluded.

· · ·

There were three choices, he finally decided. Forget about it, go to the police, or talk to Catherine Deegan himself. Following one sleepless night, he surprised himself by choosing to talk to the woman. Telephone was safer, but had an air of crank caller to it. With a sense of righteous nobility, he decided to go in person. It took another three days to work up the courage, now sixteen days since the funeral.

He drove up Silverton Hill Road, turned left into the apartment complex, and found a spot in the visitors parking area. After checking mailboxes in the lobby, Ollie climbed the stairs to apartment 5E. He took a deep breath and knocked. A boy of ten or eleven answered. He had reddish-blond hair and was wearing a Denver Broncos sweatshirt.

"Is your mother home?"

The boy turned. "Mom! There's a man here to see you!"

Ollie could hear a woman's voice in another room as he stepped inside. The boy looked at him intently, a mix of curiosity, fear, and suspicion on his face.

Catherine Deegan suddenly appeared from around a corner. The thin figure and dark blond shoulder-length hair were exactly as he remembered.

"Yes? What can I do for you?" she asked.

"I'm Ollie Mendenhall, Mrs. Deegan."

"*Ms.* Deegan."

"Sorry."

"Are you from the bank?"

"No, nothing like that," Ollie said, flustered. He looked uncomfortably at the boy, still eyeing him with suspicion and curiosity. The woman noticed the glance.

"Tommy, go wait in your room with your brother while Mr. Mendenhall and I are talking. Tell Susie to stay in her room, too."

The boy slunk away, looking back at them once.

"Ms.Deegan," Ollie continued, "I was watching a baseball game at the Babe Ruth field the day your daughter . . .died."

She nodded patiently.

"I was watching through *binoculars.*"

She looked at him blankly, a polite smile still in place.

"I happened to look up at the apartments through the binoculars."

"Yes," she said, a slight impatience surfacing.

"I saw you, Ms. Deegan." He hesitated. "I saw what you did."

The woman's face turned serious, seemingly annoyed. "Saw *what?* What is this all about?"

Ollie took a deep breath. "I saw you drop the doll."

She squinted her eyes, raised her hands in confusion. "You saw me—*What* doll?"

Deny it all you want. I know what I saw. "Ms. Deegan, I saw you drop the doll from the window. You told the police your *daughter* may have dropped it, causing her to fall. But *you* dropped it. I saw you."

The woman stood, hands shaking. Her eyes blazed with anger and indignation. Ollie's eyes widened. He had conned himself into thinking that Catherine Deegan would fold like a house of cards.

"You listen to me," she snapped. "I've been through hell the past three weeks. I don't need to hear anyone practically accuse me of killing my own daughter! I'm going to set you straight on a few things, and then you'd better leave before I have you arrested!"

Still shaking, she grabbed Ollie by the arm, leading him down the hallway.

Oh my God, he thought. *What the hell have I gotten into?* They marched to the far end of the apartment. At a door at the end of the hallway, she knocked loudly, and without waiting for an answer, opened it.

Ollie tried to absorb what he saw inside. There were the usual trappings of a child's bedroom, with posters of Sesame Street characters, and a large wall hanging of a cow jumping over the moon. The Lord's Prayer was embroidered on a cloth on the far wall. In a corner, a disassembled bed leaned against the wall. A young girl sat on the room's other bed, her eyes wide at seeing a stranger.

Ollie focused on the child safety bars at the window. *Yeah, NOW you install them. Well, I'm sure there's still plenty left to live the good life.*

Catherine Deegan's voice shook. "Kristina had her bed against that window. She liked to crawl to the foot of it and look

out. After she fell, I took it down and had the bars installed."
She paused. "Take a look out the window, Mr. Mendenhall,
and tell me what you see."

Ollie froze, and looked back at her, genuine fear in his eyes.

"Don't worry, I'm not going to *push* you," she said
sarcastically.

Ollie went over to the window and looked out. He was
confused and disorientated by the view. He was looking at
the side of the other apartment building. He looked to his left,
towards the highway. The Babe Ruth field was not in sight. It
would have to be around the front corner of the building. He
had not been looking into *this* window with the binoculars.

"Do you see the baseball field?" came a choked voice
behind him.

"No . . .but I *saw—* "

"I'll *tell* you what you saw! You saw me at *my* bedroom
window. Kristina and her doll were found on the sidewalk
below *this* window."

Ollie wrinkled his face, trying to get this mismatched
puzzle together.

The woman exhaled deeply, and made hard eye contact. "I
did drop a doll from my bedroom window that afternoon, but
it had nothing to do with Kristina. It was a different doll."

"I don't understand," Ollie said, still stunned.

"It's none of your business, but I'll tell you anyway. My
whole life seems to be a matter of public record these days."
She sat on the bed next to her daughter. "A few months ago,
my husband ran off. Left me with four kids and no money.
That day you saw me, I got a letter from him. He was back
with his ex-wife in Texas, living in a motor home. He said
he'd never be back, and I'd never get a cent from him."

"I'm sorry, I had no idea—"

"Oh, shut *up!* That's all I ever hear from you people. You're all *sorry!* And what do I have to show for it? A free funeral and child safety bars."

Ollie found it impossible to look at her.

"My husband bought me an expensive doll on our honeymoon, said it reminded him of me. I saved it even after I'd gotten rid of everything else he left behind." Her voice became choked and raspy. "When I read that letter, I was so bitter, I had to get rid of it. It wasn't enough to throw it in the trash, so I dropped it out the window." She squinted hard at him. "*That's* what you saw, you nosey, stupid man."

As embarrassed as Ollie was, he wrinkled his face again. "But when I mentioned a doll—"

The woman exhaled in disgust. "Do you honestly believe I think about a doll my no-good husband gave me after what happened that afternoon?" Her voice became bitter. "I don't sleep at night any more, Mr. Mendenhall." She hugged her daughter, still silent and wide-eyed.

Ollie worked up his nerve enough to make eye contact, as her eyes bore into him, more inquisitive than angry.

"What made you come here, instead of going to the police?"

Ollie's face wrinkled again. "I'm not sure, really. They would have wanted proof, or a sworn statement. The whole thing would have become just more police work. *I* was the only one who saw. I *needed* to find out for myself. I was trying to do something good." He shrugged.

She looked at him intently, trying to comprehend, then walked over to the barred window and looked down.

Uncomfortable, Ollie stood. "I guess I'd better be going. I'm very sorry about all this."

She straightened and turned toward him. "I'm trying to understand what you did, Mr. Mendenhall, but I honestly don't." She motioned for him to walk ahead of her.

When they reached the front door, she said, "Mr. Mendenhall, I'm curious. What were you doing with *binoculars* at such a small place as the Babe Ruth field?"

Ollie hesitated. "I like to see things up close. It's sort of a hobby."

She closed her eyes and shook her head, as if in disbelief. "Be careful what you look at, Mr. Mendenhall. You might see something that's not really there."

He nodded, embarrassed, and looked at the doorknob. She opened the door for him. Without another word, Ollie left, descending the five flights of stairs out to his red Ford. As he opened his door, his eyes fell on the Taika binoculars on the passenger seat. They had been there since that afternoon at the baseball game.

From a fifth floor bedroom window, the woman watched the red car head down Silverton Hill Road. She could still see it as it rounded a bend, looking like a child's toy in the distance. A small black object flew from the driver's side window, bouncing among the scrub, before sliding down the embankment.

The woman allowed a trace of a smile to appear.

"Mom, " sounded a timid voice behind her.

She turned, looked at the boy, his reddish-blond hair catching sunlight from the window.

"Mom, was that man from the police?"

"No, Tommy. He was just . . .a man."

"What did he want?"

"He wanted to talk to me. He thought he saw something the day your sister died."

The boy's eyes widened. It was the look of a trapped, defenseless animal.

"What did he see?" The eyes grew wider still.

"Nothing. The man didn't see anything."

"You didn't—"

"No, Tommy, I didn't.

The boy hugged the woman around the waist, a firm, relieved hug.

"LUCKY FRIDAY"

There was a certain "feel" about Fridays that Scott Verlik could sense from the moment he awoke. Friday was *his* day. Just about everything he touched on Fridays turned to gold.

Since his sophomore year started nearly three months ago, almost every Friday contained cancelled tests for which he was unprepared, money found in the school parking lot, his younger brother getting in trouble, thereby setting him up as "the good son," and a host of other fortuitous happenings.

Today, he *needed* Friday to come through for him. When the boy-girl stuff evolved, his shyness had caused him to miss out. He was gradually becoming someone included in "guy stuff," but cast aside when the girls showed up. Today, though, he would *use* Friday's magic. In yet another stroke of good luck, two seemingly non-related aspects of his life were about to collide, and he would come out smelling like a rose.

This afternoon, as on every Friday, the usual football game would be played in Basson Park with Scott and many of his long-time friends. And, by some stroke of Friday Magic, the girls would be there, watching. He had crushes on all three since seventh grade, but his shyness precluded anything more than a simple hello.

He couldn't decide which one he liked best, but right now Jessica Moser was the most important. She was having a party at her house after the Thanksgiving dance at the high school. Scott liked her pleasant manner, and her shiny, shoulder length red hair. Kathy Hermeneau was nice, too, more outgoing than Jessica, with light brown hair that had darkened over the years. And there was Carole Burns, a black-haired firecracker; loud, but nice. Any one of them would be worth having as his first serious girlfriend. And they would be watching the boys today at Basson Park's weekly football game.

Even the calendar was with him today. There were teacher workshops at the schools, so there would be no classes. He had all morning to get ready. They would play at one o'clock in Basson Park and be home in plenty of time to have dinner and get ready for the dance. And hopefully, Jessica's party, to which he had not been invited . . .*yet.*

But that was why the girls were coming to watch. Jessica wanted to invite some of the boys to her party. Anyone who happened to catch her eye could get an invitation. All he needed to do today, he calculated, was have the game of his life, and he could get an invitation to his first boy-girl party since grade school. *No problem,* he thought. *It's Friday.* Friday was the day when everything he touched turned to gold.

. . .

It was nearly a mile walk from his house to Basson Park, next to the new shopping center. Scott didn't mind. It gave him time to think of ways to get the girls' attention. He had rehearsed a number of witty lines, but minutes later they seemed trite and tired. He would just be himself, and let his performance on the makeshift football field do the talking.

When he arrived, several of the guys were already there, tossing footballs around. Scott carried his lucky red hooded sweatshirt, as the late November day was unseasonably warm. He appraised the other boys, any one of whom could be an ally or an enemy, depending on how the sides were chosen.

Down by the Civil War statue he saw three girls walking slowly towards them. The sun caught the red hair of the girl on the left.

There were a dozen boys gathered now, with a couple of younger brothers tagging along. Usually one of them was given a watch, and the title "Official Timekeeper."

Freddie Coosta and Peter Wansick, the two best players, agreed to choose sides.

"I'll take Digger," said Coosta, pointing at Tom Terenzini, a huge, silent hulk whose father was a funeral director.

"Mike Pace," countered Wansick.

"Bird Man," said Coosta, indicating Jimmy Byrd.

"The other Mike."

"Craig," said Coosta.

"Jerry."

"Shit on you, Wansick. Okay, I'll take Verlik."

"Bob, get your ass over here."

Freddie Coosta looked at the two remaining boys; scrawny, chicken-limbed hopefuls. "Okay, I'll take the Jerry Lewis look-alike," he muttered, indicating Will Sileo, wearing his customary black horn-rimmed glasses and plaid shirt.

"*Him,*" said Wansick with disgust, pointing at Louis Howard.

"We get the ball first, " said Coosta firmly.

"Like hell, Fred!"

"You got *both* Mikes, Wansick! You want the *ball,* too? How about you start on our one-yard-line while you're at it?"

"Odds or evens, Fred," countered Wansick. "Winner gets the ball."

. . .

Half an hour into the game, Scott Verlik crouched in his team's huddle, ten yards from a touchdown that would give them the lead. He was having a decent game, but nothing that would get the attention of the girls, who had taken up positions on the sideline, at midfield.

On defense, he was assigned to cover short passes, of which there were few. Basson Park football was a long ball game. So far he had mostly pass-protected on offense, no bed of roses with Mike Burrell to block. Twice, Burrell had picked him up and thrown him like a sack of flour. Then he started blocking him low, and discovered that Burrell couldn't jump over him.

Scott nearly pinched himself. Freddie Coosta was giving him a chance to make a play. "Scott, you been doin' a good job. Line up next to center like you're gonna block, then slide off into the flat and I'll hit you."

"And don't screw it up," whispered Craig Wargot.

Scott faked a block when the ball was hiked, and slipped downfield a few yards. Peter Wansick grabbed the hood of his sweatshirt to hold him up, but it ripped off, sending Wansick sprawling, allowing Scott to rush to the corner of the end zone, by the chain link fence.

He was wide open. As the ball arced its way toward him, Scott could see a shape coming from the corner of his eye. Jerry Granger bore down on him, looking for an interception. Granger stepped in front of him and extended his arms. There was a thunk of pigskin hitting flesh, and a tannish blur as the ball deflected. Scott reached in the general vicinity; more of a half-hearted attempt than anything, and felt a strange stinging sensation as the ball, point first, seemed to *insert itself* into his hand.

Bellows of approval sounded, with an equal volume of groans and curses. Jerry Granger looked at his hands as though betrayed, then scowled at Scott. "Lucky asshole."

Scott trotted upfield, glancing at the girls, trying to be nonchalant. All three were still applauding. "Nice catch," he heard one of them say.

They played for a few more minutes, then called a ten minute halftime after Freddie Coosta and Mike Pace got into shoving matches on consecutive plays.

Both teams gathered on opposite sidelines, resting or discussing strategies. Scott sat and listened, then realized that among the sneakers surrounding him were three sets of penny loafers. He looked up at Jessica, Kathy, and Carole. Jessica smiled at him. "That was a nice catch, Scott. Did you play on the high school team?"

"No," he answered shyly.

"I'm having a party tonight after the dance."

Thank you, Lucky Friday, he said to himself.

"You're invited if you can make it. I live across from Jerry Granger."

"I know where that is. I'll be there," he said, smiling up at her. High on his own adrenaline, he bolted up and started jogging around the park under the pretense of "loosening up." He looked back occasionally to see that the girls had taken a couple of others aside.

Both teams wandered back onto the fifty-yard stretch of open grass, ready to start the second half. Freddie Coosta and Peter Wansick argued over wheather the teams should switch directions.

"But you'll have the wind, Coosta."

"You had it the *first* half."

"There *wasn't* any wind, then."

Scott barely heard. He was daydreaming a scenario of new-found popularity at the dance, explaining to the girls yet again how he wrestled the ball away from both Jerry Granger and Peter Wansick in the end zone. Later, at the party, Jessica walked over to him, and amid the blaring music and laughter of the party, whispered in his ear . . .

"Verlik! Ya deaf or somethin'? Get the hell down here! We gotta go the other way this half."

. . .

The game evolved into a defensive struggle in the second half. Peter Wansick hit Bob Denninger for a tying touchdown, but neither team threatened to score after that.

Scott checked the sidelines regularly to see if the girls were still watching. They alternated sitting cross-legged on the grass, or standing. Occasionally they took turns teasing Neal Pace, Mike's eight-year-old brother, who was timekeeper.

Just after two o'clock, Scott glanced over to see a white station wagon parked by the sidewalk. A woman had gotten out and was talking to the girls. Scott could not hear, but could see serious expressions on all four faces.

"What's going on over there?" he asked.

"That's Jessica's mother," replied Jerry Granger. "Her grandmother's been sick. Maybe she died."

The woman and the girls piled into the wagon and drove off.

Don't let the old bat die TODAY and ruin everything, Scott pleaded. Neal Pace and the other boy were running towards them. *This can't be good,* Scott said to himself. *C'mon, Lucky Friday, work your magic,* he implored.

"Wadda you jerks want?" snarled Peter Wansick. Scott saw looks of unbelieving shock on the two young faces.

"Someone shot the President in Dallas," Neal Pace gasped.

"He died a few minutes ago," the other boy added.

There was a second of complete silence. Twelve minds struggled to comprehend the impossible. "What the *hell,*" someone said.

"Are you guys pullin' my leg?" Wansick bellowed.

"No, honest," Neal said, holding his hands up protectively. "That's why that lady came to get those girls. I heard her car radio."

There was another interlude of silence.

"I'm goin' home," said Tom Terezini. A full head taller than the others, he walked through the assembled boys, his eyes red-rimmed. Everyone in his path stepped aside, staring. Jerry Granger followed, crossing the street and entering the shopping center.

"Where's *he* goin'?" demanded Peter Wansick.

"His father works in the TV store there," Freddie said.

Wansick looked down at the dying grass. "Let's finish the damn game," he said quietly. "Next touchdown wins it."

. . .

As the ten remaining boys went through the motions of playing football, thoughts of the tragedy tried to force their way into Scott's brain. But anticipation of the dance and Jessica's party refused to give them center stage. His mind was aswirl with images of both. One strange side-effect was that he had no grasp of what was supposed to happen, now.

In the huddle, he asked, "Do they have another election now, or what?"

"Are you *stupid,* or what?" answered Jimmy Byrd. "The *Vice*-President takes over."

Scott looked down, embarrassed. He had known that the Vice-President was next in line. Somehow, it had left his store of information, along with the man's *name.* He was about to ask *that,* then thought better of it.

The half-hearted game continued, without the banter or raucous insults. It was as if ten boys from a school for the deaf were playing football. Peter Wansick finally managed to lead his team into scoring range, using short sideline passes which no one on Scott's team seemed willing or able to defend against.

On third down, scrawny Louis Howard cut across into Scott's sideline zone, and Wansick fired a high, hard pass to him. Howard, wearing leather-soled shoes, had his feet simply disappear from under him as he fell. The ball continued, unimpeded, into Scott's waiting hands. He caught it on a dead run and raced down the sideline, knowing he had a chance to score the winning touchdown. He looked ahead and to his right, expecting to find Peter Wansick about to make a punishing tackle, only to see Wansick running savagely in the opposite direction, screaming one obscenity after another.

Scott cruised into the end zone untouched. "Game's over, boys!" he shouted gleefully, as he turned and headed back upfield. He expected to find his teammates heading toward him, hailing him as the hero. What he saw instead, were seven boys gathering up their various belongings, quietly.

Two others, however, were not. Peter Wansick had taken off after the luckless Louis Howard. He had caught him and thrown him down, attacking him mercilessly. "Stupid, clumsy asshole!" he screamed. "You *had* to fall, didn't you?"

Howard lay on his back, his legs in the air to fend off Wansick, who now twisted off Howard's offending shoes and flung them at him, trying to find a hole in the boy's defenses. He picked up the shoes and threw them repeatedly, as Howard begged forgiveness, adjusting his prone body to the ever-changing angle of attack.

"Leave him alone, Wansick," someone said disinterestedly.

Scott knew Peter Wansick had a short temper, but was amazed at the sudden display of brute force. As of this afternoon, though, such violent outbursts were not limited to boys playing football anymore.

Then he remembered that he had made the game-winning play. "Hey Freddie, we won! I drew a bead on that ball and—"

He stopped in mid-sentence. Everyone was looking at him, frozen. Even Peter Wansick had stopped his furious assault.

"Shut the hell up, Verlik," Freddie said.

Peter Wansick glared at him. "Like winning *means* anything *today.*"

The group seemed about to melt away when they noticed Jerry Granger approaching from the shopping center. He ran across Main St., talking as he ran. "They caught the guy that did it. His name's Oswald."

"Who's *that?*" Scott asked.

Peter Wansick furiously grabbed the nearest football. "The one who *shot* him, asshole," punctuating the word 'shot' by throwing the ball and hitting Scott in the arm.

Granger filled in more details of the assassination, seen on the television sets at his father's place of business. Scott drifted away, the conversation fading as he made his way towards the Civil War statue. For the entire walk home, his mind played mismatched scenes of the assassination, the football game, the dance, and the party in no discernible order.

· · ·

This must be how it is when there's a death in the family, Scott thought. His dad was grim and sober, watching TV in his chair in the living room. His mother stood in the entryway between the living room and the kitchen, choking back quiet tears, her face red. His nine-year-old brother sat in front of the TV, his mouth forming an oval.

Scott picked up the afternoon paper, which had been going to press as news of the shooting was broadcast. "PRESIDENT SHOT!" it screamed, in two-inch high letters, followed by a brief, sketchy report. There wasn't even any mention of Oswald.

The rest of the newspaper was regular day's events. There had been a fire in a nursing home in Ohio, killing sixty people. Secretary of State Dean Rusk was on a trip to Asia. The New York Giants were preparing for a big showdown with the St. Louis Cardinals at Yankee Stadium Sunday.

It was as though the Kennedy headline was a hoax. Someone at the newspaper had a sick sense of humor, possibly.

Scott didn't think he could bear to sit through dinner listening to it discussed endlessly. He told his mother he wasn't hungry and asked if he could go to his room. She looked thoughtfully at him and said yes.

He sat on his bed after laying out his clothes for the dance, wondering if he should tone down his football heroics when he saw the girls. It *would* be a temptation to tell them all about the interception return to win the game. Maybe the girls would be sad, though. He could console them. Yes, he decided, he would be the sympathetic and understanding one, while other guys would be talking about "massive head wounds" and other gory details.

His heart jumped as he realized there was a possibility that Jessica's party would be off. His face-to-face shyness with girls had never carried over to the telephone. He looked up her number and called. A choked, sniffling voice answered.

"Is Jessica there?"

"This is Jessica."

"Oh, I didn't recognize you. This is Scott. I was, uh, wondering if you were still having your party." There was a pause at the other end.

"Are you serious?" The voice's choked quality had been replaced with an impatient anger.

"Well, I wasn't sure, since—"

"Of *course* I'm not having a party tonight! How could you even *ask* such a thing?"

"Oh, okay. Just makin' sure." He needed to end the conversation on a positive note. "I guess I'll see you at the dance, then."

A loud exhaling in his ear startled him. "The dance is *cancelled.* It was on the radio. Why would you think there would even *be* . . .Don't you *care* about what happened?"

Scott could sense that the *S. S. Lucky Friday* was sinking. "Well, of course, I was just—"

"Scott," interrupted a hurt, angry voice, "don't ever call me again. In fact, don't even *talk* to me again."

He stood there, mouth open, hardly believing what he heard.

The voice choked up again. "You insensitive *jackass!*" There was a loud click in his ear.

Scott felt a lump in his throat. Tears burned his eyes. Again, images of the football game, the shooting, the dance, and the party, his personal four horsemen of the apocalypse, played in front of him.

He looked at today's date on the wall calendar. Friday, November 22nd. How could something so *lucky* become so *unlucky. . . so fast?* He grabbed a pen from his nightstand and scribbled violently across the date, bringing to mind Peter Wansick's blind rage at Louis Howard. He scratched out next Friday's date. His rage grew. He flipped the calendar page to December, 1963 and ripped the pen across all four Fridays.

He threw the pen across the room and collapsed on his bed. He was ruined, socially, for the rest of his high school years. Of that, he was positive. Word would spread quickly about his phone conversation with Jessica. All because the President had to go and get himself killed on *his* lucky Friday.

"It isn't *fair,*" he wailed. "It *isn't!*"

Victor Verlik, halfway down the hallway to Scott's room, heard the plaintive words, followed by quiet sobbing. He wanted to knock on the door, but sensed this was a private moment for his son. It could wait. Today, *everything* could wait. He retreated to the kitchen, where his wife was clearing the table.

"Victor, did you talk to Scott?"

"Not now, Marion. He skipped dinner, and now he's in his room, crying."

Motherly anguish appeared on Marion Verlik's face. "Should I—?"

"No," he replied, thinking of the burden nearly everyone bore this day. "Let him be for now. He's taking the President's death awfully hard."

"A STONE'S THROW"

Some things never get paid. Thirteen years and twelve thousand miles later, an ugly part of my past reared up and bit me tonight.

At halftime of *Monday Night Football* my New England Patriots were actually winning, so I was still awake a half hour after my wife and sixteen-year-old son had turned in.

Just before the second half they aired a news spot. Vietnam had released an American POW they had been holding for thirteen years, Marine Pfc. Art Brombaugh. It showed him deplaning in San Francisco. His hair was streaked with gray, and he looked at least twenty years older than his thirty-five years.

I looked carefully at his demeanor. Usually these guys had that so-happy-I-could-cry expression, or one of extreme pride. Art Brombaugh looked like an extra from *Night of the Living Dead.* He stared straight ahead, not acknowledging any of the people cheering. His parents and brother ran up to hug him. His arms never moved as they took turns embracing him vigorously. If they had let him go, I think he would have just toppled to the pavement.

I was counting to ten for the phone to ring. I had gotten as far as eight when it did.

"Hello," I answered.

"Vinnie, this is Mike Perret."

"I just saw him, Mike. Like looking at a ghost, wasn't it?"

"I don't like this, Vinnie."

"You call the other guys, Mike?"

"No, I was hopin' *you* would."

"Okay."

"Vinnie, you gonna call *him?*"

"Are you kidding?"

"No. He's gotta figure one of us would see him. If nobody calls him, that could make things . . . worse."

"Mike, can it really *be* any worse than what happened that night?"

After I hung up, I made calls to Don Stegmeyer in Virginia, Chip Blake in Iowa, and Jesse Lynch in South Dakota. They had all seen Art Brombaugh at one point during the day or early evening. They nominated me to represent them in welcoming Art Brombaugh back to civilian life. They were all scared, too. Who could blame them? How can you put a fellow Marine in hell for thirteen years, and expect him to be forgiving about it?

. . .

On March 26, 1972, I, Sgt. Vincent DiVito, Cpl. Mike Perret, and Privates Brombaugh, Stegmeyer, Blake, and Lynch went on dusk ambush patrol up in Quang Tri Province. Word from intelligence was that a brigade of NVA were moving through. Our job was to ambush their recon parties.

We would traverse an area, looking for the best cover. Then I would walk the patrol across, dropping off one man every sixty feet. I had already dropped off Art Brombaugh at the left end and was about to leave off Don Stegmeyer at the next position when we heard our radio crackle to life. Those guys back at Battalion could get us killed breaking radio silence.

They were trying to save us, though, screaming for us to pull out. They had gotten some updated reports. The NVA was rushing the *entire* brigade south. The six of us were about to be engulfed by several hundred enemy regulars. Not five seconds later, we heard them. They couldn't have been any more than thirty yards away.

I made a snap decision, one I regret to this day. It was pitch dark now. I picked up a stone and threw it away from us to mislead the enemy. I threw it directly back toward Private Arthur Brombaugh. God forgive me.

I have replayed that moment thousands of times since. Why didn't I throw it in the other direction? That was our escape route. Maybe I actually *forgot* that Art was back there. It happened so fast.

The enemy must have heard the stone hit to our left, and opened up with small arms fire. We ran at least three hundred yards before stopping to regroup. On my orders, Chip Blake called in a mortar attack on that sector to buy us some time.

Even then I thought how ironic it would be if Art had somehow survived their onslaught, remained undetected, and then got pasted by one of own mortar rounds.

We five made it back to Battalion. Art Brombaugh was listed as "Missing in Action." There was no search. That area was now "hot" and under enemy control.

All four of the others realized that I had made an error that cost a man his life, so we thought. But none held it against me. In the past, I had gotten them out of tighter spots. We quietly agreed to speak no more of it. Our secret acted as a bond, and we spent the rest of our tour as comrades and friends.

All of us, Art included, had exchanged addresses and phone numbers over there, intending to remain close when we came home. What happened on patrol that night put an end to all that. We kept in touch a couple times a year by letter and phone, mostly updates on our civilian life. There were no reunions. Nobody had any good war stories to remember. We all had one we were trying to *forget.*

Where are they now? Thirteen years later, Mike Perret is a truck driver out of Cody, Wyoming, married with a young daughter and another on the way. Chip Blake owns a bookstore in Dubuque, Iowa. To his credit, he refuses to carry any books on Vietnam. Jesse Lynch resides in his native South Dakota, working for the National Park Service at Mt. Rushmore. He was married and divorced within two years. He tells me he never got Vietnam out of his system, whatever that means. Don Stegmeyer is single, and a music teacher in Roanoke, Virginia. He took up drums after the war. I think he just wanted to hit something that had no chance of hitting back.

And I, Vinnie DiVito, cover high school sports for a newspaper here in Providence, Rhode Island. I'm comfortable, have a great wife and son, and am basically happy, except for the occasional nightmares. They all involve me tossing a stone in the direction of Art Brombaugh. The stone has grown in size over the years. In the last dream, it was about three feet across and weighed over four-hundred pounds.

Art Brombaugh was from Santa Fe, New Mexico. His father owned a hardware store, and wanted him and his older brother to take over when he retired. I noticed that he walked with a limp, and the commentator stated that he has only partial use of his right arm. I assume he was hit by a couple of rounds in that barrage I caused to come his way. Even if he wasn't, the Vietnamese were brutal in their treatment of Americans.

But to them, he was the enemy. What's *my* excuse?

. . .

Bravery comes in many forms. I've been in combat, faced enemy fire. That was nothing compared to what it took to dial out-of-state information the next day to locate Art Brombaugh.

I had long since thrown away his address and phone number. It felt like destroying evidence at a crime scene.

The operator read me three listings for 'Brombaugh' in Santa Fe. One of them, Hector Brombaugh, sounded familiar. I assumed it was Art's father. An older-sounding man answered the phone.

"Hello, I'm looking for an Art Brombaugh. Is this the correct residence?"

"Yes, but he's asleep. Who's calling?"

"Vinnie DiVito. I was in his unit in Vietnam."

"*Sergeant* DiVito?"

"Yes."

"He mentioned you in letters years ago. I'm sure he'll want to talk to you. Hang on." There was a dull clunk as he put the phone down.

It was a minute or two before the phone was picked up, and in that interval I thought about the two hells I faced. In one, I stood accused of betraying a man under my command, endangering his life, and causing a sizeable portion of it to be wasted. In the other, I was consumed by the secrecy of a deed so vile that I could hardly speak of it.

"Sergeant DiVito?"

I waited to see which hell it would be.

"Art, is that you?"

"It's me Sergeant. I finally made it home."

He sounded relieved and happy. The second hell, then. "Mike Perret called as soon as he saw you, Art. I called the others. They all saw you and send their warmest regards."

"Sergeant?"

"Yes, Art?"

"I've had a lot of time to think these past years."

That didn't sound promising. "Think about what, Art?"

"About that night."

I froze. He *did* know, then. Even though he still thought of me as his Sergeant, he was going to call me on it.

"Sergeant, this may sound corny, but there's some unfinished business between us that can't be settled over the phone."

Part of me was telling myself to come clean with him. He'd earned that much. But I still didn't have the guts to admit what I'd done. I did what I'd become best at. I played dumb. "What are you talking about, Art? What unfinished business?"

"I can't talk about it now, Sarge. I'm gonna rest a week or two, then I'm gonna come and see you. I hope you don't mind, but I *have* to."

I was grateful he couldn't see the shock and shame on my face.

"You still live in Providence, Sarge?"

Maybe if I told him I lived in Vietnam he'd stay away, but I was getting used to the idea that the secret was over. "Yeah," I said. "I still live in Providence, Art."

"Take care, Sergeant DiVito. I'll see you soon." He hung up.

. . .

If Art Brombaugh lived in a physical hell the past thirteen years, I was living in a psychological one the next few days. I considered every option, from moving, to hiring a bodyguard, to calling and trying to stop him from coming. But like that night back in 1972, my mind just seized up.

I called everyone and told them of our conversation. Don Stegmeyer advised me to meet him in a public place. Chip Blake said I should have a gun on me. I'm sure they meant well. Jesse Lynch told me to spill everything to my family. That I rejected out of hand. I could barely admit to myself what I'd done.

Six weeks passed. He said he was going to rest a week or two, then come to see me. As the days mounted, I began to wonder what happened. Had there been medical complications? Had he reconsidered and decided to bury the past? He couldn't have simply forgotten.

I made the phone rounds of the others weekly. In my paranoid condition, I pictured him working his way east, exacting revenge on all five of us. But none of them had seen or heard from him, and they weren't about to make contact. I tried to get a volunteer to call, feel him out, maybe get him to tip his hand.

"We aren't in 'Nam, Vinnie," Chip Blake scolded. "We don't *volunteer* for dangerous missions any more. Ain't it enough we kept our mouths shut all these years. *We* weren't the ones who gave him away."

That hurt. But it was the truth.

One rainy night a few days later, the phone rang. "Sergeant DiVito, this is Art Brombaugh calling."

I could hear bustling in the background. "Where are you, Art?"

"Right here in Providence, at the airport. I'm about to rent a car."

Curiosity got the better of me. "You said a week or two, Art. What happened?"

"Had to get a new driver's license. My old one expired. They made me take the driving test, because of my . . .injuries. Took about a month. I'll be needing your address, Sergeant."

He was so close, now. "Art what the hell is this all about?"

"Sorry, Sergeant. I promised myself if I ever got back, I would settle with you in person. It helped keep me alive all those years . . . back there."

Feeling like a condemned man ordering his last meal, I heard myself giving Art directions to my house.

· · ·

I made final preparations to meet this ghost from my past. I went upstairs and told Vinnie Jr. that a fellow Marine from Vietnam was coming over. I wanted our reunion to be private. I tossed him my car keys and a twenty.

He winked at me as he was leaving. "So Dad, how long does it take two ex-Marines to name every whorehouse in Saigon?"

I smiled a little. "About two hours." It was just after eight. My wife, an investment advisor, was paying a house call on a client, and wouldn't be back until nine-thirty or ten.

After my son left, I got out my Colt Trooper, loaded it, and put it under the couch cushion next to where I planned to sit. I was guilty, no argument, but I wasn't going like a lamb to the slaughter. I reserved the right to defend my life, no matter what I'd done in the past.

A car pulled up at eight-thirty. I heard the door slam, and an uneven scraping of someone coming up our walk and porch steps. The doorbell rang. I peered through the curtains as a precaution, and saw him standing there. His hands were visible and empty. I opened the door.

He looked somewhat healthier than the walking corpse I'd seen on the news, but he still carried signs of suffering in his posture and face. Two lower front teeth were missing. As he limped across the threshold, I stuck out my right hand. "Welcome home, Art."

He grabbed my outstretched hand with his left and shook it in a weak, ragged motion. "Excuse the handshake, Sergeant. My right arm—"

"It's okay, Art. I forgot." I showed him to a cushioned chair across from the couch, and asked if he wanted a beer, or something stronger.

"No thanks, Sarge."

I settled onto the couch, placing my hand on the cushion next to me, pressing down until I could feel the revolver beneath. I spoke first, defending myself, although deep down I knew I had no right. "Art, we're civilians now. Vietnam was a long time ago. Anything that happened in combat back then has to be viewed separate from our lives now, I think."

His jaw trembled. "A Marine is supposed to look out for his buddies. Right, Sergeant?"

He *did* know, then. "Yes, Art, but—"

"And the last thing a Marine would do," he continued, his voice shaking, "is to give away his buddies to save himself. Isn't that right, too, Sergeant?"

"Yes, Art, it is." I replied softly.

"I was alone over there, Sarge. There were five of you. You at least had a fighting chance!"

I hung my head, waiting for him to come right out and say it. He stood suddenly, wobbled a bit and looked me in the eye, as my hand reached ever-so-slightly under the cushion.

"Sergeant DiVito, when I heard what seemed like a large body of the enemy bearing down on our positions, I grabbed a metal tube of camouflage paint and was about to toss it in your direction when they opened fire."

There was silence in the room. Had I heard correctly?

"I have come here Sergeant," he continued, his voice cracking, "to ask your forgiveness."

I stared at him in disbelief. Here I sat, with one last chance to confess, and possibly come out all right. He apparently, felt guilty enough for what he merely *intended* to do. Or I could keep my secret, and let him take the brunt of the suffering, as I'd done before. It didn't take long to choose. I merely reverted to form.

I waved away his admission as if it were nothing. Trying to look puzzled, I asked, "Art, why do you think the enemy opened up on *you?* They were closer to *us.* Did you hear—I mean, did you make a sound?"

His voice remained choked with emotion. "I'm not sure how they got a fix on me. Maybe when I did *this.* " He raised his left arm as if to throw something, demonstrating what the enemy might have seen. "It was fate, Sergeant, or God punishing me for being a bad Marine."

I walked over to him, putting my hands on his shoulders, and acted out this new part that had fallen in my lap. "Art, I don't consider you a bad Marine. You're a damn fine one, in fact, to come here and admit what you did." I paused, as though searching for an irony, but I *knew* what my next line was. "Sometimes, Art, I feel as though *I* was the one who let *you* down."

He smiled through teary eyes. "Just *like* you, Sarge, to put your men first."

I did a casual 'think nothing of it' toss of my head. "Tell you what, Art. To show there's no hard feelings, I give you my word I'll never mention this to the other guys."

His face lit up in gratitude and awe. "Sergeant, you are definitely the most class 'A' Marine a guy could ever serve with."

When he had composed himself, he said goodnight and thanked me again as I walked him toward the door. As I opened it, he broke into a wide grin, looking like a kid on Christmas morning.

"I had faith, sir, that you would understand."

"You know I do, Art."

"I'm forever in your debt."

I nodded humbly.

"Before I came out here, sir, I had the VA find me a job."

"Good, Art. What is it?"

"I'm a counselor for disabled vets, guys like me. Waddaya think?"

"They couldn't have picked a better man," I said, with false enthusiasm, trying to move him along.

"And it's right here in Providence, Sarge."

"What?"

"That's right. I brought all my stuff. They found me a furnished apartment not ten minutes from here."

"That's . . .that's *great*, Art."

"It's the *greatest,* Sarge."

I'll swear on a stack of Bibles that his entire demeanor had changed. He looked like a cat who's found a wounded mouse. He clapped his left arm around my shoulders, a gesture way out of character for him.

"From now on, Sarge, we're gonna be like *this,*" he said, crossing his index and middle finger, his voice filled with exaggerated charm. "The best part is . . ." he winked. "I'll only be a stone's throw away."

"CRAWLY STICK"

D. J. Galley looked at the newly-occupied apartments from his perch in the old tree fort, some thirty feet above the pine needle carpet.

He was paying closer attention these days to what his father called "external influences." He still wasn't sure what the words meant, but he knew they were bad. Dad had said so. It had to do with what he called "Northern trash movin' down here and takin' our jobs."

Last night, the *South Sullivan Daily* had an article about the new apartments, and how they were being occupied by workers from a bankrupt plant in upstate New York. At dinner, Dad and Mom had discussed it.

"You read the article I showed you, Mel?"

"Yeah. Damn shame, that's what it is."

"Them people need jobs too, Mel."

"Then let 'um have their jobs up North. There ain't enough to go around no more, Linda."

"Their union was pretty smart, havin' a relocation clause in the contract."

"Pretty smart, all right. There's word goin' around that some of *us* might get bumped 'cause of *them.*"

D. J. took a last look at the apartments before settling down to the pile of Dad's comic books he was allowed to bring to the tree fort since turning nine last month. He had been watching to see if there were any kids his age. It could get lonely on the outskirts of South Sullivan.

The only kids he had seen were the pesty four to six-year-olds. The kind of kid that could ruin a guy's secret hideaway. "External influences," he muttered.

For a while D. J. was lost in the comic book world of a generation past. A crunching sound snapped him back to reality. Looking down, he spied a small boy, about five, wandering at the wood's edge, a hundred feet away. He wore a faded red T-shirt and blue shorts.

D. J. squinted hatred through hazel eyes. What if he told the other pests what great woods these were? They would overrun the place in no time. His one sanctuary would be ruined. Dad was right. These Northerners brought nothin' but trouble.

He kept an eye on the boy as he descended the wooden rungs. *Got to get rid of him*, D. J. thought. He *could* just bully him into leaving. But the kid might tell his parents. No. He had to think of something that would make *all* of them *want* to stay away. Maybe even move back North, and save his dad's job.

As he made his way down, he caught sight of the pond fifty yards farther into the woods. He had been warned about it ever since his dad helped him build the treehouse. Even now, he never even *considered* going near it. D. J. smiled. He reached the ground and regauged his bearings, looking for the boy. Noticing a patch of red behind some bushes, he approached, still smiling.

"Hey," he said, startling the youngster. "Watcha all doin' here?"

"Nothin.' Just lookin' around."

Plan 'A', D. J. thought. "You shouldn't be here, ya know. There's lots of dangerous wild animals."

The boy's eyes widened, but an excited smile accompanied them. "There are? Can we see some?"

D. J. swallowed his own smile. If anything, he had made the woods *more* attractive to him. "What's your name, kid?"

"Todd. What's yours?"

"Harold," D. J. replied. "How come you ain't ascared of the wild animals?"

"I like 'um." His face dropped. "But my mom says I can't have none 'cause we live in a 'partment now. There's *lots* of kids, but no animals."

"Don't remind me," D. J. mumbled.

"These are nice woods," Todd said. "I'm gonna come here from now on."

Plan 'B', D. J. thought. " The woods are okay, but the pond over yonder is even *better. That's* where all the wild animals hide."

Todd's head sank in further disappointment. "I guess I won't be seein' them, then. I ain't allowed to go near water. I can't swim."

Damn it all, D. J. said to himself. *I ain't even GOT a Plan 'C' yet.*

"Todd!" called a woman's voice in the distance. The boy snapped to attention, looking guilty and scared.

"I gotta go."

"Don't tell nobody about the woods, okay?" D. J. said. The boy didn't answer, continuing to run until he was out of sight. D. J. headed back to the tree fort. He had time to read a few more comic books. *And* come up with Plan 'C'.

. . .

The brown paper sack beside him in the tree fort held three small bottles of paint, paint thinner, brushes, and a dozen foot-long round wooden sticks, formerly logs in D. J.'s toy construction set. He still used the set, but had decided to sacrifice the logs.

He placed the sack's contents in a neat assembly line order; the black, red, and yellow paint lined up in the correct sequence Plan 'C' required. He chuckled and repeated the adage his mother made him recite whenever he came out here. "Black on yellow can kill a fellow."

When he had finished painting, ninety minutes later, each former log was decked out in wide alternating bands of black and red, separated by narrower bands of yellow. As he admired his work, he heard rustling below.

"Harold," called a tiny voice. "You out here? It's me, Todd."

D. J. hunkered down in his stronghold. "It's not time for Plan 'C' yet, you little booger," he said softly. The tree fort was nearly undetectable from the ground. D. J. continued to lay low, waiting for the five-year-old to tire of his search.

Todd wandered haphazardly for a few more minutes, calling for "Harold," before giving up and heading towards the apartments.

D. J. stood and watched the distant figure. "Next time, we'll have some fun, looking for. . ." he glanced at the colored wood. ". . .magic crawling sticks."

. . .

Donald James Galley stood in his tree fort, watching the distant apartments, ready to drop down if he saw Todd approaching. Next to him was yesterday's handiwork, the paint now dry. "Stupid kid's gonna come 'round lookin' for *Harold.*" He was quite pleased for having given a fake name, on the almost certainty that Todd would mention him at home. "Unless," he mused, "he wants this to be a secret from his parents. In that case, even better."

He climbed down and quickly "hid" the colored logs so as to be easily detectable. "Just enough so he'll have to work a little," he said aloud. Then he climbed back up to watch.

Minutes later, he observed a young boy resembling Todd hitting a whiffle ball in his apartments' small backyard lot. A woman's head appeared at a nearby window. The boy waved at her. As soon as she disappeared, he dropped the bat and ran nonstop for the woods, as though legging out the world's longest single.

"You little sneak," said D. J. He hurried down before Todd could discover his secret whereabouts and positioned himself about twenty yards away.

"Harold, you're *here!*" Todd said brightly, finding D. J. by the bushed he had rounded.

"That's right. This is my favorite place."

"Mine too."

"Ya know *why* this is my favorite place?"

"Why?"

"Cause it used to be a *magic* place."

Todd looked fascinated, but puzzled.

"There used to be magic colored trees here long time ago, but they're gone now."

"What happened to them? Did they die?"

"Somethin' like that. All that's left of them are a few pieces of their branches. They're hard to find. But I found one today." D. J. reached behind him and removed the remaining colored log from his back pocket, holding it near Todd's eyes.

The bright colors mesmerized him. He reached for it, but D. J. pulled it away, looking at Todd's shabby T-shirt and ripped jeans.

"I'll give you a whole quarter for every magic stick you find me."

Todd's eyes widened. "Really? Where should I look?"

D. J. feigned deep thought. "Well, I been lookin' 'round here, but all's I could find was this one. Maybe if you looked over yonder there," he said pointing in the opposite direction.

"Okay!"

For the next ten minutes, D. J. pretended to look in places he knew were barren, at the same time suggesting certain rocks, bushes, and clumps of grass to Todd, several of which concealed a colored wooden stick. D. J. laughed to himself. He could actually *see* some of them sticking out as he directed Todd to their location.

"Another magic stick!" Todd shouted, bending down and snatching his latest find from between two rocks.

"Boy, you sure have a knack for findin' 'em," D. J. said good-naturedly. "That's six, now." *This is perfect,* he thought. *He's grabbin' 'em before he can even tell what they are.*

"I'm tired, Harold. Can we rest?"

"I think that's enough for today."

"When do I get my quarters?"

"Right now," said D. J., reaching into his jeans pocket. He had been saving to buy a model car, but like the wooden logs, had decided to "invest" in a more important undertaking. He smiled patronizingly as he handed over the quarters. "Here you go. Buy yourself some decent clothes."

"My mommy and daddy do that," Todd said innocently. "But they said they don't have much money right now."

"Next time," D. J. stated casually, "maybe you can make five whole dollars."

"How?"

D. J. sat down on the pine needles. Todd copied him. "Ya see, sometimes the magic sticks can come to life. They turn into magic crawling sticks."

"Crawly sticks?"

"Yeah," D. J. said, chuckling at the mispronunciation. "Crawly sticks. And you know what?"

"What?"

"If you catch one before it gets away, it will give you anything you want."

Todd's eyes turned to saucers, his mouth formed an oval. *"Anything?"*

"That's right. When I was little, I caught one, and it gave me lots of money and toys."

"Can I see it?"

D. J. dropped his head in mock sadness. "It crawled away one day when I left the door open. But there might be another one around here."

"Let's look. I'm not tired any more."

D. J. glanced at the sun. Todd did the same. "They only come out on cloudy days."

"Oh." Todd closed his hands and jiggled the six quarters.

"Remember, don't tell nobody, or you'll have to give the money back, and I won't help you look for a crawly stick," D. J. warned.

"I won't."

"You better get on home before your mama comes lookin' for you."

"Okay. Bye, Harold." He ran out of the woods as quickly as he had run in.

D. J. remained on the ground, idly banging two of the sticks together. He snorted with contempt. *"Crawly* sticks!"

. . .

The day was perfect. At eight in the morning the cloud cover was so thick and dark it seemed like late afternoon. D. J. had arisen early, left a note to Mom that he was taking a hike out on Highway 72, and gone out to the garage for a bucket and the long metal strip Dad had bent at the bottom to form an 'L'.

He was going to the pond. He had never even gone close to it before, but today he *had* to. A lot depended on his bravery and success. Maybe even Dad's job at the mill. Today he would do what no one in South Sullivan, Georgia would even attempt. He was going to capture a Harlequin, the Southeastern coral snake.

He had always paid attention when the teacher talked about poisonous snakes. He knew they were shy and wouldn't strike unless stepped on or handled. And he knew their fangs were so small that nearly half those bitten were not poisoned because the skin was not broken.

He was confident that the plan would work if he could capture a Harlequin. His heart pounded. He had never felt so *scared,* or so *invigorated.*

He passed by the tree fort, yearning for the times he could just idle away the day there. Not today, though. There was dangerous, important work to be done. His musing had caused him to temporarily lose his vigilance. He didn't see the black, red, and yellow shape until he had stepped on it, that last instant seeming to play out in slow motion as he watched his foot come down.

He shrieked, trying to move every muscle at once, in every possible direction. The hard shape gave way, as he sprawled on the ground, the bucket and metal rod clanging against each other as he rolled , heart jackhammering. He leaped up to determine the snake's location.

The colored bands *rolled* down the slight incline, then stopped. It was one of the logs he had hidden. D. J. wanted to laugh at his foolishness, but couldn't. He put a hand over his pounding heart. "Damn it all," he said. He rounded up the bucket and rod and continued toward the pond.

He approached slowly, one step at a time, as though sneaking up on an enemy. Ten feet from the mushy, reedy shores a bullfrog sprang into the water, followed by other splashes around the pond. Circling, he watched the water's edge intently. "Gotta be careful," he reminded himself. Dark shapes revealed themselves in the shallow water, most of them apparently in flight. Halfway around the pond he came upon several sheets of long-rotted plywood, possibly discarded by a builder of the houses on the other side of the pond.

He laid the bucket down and eased the bent section of the metal rod beneath the plywood. With all his might, he lurched up and away, lifting the plywood and flipping it end over end. Part of him wanted to attack instantly, but was overruled by the awe at seeing the largest coral snake he could imagine. In a second, *half* of it had taken off in the direction he had come. There were *two* of them.

D. J. grabbed the bucket and rammed the metal rod onto the remaining Harlequin, but it wriggled free and took off in the opposite direction. D. J. gave chase, careful not to fall into the water or onto his prey. Several times he caught up to the coral, pinning it. But each time, after initially rearing back and biting the metal, the snake was able to escape, aided by soft, uneven ground, a loose rock, or D. J.'s reluctance to press down hard enough to hold the snake's furious movements.

Finally, at the head of the pond, where the ground was harder and less sloped, he pinned him two inches behind the black head. The snake could not reach up or around to bite, and the boy's resolute pressure on the rod held it fast.

He dropped the bucket, and gathering all his resolve, stepped on the thirty-nine inch serpent at its midpoint, sliding the metal rod up until its head was pinned. For the next five minutes, he prayed for the nerve to grab the snake behind the head.

"Please, God, don't let nothin' happen." He held his breath and picked up the snake, holding it at arm's length. The mouth was open, the body whipsawed beneath his arm.

He squatted, grabbed the bucket, and eased the snake to ground level, pointing its head directly up to prevent it taking off immediately. When he had jockeyed the opening directly over the coiled reptile, he released his grip and slammed the bucket down. Keeping one foot on it, he reached for a nearby rock and placed it on top. He could hear thrashing and scraping sounds, but the bucket didn't budge.

D. J. waited for his breathing to return to normal, then looked admiringly at the fruits of his cunning and bravery. A slow, simmering smile appeared. He walked back towards the tree fort, carrying the metal rod. "Oh, To-*odd*," he cooed, "I've got a *surprise* for yoooooou."

. . .

D. J. held the five dollar bill lengthwise. "Here it is. It's all yours if you find a magic crawly stick."

"Think we'll find some today, Harold?"

D. J. fought back a smile. "Well, maybe *one,* anyways."

They walked towards the pond, D. J. pretending to look at the ground, raising his eyes to locate the bucket in the distance. Todd dutifully imitated him.

"Remember, Todd, crawly sticks *look* like snakes, but they ain't."

"How come they look like snakes, Harold?"

"Uh . . . so's not *anybody* will pick 'um up. Just kids like us."

"Oh."

They were fifteen feet from the bucket, the pond in full view. Todd halted. "Uh oh."

"What?"

"I ain't allowed to go near water, 'cause I—"

"Can't *swim,* I *know.*" D. J. realized he had to handle this carefully. "You don't have to get any closer than that bucket there, okay?"

"I guess."

They approached the bucket. D. J. stopped, held his arms out as though asking for quiet. "I think I hear one, Todd."

"Where?"

"Somewhere right around here." He pointed at the bucket. "Crawly sticks *like* to hide under buckets and stuff. Tell you what. I'll go on down by the water and look, and you look under there."

"Okay!" Todd started to rush forward, but D. J. caught him by the arm.

"Hold on there, Todd, old boy. Let me get down there in case he gets away from you."

"All right."

D. J. walked past the bucket, then turned and pointed at it, eyes wide, in a pantomime of discovery. In truth, he had no desire to watch. If by chance he was questioned, he could always say, truthfully, that he hadn't *seen* the snake. The trusty old bucket, of course, would have to be tossed into the pond. Facing the water, he heard Todd's footsteps.

"Harold! A crawly stick! I'll get him!"

Any second now, D. J. thought.

"No you don't crawly stick. Get back here!"

Yeah, get back there, crawly stick.

"I got you *now,* you little—"

The shriek that pierced the air gave D. J. an instantaneous jolt. He was sure he had jumped. He turned to take in the scene he had orchestrated.

The bucket remained upside down, the rock still in place. *Bet he only lifted it an inch before that devil came flying out of there.* Todd was uphill about ten feet away, seated, wailing loudly. Twenty feet to the right, the grass was a kaleidoscope of black, red, and yellow as the Harlequin made its escape toward the far end of the pond.

"Nice goin', big guy," he whispered. He ambled up the hill, smiling at the stricken boy. He bent and looked into the pale, frightened face, snapping his fingers in mock forgetfulness. "Oh yeah, Todd, I forgot. Crawly sticks *bite* sometimes. *And,* they're *very* poisonous.

Todd struggled to get his voice under control. " I d-don't like y-you Harold. You're *mean!*"

D. J. smiled a pitying smile. "Todd, old boy, I'd say you had more important things to worry about right now." Todd remained sitting, engaged in a new round of sniffling. "Well, Todd, gotta run. First, I better toss this old bucket in the pond."

He walked over to it, threw the rock aside, and grabbed it, in the same motion walking over the spot it had occupied. For the second time, his heart leaped as his foot came down on the black, red, and yellow color pattern.

The furious Harlequin struck, sliding up between the billow of D. J.'s jeans and his bare leg. He felt the stinging pierce in his leg; felt it again, and felt it a third time before his brain signaled to shake his leg vigorously. The coral was flung several feet away, making a mad dash around the pond.

No words came immediately. D. J. pulled up his pants and stared at his lower leg. Three neat sets of puncture wounds marked it. "Oh, *JESUS!* There were *TWO* of them!"

Todd had stopped crying, stood, and walked over to D. J. "Ha ha, you got bit by a crawly stick, too." He peered at the wound, then seemed to lose interest in the entire episode. "I'm going home now."

Although numbness was already setting in, D. J.'s brain was still processing information. "But *you* got bit, *too!*"

Todd lifted his foot and pointed. "The other crawly stick bit my *sneaker.*"

"You're not poisoned!" D. J. shouted. "Todd, listen to me. I need—"

"I'm not playing 'crawly sticks' any more, Harold." Todd turned and walked uphill towards the woods entrance.

D. J. attempted to rise, found his limbs unwilling. "Wait! Go get help! I'll *die!*"

Todd looked down at the older boy. "No! You lied!" He turned and ran out of the woods.

D. J. could feel his breathing becoming labored, his chest tight and burning, and the numbing sensation in his limbs growing.

His brain, in its last stages of usefulness, was reminding him that captured "crawly sticks" gave off a distress scent, often picked up by their mate.

"EIGHT-TRACK"

It was one of those neighborhoods where the 'Have's' and 'Have-Not's' lived side by side. Oddly enough, the rich family, the Redmers, bordered on the property of Del Strobeck, the neighborhood Have Not.

We called him Eight-Track, after the obsolete tapes he collected, and spent as much time hanging out there as we did at the ball fields or each other's houses.

I know that a bunch of eleven and twelve-year-olds palling around with a guy in his late sixties seems kind of odd. But Eight-Track was more like an *advisor* to us. We'd go over there, six or seven of us, complaining about our parents, and nine times out of ten he'd take *their* side. But he'd *explain* it to us, at least. Most of the parents didn't care too much at first for us going over there. Eventually, they realized that he was okay. After that, they weren't suspicious, although I don't think any of them were really crazy about it.

Richard Kane, the eighteen-year-old half brother of Mike Pfleuger, one of our gang, always gave us a hard time about it, though. "You guys oughta stay clear of that old coot!" he'd say. Richard had grown up bitter. His father was actually the fourth-to-last man killed in Vietnam. He took it out on the world in general, us in particular. We'd be sitting on top of the hill where Eight-Track's house was, and Richard would walk by, shaking his head and giving us dirty looks.

Marcus Wesley, a kid that liked to talk as if he was from King Arthur's time, would say, "Ah, Richard the Fatherless passes."

Mike would whisper, "You mean Richard the *Asshole.*"

. . .

What did we do at Eight-Track's house? Mostly we listened to him tell of his life experiences. He had tons of fascinating stories, many involving some weird conspiracy to take over the country. We didn't understand any of it, but it was fun to hear.

He claimed that one of his friends was there at President Kennedy's assassination. That got him going on this theory as to who was *really* behind the shooting. According to Eight-Track, it was a dairy corporation in Wisconsin and two infielders from the New York Mets. And don't even *ask* what the war in Vietnam had *really* been about.

"Tungsten mines!" he would exclaim. "We didn't want the Communists getting their hands on all that tungsten!"

All of his tapes were homemade narrations of his philosophy and stories. He tried a couple out on us, but they didn't hold our attention. Why listen to a tape of him when it was more fun when he talked live? We would interrupt with questions and objections to his weird theories.

For a retired truck mechanic with a bad back, a wife who had run off with a school custodian, and not much money, he seemed pretty happy. He still drove his sapphire-blue 1976 Plymouth Volare`, which he kept in great running condition, despite his back. Everything with him, everything *about* him, seemed just right. But, as he himself used to say, "Nothing in life remains static for very long."

. . .

We went over to his house one morning during the first week of summer vacation.

"Somethin' happened over there," he said grimly, pointing down his slope towards the Redmers. Their back yard, containing a luxurious built-in swimming pool, was visible even over the seven foot stockade fence separating the two yards.

"What's goin' on, Eight-Track?" Lance Derwish asked.

"I don't know, but there's cops and ambulance guys there."

We tried to get a better look, but that's when he kicked us out. No big deal. We ran around the block to the front of Redmer's property. Sure enough, there were two police cars, another marked "County Medical Examiner," an ambulance, and a couple dozen people standing around on lawns and sidewalks.

"What happened?" we all asked, clamoring about.

The stern adults told us to simmer down, so we listened in on various conversations.

"Mrs. Redmer drowned in her pool last night," said one woman.

"Probably had too much to drink, as usual," added an older man.

"You don't know any such thing, George," someone scolded.

"I heard she had lung cancer," said the first woman. "Smoked like a fiend. Probably didn't have long, anyway."

We were shocked . Nothing like this had ever happened before. We didn't really *know* the Redmers. They owned several dry cleaning stores, and mostly sat by their pool drinking all day. Finally, the ambulance guys wheeled a stretcher down the driveway. There was a long dark green bag on it.

We drifted over to Marcus's house for a while and talked about what it must feel like to drown, then headed over to Eight-Track's again. His old Plymouth was there, but he didn't answer the door. We yelled for him and everything. Norm

Sutter even tried his back door, but it was locked. Marcus had that thoughtful look on his face. "Perhaps Eight-Track is disturbed by the untimely passing of Lady Redmer."

The drowning was front page news the next morning. Mr. Redmer told police that he and his wife had a few drinks by the pool before he went to bed around 12:30. She was going to take a short swim, then join him.

The next thing he knew, it was eight A. M., and he was alone in bed. When she didn't answer his repeated calls, he went out to the pool and found her at the bottom of the deep end. He jumped in and hauled her out, but she was already dead.

The story mentioned that her blood-alcohol level was high, and was probably a contributing factor in her death. My mother was reading over my shoulder at the kitchen table. "Fifty-nine years old," she said. "What a shame."

"Mom," I replied, "that's *old.*"

. . .

"Somethin's goin' on with Eight-Track," Mike Pfleuger said, as we sat around home plate in one of the vacant lots we used. "Yesterday he wouldn't answer the door. Today he's not even home. His car's gone."

"Can't he go to the grocery store?" demanded Lance.

"He's been gone over seven hours!"

"Maybe he's *really* hungry, Mike."

Mike couldn't let *that* one pass. He chased Lance all over the outfield, with Lance laughing and managing to keep one step ahead of him.

The car that went by just then hadn't gone another twenty yards when the rest of us jumped up. "Eight-Track! Hey, you guys," we hollered into the outfield, "Eight-Track just drove by!"

Mike took off toward us. "Remind me to kill you later," I heard him yell at Lance. We sprinted towards Eight-Track's house, nearly a half mile away. It looked like a road race in progress. We passed by Mike's house, where his half-brother Richard was sitting on the porch. He looked us over, scowling as usual, and picked out Mike bringing up the rear.

"Don't be late for dinner, jerk!"

Marcus nudged me. "Richard the Fatherless will make a fine mother someday."

We got to Eight-Track's house a couple minutes later, saw the blue Plymouth at the top of the steep driveway.

"Knock on the door, Marcus," I urged.

"Perhaps Eight-Track is deep in—"

"Oh, shut up. I'll do it myself." I knocked. After a couple of seconds we could hear him coming down the long, steep stairway that led to his second floor den, where we usually hung out with him among his piles of tapes. We weren't sure what to expect. It was a pleasant surprise when he opened the door smiling.

"Come on in, boys. I've got ice cream sandwiches and soda for everybody."

We piled into his hallway, grinning ear to ear. Eight-Track was one of the guys again. Amid all the slurping and gurgling, Marcus asked, "Where were you, Eight-Track, pray tell?"

He leaned back, looking quite satisfied. "Well, I had to go pick up some groceries, for one."

"See, Mike, I told you," Lance said.

"And I had a little business decision to make. Needed some time to think it over."

"What kind of business?" I asked.

He gave me an odd sideways glance, as though he was stalling for an answer. Right then, Phil Chandler, who had gulped down a whole can of soda in one breath, let out a belch so long and loud it echoed and forced tears from his eyes.

The room erupted in laughter and insults. Ice cream wrappers and a couple of empty cans were thrown in his general direction. Eight-Track gave me another look. I was about to repeat my question when he jumped in with stories about guys he served with in Korea who were loud belchers.

Within seconds, *everyone* was trading stories or trying to imitate Phil. Eight-Track often joined in our silliness, but it seemed that *this* time he did it to avoid answering me..

For a couple of days, things seemed normal. No more nosy questions for me, but I was still wondering why he didn't answer.

Then, of course, things changed again. Like he said, nothing in life remains static for very long.

. . .

We were playing baseball in one of the vacant lots. About the time when everyone was tired, Tony Ondifer hit a foul ball in the woods behind home plate. No one except me moved a muscle to look for it. I never found the stupid ball, we all left, and the next day I was covered with poison oak.

I was confined to the yard, something that normally would have been torture. But I couldn't do anything except scratch myself, anyway. To make things worse, that night was the annual Fourth of July fireworks at the park.

In a dull Ohio town of five-thousand, nearly everyone attended. A house-breaker could have had a field day on our street alone. Around eight, I could hear the explosions and cheers of the crowd. Feeling sorry for myself, I took a walk over Eight-Track's. He never went to stuff like that.

The itching had let up a bit, although my hands were still quite swollen. I was hoping Eight-Track and I could just shoot the breeze. And I would *bet* he had a theory about enemy agents planting poison oak.

About fifty yards from his house I saw someone coming out his side door. Although it was twilight, I could see the hands stuffed in the pants pockets, head down; that prowling walk. It was Mike's half-brother, Richard the Fatherless, the guy who always griefed *us* for hanging out there. I didn't want him to know I'd seen him there, so I ducked behind a hedge opening until he was off the property. As we moved closer he looked up.

"Well, if it isn't little Eddie Cordelico," he said, with his usual nastiness. "Why ain't you down at the fireworks like a good boy?"

"I got poison oak. I itch all over." I scratched myself for effect.

He shook his head in disgust. "You guys. Every one of you is dumber than the one before, I swear." I looked at the ground. "Where you goin' Eddie? To see old man Strobeck?"

"I thought I might—"

He walked away, mumbling. It was so tempting, but I kept my mouth shut. Nobody wanted to rile Richard Kane. We all felt he was capable of killing somebody.

I headed up the hill toward Eight-Track's. The only light on was in his kitchen. As I walked by his side door I caught sight of him inside, his back to me, the telephone receiver to his ear. Don't ask me why, maybe nosiness, or maybe because he avoided my questions that other day, but I stepped back against the side of his house and stood there, listening.

"That's right. Just a little piece of the pie for myself," he said. "No, don't worry about that. Just bag it and toss it over the fence. You know what they say. Good fences make good neighbors." He laughed.

I was pretty darn confused. Was someone going to throw *pie* over the fence to him?

"You just do that, now," he continued, "and I'm sure my memory will get fuzzy concerning . . .certain things. Fine. Five minutes, then."

He hung up and began to turn around. It was too late to pretend I just arrived. I dashed to the side and hid behind his baby pine tree. It was about as thick as my arm, but had full branches, like a miniature Christmas tree.

A couple of minutes passed. Then, he went out his back door, the one facing down the hill. I heard it shut, and could see his shadowy figure walking down the slope towards the fence separating his property from Mr. Redmer's. The lights were off by the pool, but I figured since his wife died, maybe he wasn't up to keeping them on.

I lost Eight-Track in the darkness, but I heard this crinkling sound, then footsteps as he materialized and went back inside. Wouldn't pie get wrecked being thrown over a fence? What was the big deal about it anyway? Sneaking back to the side of the doorway, I saw him sitting at his kitchen table, the bag open. But what he took out wasn't pie. It was *cash,* wads of it. I was scared, now. Dad once told me that when large amounts of money changed hands, something was rotten. I slid along the side of his house and ran home. Luckily, my parents were still at the fireworks. I needed to do some hard thinking.

. . .

It was tough pretending everything was normal, and not telling any of the guys what I'd seen and heard. The hardest part was hanging out at Eight-Track's and trying not to look guilty or suspicious.

About two weeks later I went over to Mike's house to see if he wanted to do anything. Just my luck, Richard answered the door. The instant I laid eyes on him it reminded me of the night of the fireworks. With all the turmoil inside over Eight-Track and the bag of money, I had almost forgotten the *other* mystery; Richard leaving Eight-Track's house.

"Nobody's home, runt," he said.

I was staring at him, possibly looking for some clue to all my confusion. Eight-Track was living some deep, strange secret, and so was Richard.

"You deaf or somethin'? I said he's not home. Beat it."

Maybe holding so much inside gave me the nerve to do what I did. "Richard."

"What?"

"I saw you that night."

"Saw what, you little moron?"

"I saw you coming out of Eight-Track's the night of the fireworks." He opened his mouth on impulse as if to deny it, but I could read something else in his eyes, a *trapped* look.

"So you saw me. Big deal. I do odd jobs for the old geezer. He doesn't know his ass from third base."

"Oh," I turned to leave, but he spun me around, his fingers digging into my shoulder.

"I get paid under the table from him, so you keep your fat mouth shut about me workin' there and you seein' me. Got it?"

"I got it."

Nice try, Richard, I was thinking on my walk home. Doing odd jobs, huh? The man had been a master truck mechanic, and could *still* make a living as a plumber, carpenter, or electrician if he wanted. He was about the handiest guy in Ohio.

So Richard the Fatherless now had *two* secrets. He regularly went over to Eight-Track's, presumably when the rest of us were home. The big secret was *why.*

. . .

For Marcus, Mike, Lance, Phil, Tony, Norm, and me, it was like seeing a nightmare acted out. And the worst part was, you knew the ending. On the morning of July 21st, three days after my conversation with Richard, the same ugly scene played itself out in front of Eight-Track's house. The police. The ambulance. The crowd. The stretcher with the dark green bag wheeled down a steep driveway. We didn't have to ask. We knew he was dead. But this time there were no rumors.

I looked around at the guys, all of us standing together, a couple of our parents among us. I saw the same thing on all their faces: shock, grief; the end of innocence, I suppose.

I thought about that bag on his kitchen table that night, remembering what my father once said. When large amounts of money changed hands, something was rotten.

Across the street, by himself, stood Richard Kane, his fists clenched in front of him. The look in his eyes was one of pure rage. I shuddered. He ran toward his house.

. . .

I followed him, keeping my distance. When he got home, he headed for their garage. I heard its side door slam. With my heart in my mouth, I opened it and stepped inside. He was sitting on an old storage box in the far corner.

"What the hell *you* want? Get outta here!"

"Richard, I've got to talk to you about Eight-Track."

"You gonna leave, or do I have to wipe up the floor with you?"

"No. I won't tell anyone about this, honest." He glared threateningly, but I just stood there. It wasn't all bravery, I don't think. I was sure he *wanted* to talk, he just had to overcome the tough-guy image.

"Shut the goddam door at least. You think I want the whole neighborhood to hear?"

I shut the door, and sat next to him. I was right. There was a lot more to him than he let on. His anger over not knowing his real father was starting to overcome him. Then, by some odd twist of fate, he met Eight-Track. He had been going over there on the sly since he was fourteen. It wasn't the fun relationship that we had with him. It was more like going to see your guidance counselor, or one of those Big Brothers.

"He couldn't help me control anger," Richard said, "but he gave good enough advice to keep me out of serious trouble, even helped with schoolwork sometimes. He was the closest thing I ever had to a *real* father."

"What about your stepfather?" I asked.

"Pffffft! Him? All he ever cared about was Mike, *his* kid. I was the *other* kid, the one that came with the house when he married my mother."

"What are you gonna do now?"

He rose suddenly, shoved me off the storage box, and opened it. Digging down, he produced a small paper bag. *Oh, no,* I thought. *Not another paper bag.* He removed a red, oblong plastic object from it. It was an eight-track tape. "I'll tell you what I'm gonna do. Just what he told me when he gave me this two weeks ago."

"What?"

"He said if anything . . . *strange* ever happened to him, to play this tape he made."

"What do you mean, 'strange'?"

"*Dying,* or disappearing without a trace! Jesus, how stupid *are* you?"

I shrugged.

"Tomorrow, when the paper tells what happened, if there's anything suspicious about it, I play the tape."

Did he say *suspicious?* "Richard, the night of the fireworks, I overheard him talking to someone on the phone, telling them to bag it and throw it over Redmer's fence. Then I peeked in his doorway. The bag he got thrown was filled with money."

He looked surprised, then his eyes narrowed. He reached back in the box and pulled out a square, metal device with a slot and buttons on it.

"What the heck is *that?*"

"It's the extra eight-track player he gave me." His eyes narrowed some more, and I could see the rage building again. "We're gonna play that tape *now.*"

. . .

For the next ten minutes, we listened to the tape.

Eight-Track, looking out his second floor window one night while recording, had seen Marv Redmer murder his wife. He got her stinking drunk, then teased her into taking a dip in the deep end of their pool, promising he would be right in.

In her condition, and with her lung problems, she was in trouble in no time at all. Redmer pretended to hold out the pool's skimmer for her, then would move it just out of reach. Within minutes, the exertion left her exhausted; too exhausted to even yell, and she sank like a stone. Redmer shut the lights and went to bed.

There was no evidence of foul play,and nothing in his past to suggest a motive. He was just one greedy SOB who couldn't wait for her to die, which was probably only a year or two more. The dry cleaning stores were in her name, as she had inherited them from her father. Only by her death could he own them. And he had found a buyer who could make him fabulously wealthy.

Eight-Track, apparently, was told all this when he contacted Redmer the first time, informing him what he had seen that evening, and offering to forget about it in return for "a piece of the pie for himself."

"I don't condone what Redmer done," he said, "but I been poor my whole life. This way I can live comfortable, and Redmer can *pay* for his crime. He'll get his money, but I doubt if he'll ever enjoy it. *I* will, though."

The tape stopped.

"So *that's* why he wanted me out of there that night," Richard said bitterly. "So he could collect his payoff."

"I guess he wasn't *perfect,* " I offered, "but he *was* a pretty decent guy."

"And that bastard Redmer killed him," Richard said. "I *know* it!" He rose, and his fists were clenched like when I had seen him across the street earlier. He walked over by one of the windows, his face red and quivering. I looked down, embarrassed.

The sound of shattering glass snapped my head up. Richard was taking aim at another window pane. As I watched, feeling glued to the floor, he put his fist through all of them. He turned toward me, that expression still there. I opened the garage door and bolted.

I looked back. He was still in the garage, standing by the *other* window. All the way up to Liberty Street I could hear glass breaking.

. . .

"It's for you, Eddie," my mother said, after she had answered the phone around seven that evening. She looked puzzled. "It's that Richard character." She handed it to me and went into the living room.

"Eddie, it's Richard Kane."

"How *are* you?" I asked nervously.

"How *am* I! My *hand* hurts, you shit-for-brains. I hadda have over thirty stitches at the emergency room."

"Geez."

"You didn't say anything to anybody, did you?"

"Of course not."

"Good. You ain't half bad for a stupid runt, ya know?"

That was the first kind thing he had ever said to me. "Richard, what do we do about. . .you know, what's on the tape?"

"Wait for the newspaper. If he died of natural causes, we do nothing. But if somethin's fishy, then . . ."

"Then *what?*"

"Then we have to decide. And we both have to agree to do the same thing, or we'll look like liars and idiots."

I understood right away. With Eight-Track dead, there was no proof Redmer killed his wife. They would never believe a tape made by someone who was now dead. But if Eight-Track's death was murder, *then* the tape might help prove that Redmer *did* kill his wife, and murdered Eight-Track to protect himself. Or save money. Take your pick.

. . .

On page two of the paper the next morning, a headline read, "Police Investigate Death." Eight-Track had died of injuries suffered in an apparent fall down the stairs that led from his upstairs den into his hallway. What caught my eye was the line, "Foul play is not suspected, but investigating officers have yet to rule it out. Detective Sgt. William Tellerson was quoted, "It *looks* like a simple home accident, but there are inconsistencies." He refused to elaborate.

I was sure Richard thought Marv Redmer had *pushed* him down those stairs. Not twenty minutes later, he was in front of my house in his mother's car, honking the horn.

I got in, and the first thing he said was, "We've got him, that murdering bastard." In all fairness, he *did* ask me if we should go to the police, or right to Redmer himself and "make him sweat."

"Are you nuts?" I screeched. "That's what Eight-Track was doing, and look where it got *him!*"

"Simmer down, runt. I was just makin'sure." The next thing I knew we were at the police station. From under the front seat he produced the tape and tape player. "Well, I guess this is where I pay him back for everything he did for me."

We went in, stated our business to a desk officer, and were shown to Detective Tellerson's office. I acted like a scared kid about to wet his pants, but Richard did himself proud. He spoke clearly and simply, and asked Tellerson to play the tape. He did, right then and there. When it was finished, he asked us to leave it with him and thanked us.

"That's *it?*" Richard nearly shouted. "Ain't you gonna arrest the guy?"

"I'm not at liberty to discuss an investigation with you boys. But this tape should be a *big* help in pursuing a theory I've had. Leave your phone numbers with the Sergeant."

. . .

Marv Redmer was arrested the next day and charged with the murder of Delvin Strobeck. A small cut on the side of Eight-Track's hand was very different from what he might have gotten in the fall. The police lab examined a college ring Redmer wore, and came up with traces of Eight-Track's blood and skin.

The tape was inadmissible as evidence, so Redmer was never charged with killing his wife. But they had him cold on the other one. At some point, his attorney advised him to make a deal. Redmer pleaded guilty to voluntary manslaughter. He eventually went to prison. The money Eight-Track got from Redmer was never recovered.

Despite our brief alliance, Richard went back to his old ways, brooding and glaring at everyone. If anything, he was worse after that. But I figured that had to do with losing his friend and advisor, Eight-Track.

And us? After a few days we started hanging out again, only not at Eight-Track's, of course. For a while I was the hero, having helped solve a murder case. Almost every day the guys made me go through the whole story again, nearly word for word. They all liked the part where Richard was punching out the garage windows, except for Mike. He had to help his father replace them.

Yes, everything went back to the way it was before. But like Eight-Track used to say, nothing in life remains static for very long. We were all sprawled in the outfield one very hot day in August after a baseball game, picking out shapes among the clouds when footsteps sounded. We figured it was someone's little brother and ignored it.

"What're you idiots doin'?"

We all sat up, staring at the unlikely sight of Richard Kane, Richard the Fatherless, the neighborhood hoodlum. No one said a word.

"Whattaya all retards or somethin'?"

Finally Mike spoke up. "We were just—"

"You were just shootin' the breeze like you used to at Eight-Track's."

We studied his face closely. For all we knew, he had decided to beat the crap out of the whole bunch of us. But Richard didn't look *angry,* he looked like he was doing something he *needed* to do, but to him was like taking a large dose of bad-tasting medicine.

"Eight-Track only told you guys stupid stuff," he declared.

No one dared to disagree.

"He saved the good stuff, the valuable stuff, for me," he continued. "I figure even a pathetic bunch of losers like you guys might learn somethin' from it."

It must have dawned on us that Richard the Fatherless had appointed himself as Eight-Tracks's successor. One or two of us may even have smiled, probably the same smile Eight-

Track had seen on our faces countless times. Richard returned the smile with a contemptuous sneer of disgust.

"You assholes know where to find me," he said, turning and sauntering across the outfield grass, head down, hands jammed into his pockets.

"BROTHER PACT"

I am called Mishanook by those who know me. In Shoshone it means "morning star." My mother said I was born as the first star appeared over the Lake Shaped Like A Heart.

We do not keep written records, but the things we pass down are true. This story is not about me, but I got in its way. I pray to the Gods for an answer, but I fear the answer is my own death. Or worse, my living.

I will tell you what happened, but I will not say where. No more of you should come here.

. . .

He called himself Brother Pact. Many years ago he came here from New Catenia, in the Ohio Place. He had been branded a false prophet by the people there, he said, and that they would hunt him down.

These people, he said, had many secrets they did not want known. For this reason, Brother Pact, although a white man, painted his face to fool those who hunted him.

How he became the leader of our people is not known. He spoke fearful truths. Perhaps this was enough.

What Brother Pact, the Man, gave us was the Brother Pact, an agreement among people to avenge any wrong done them. The people believed in Brother Pact, the Man, and heeded his words. Before long, no one would lie, cheat, or steal for fear of the Brother Pact. You would not even dare to laugh at another's foolish mistake.

Men would not say that if Joseph Lightfoot's wife jumped into the Lake Shaped Like A Heart, all the water would come out. Our people, who had always lived for their own selves, began to live for the others around them. Yes, there was fear, but there was kindness, too.

The people came to realize that Brother Pact spoke the Truth, and that his way was the only way. He was treated as a God would be. His followers built him the best and biggest house. He instructed the people, giving his blessing to some, and condemning others, who learned the true ways, or soon left.

There came a time when Brother Pact grew restless and afraid. He had stayed long enough, he said. It was time to move on and spread his message before the Bad Ones from the Ohio Place could find him. But Brother Pact did not leave us alone. He had chosen a young Mexican Indian as the one most worthy to carry on the Brother Pact.

No one knows what name the Indian carried, but Brother Pact called him Centavo, because of his small size. Before he left, he gave Centavo a coin to keep as a remembrance.

Many believe the coin holds the power that Brother Pact passed on to Centavo.

Centavo went to live in the large house built for Brother Pact just outside our village. After many years, he was the only one remaining who had known Brother Pact. Some say he was over one-hundred, others say no. But everyone agreed he carried with him at least ninety trips around the sun.

No one knew what powers Brother Pact bestowed upon Centavo. Some say he can become one of the animals. A woman said she saw Centavo walk into the Lake Shaped Like A Heart until the water covered him, then appear on the lake's other side. I did not wonder about *that* so much. I wondered how the *woman* could *see* that far. And this I heard: a snake once bit Centavo, and it was the *snake* who died.

For many years Centavo carried on the work of Brother Pact, the Man. He too, gathered everyone in the village to meditate in silent prayer. The children went to his house to learn, and to play.

Centavo kept two lizards. They looked like babies of The Giant Lizards From Before Time. They were allowed to roam free in the house and yard, and grew to half a man in size. The children would make up names for them. One day I asked Centavo what their names *were*. He said, "Only *they* know, and they have not yet told me."

Like the true names of the lizards, the ways of the Brother Pact remain unknown to us. No one knows how you find your Brother. Many times there have been several Brothers of the same person. Stranger still, the person you are bound to in a Brother Pact is never bound to *you*.

When Brother Pact, the Man, lived here, he would gather the people together and instruct them to meditate and think about their Brother, even if they were not yet known. He said that when you became worthy, you would awake one morning knowing who your Brother was.

. . .

The Renegades that came that last time were from east of us. When you live out here, you cannot always tell from which direction strangers have come at you. The thing to do is watch them when they leave. If they head west, they came from the east. That is what happened this time, except that there were four that came, and only one who left.

The tan and gold license plate on their blue Pontiac said "Amber Waves of Grain" at the bottom. On top it said "Indiana."

We did not know their names, so we gave them names. The driver was a white man with long blond hair, black boots and jeans, and a big nose, like an eagle's beak. The man who rode in front with him was a black white man, with very short hair and a birthmark on his cheek. His body was thick, and he spoke softly. The third white man had black hair, much taller than the other two, with eyes that shone like sapphires. The woman was tall, too; taller than two of the men. She had brown hair to her shoulders, and spoke little. She seemed to be in much anger.

Everyone knew that there would be trouble with Big Nose, Birthmark, Sapphire Eyes, and Tall Woman. They were staying in an old shack outside of town, not far from the great house of Centavo.

The four Renegades were not harmonious with the town. They did not live for others, but for their own selves, as our people did before the Brother Pact. They stole from vegetable stands on our streets, begged for money from strangers, then used it to buy beer and cheap whiskey. They spread filthy litter across the face of the land and shot at wild animals with a rifle Big Nose had. They raided from some of the farmers, who recognized the car as it sped away in the darkness.

At the pharmacy, Sapphire Eyes bumped into Joseph Lightfoot's wife and called her a "fat squaw." He then taunted Joseph when he stood watching, silent. But Joseph was not in fear. *He* did not have a Brother Pact with his wife. He knew that others would balance the scales for the insults they had suffered.

. . .

I know I am to blame for what happened. One day, outside the hardware store, Big Nose and Birthmark came up to me, asking questions about Centavo.

They asked if he needed any hired hands. I told them I did not think so. Although he is old, he manages somehow. Then they wanted to know why his house was so much bigger. Was he rich? I told them Centavo had inherited the power and greatness from Brother Pact, the Man. Perhaps they did not understand. Their eyes jumped when they heard the word 'inherited', and 'power.'

When I realized my words could cause harm to Centavo, I struggled to work up my courage to warn him. You ask why it would be a struggle to warn the old beloved one of danger. It is because I am a coward. I did not tell you this before, because . . .I am a coward.

. . .

The Renegades had decided to move on, before their deeds could catch up to them. Greedy ones that they were, they wanted to steal the best things our town had before leaving. These things, they believed, would be at Centavo's house.

Big Nose left the others in town with instructions to buy supplies, and steal what they could. He would rob Centavo, then come back for them.

I had decided, in my coward's heart, to warn Centavo. Since I have no car or horse, I had to walk. As I approached, I could see the blue Pontiac parked nearby.

Centavo was in the courtyard with Big Nose, who pointed his rifle at him. The one time I *should* have run, I did not. I climbed a small hill, crouched down, and watched.

Big Nose waved the rifle and spoke loud and angry. "C'mon, Geronimo, I don't have all day! Where's the good stuff?" Centavo answered, shaking his head, but I could not hear his words.

Big Nose fired the rifle, and Centavo dropped to the dusty earth. It would have been better if I had run to town then. But I decided I would wait until Big Nose left, then try to help Centavo. I am not only a coward, I am a foolish coward.

Big Nose came out of the house a short time later, saying white man's swear words, carrying only the rifle, and drove away.

I ran to where Centavo lay. There was much blood from the hole in his chest. He did not breathe. I could not leave him lying there in the dust like an animal. I dug a grave in the courtyard, placed Centavo inside, and covered him, asking the Spirits to take him to the Forever Place.

I then went inside. Papers and books lay everywhere, some chairs had been knocked over. The two lizards were not to be found. Maybe they had become scared and run off, or were hiding. A small round object on the floor caught my eye. It was a very old ten-centavo coin from Mexico, perhaps the coin that Brother Pact had given to Centavo. I put it in my pocket, hoping it would bring me good luck, which I would now need.

Centavo was *my* Brother. I had caused danger to come his way. I had watched like a helpless old woman while he was killed. And I did nothing to avenge it. In my terror-filled, cowardly heart, I wondered if Centavo *knew* I was his Brother. How many *more* were his Brothers? Perhaps they, guided by his angered, betrayed spirit, would seek vengeance on *me*.

I went back to my small house on the edge of town and took what I could carry.

Justice is swift here. From a hilltop I saw as I was escaping. Birthmark, Sapphire Eyes, and Tall Woman were taken by those of the Brother Pact. They will cause no more harm in this life. Big Nose saw what was happening when he came into town. He did not try to save his friends, but turned the blue car around and drove away quickly.

. . .

I live in the foothills west of the town now, changing camps every day in case they are looking for me. Hiding from the people I spent my life with; the same thing Brother Pact, the Man, once did.

When I gain enough courage, I will head west. But I will not be trying to find and kill Big Nose. Even when a coward gains some courage, he is still a coward.

I return to Centavo's grave during the deepest part of the night to beg his forgiveness. They have put up a wooden marker there.

That last night, for some unknown reason, I decided to go inside and look through his papers, which were many. I spent hours there reading things written by both Centavo and Brother Pact. They spoke of magic things of which I had no knowledge, and could not understand.

Then I heard strange noises outside. Fearing that people from the town had come, I shut my flashlight and ran to Centavo's sleeping room and hid under the bed. I continued to hear strange sounds. After a while the noises came from farther and farther away, until they were gone.

I became bold enough to turn on my flashlight again. There was a small cardboard box next to me. Inside were more writings of the kind I could not understand. At the bottom was the letter Brother Pact gave to Centavo when he left. It instructed Centavo in what he must do to continue the Blessings of the Brother Pact.

But it was the ending of the letter that caused me much fear. Brother Pact's last words were, "Remember Centavo, that sometimes in this life *you must be your OWN Brother.*"

I knew then that this was not a place where I should be. I quickly left the house, stopping at the grave one last time.

When I did this, I was reminded of something that happened once. A white man passing through here years ago told many stories, which he called jokes. He spoke of a businessman who was hated and feared for his ruthlessness and lies. His evil heart stopped suddenly one day. His many enemies came to the funeral. This confused me. "Here," I told him, "that would show admiration and respect. Why would a man's enemies pay him such homage?"

The fat, bald white man laughed and said, "They wanted to make sure he was dead."

A flashlight's beam of light in total darkness can sometimes play tricks. I was seeing faces by the grave, and it did not look the same. I moved closer and dropped to my knees. The grave was empty, dirt tossed to both sides. The faces belonged to Centavo's lizards, whom I had not seen since his death. They looked directly at me. This I know: lizards are not supposed to *smile*.

There were no footprints nearby.

By the flashlight's beam I found my camp and gathered my belongings, ready to flee to the west.

Yes, white man, I know of your beliefs called science. He was shot by a rifle. He did not breathe. He lay underground for half a month, you say.

But listen. The empty grave belonged to Centavo, the Chosen One of Brother Pact.

Of Centavo, it was said that he could hold his breath for a *very* long time.

"TOTEM"

Stuart Fass was practically tap-dancing down the stairs of Memorial Hall to his car in the student parking lot. In his hand was his midterm exam from Dr. Dante's Concepts of Society course. His 'A+' pleasantly surprised him.

Dr. Dante was a notoriously hard marker, and the exam essays were one of the worst collections of generalizations he had turned in. Yet for some reason, Dante was falling all over himself in praise.

But then, *everything* was going exactly his way. Like the Fall Weekend semi-formal dance. He wanted to ask Gayle Roussel, an attractive brunette he met at the Orientation dance, but friends advised against it. They said she was a self-centered snob. But yesterday she came over to him in the cafeteria and asked *him* to go with *her.* He consented, of course.

And the financial situation. Since his father's death last year, money was tight. He'd had to drop out of Syracuse and transfer to Brandt College. He'd not only lost credits, making him a second semester freshman, he was on a tight budget.

But then this uncanny glut of good luck kicked in. The local hospital announced that they were hiring in non-medical positions. He knew there were dozens of applicants, though. At his interview, the woman behind the desk gushed over his records from Syracuse and his past job experience, comprised of a door-to-door sales job, and a couple of laboring stints in factories. He was hired the next day.

The extra money was a godsend, as he could run his car, cover his insurance, and with a little budgeting, continue to rent the small apartment off campus.

"Ah, life is good," he said, crossing the rows of cars to his black Chevy Corsica.

There was a piece of paper under one of his wiper blades. "Check your mailbox," it said. *Maybe a note from Gayle,* he mused. He walked the hundred yards to the student union basement, which housed a snack bar and the mailroom.

There was an envelope inside his box, his name typed on the front. He opened it, removing one typewritten sheet. *We've been watching you, Stuart. Someone with your leadership ability and other attributes could be an asset to our organization. If you're interested, come down to Messner's Men's Shop.* The typewritten "signature" said *The Lizard.*

"Cool," said Stuart, quite flattered. He *had* taken a leadership role. A year older and more confident, he was quite active in campus affairs. The letter appealed to Stuart's prowess as a *doer.* "The Lizard, huh? I gotta check this out."

. . .

Messner's Men's Shop was located at the intersection of Brown Avenue and Main St. Even this appealed to Stuart as he stepped inside. Messner's gave off an aura of old-line eliteness, not the cookie-cutter sameness of mall shops.

He observed a few middle-aged and older men browsing, a man and woman behind the main counter, and several well-dressed younger men standing at strategic positions, obviously low-pressure salesmen.

He walked over to the racks of sportcoats and dress slacks. What was he supposed to do, shout 'Is the Lizard here?' He had no sooner finished the thought when a young man, perhaps a year or two older than he, approached. He had a slight build, almost undernourished, and wore glasses. His brown curly hair was medium length.

"Are you Stuart Fass?" he asked softly.

"Yes. Do I know you?"

"That's not important. You received a letter, Stuart?"

"Yes."

"You look like a 'Forty Long.'"

"What?"

"Your suit size. 'Forty Long.'"

"That's more or less—"

"Fine. Grab one and take it into that changing stall."

Stuart, stunned at how quickly things had developed, went to the section of the rack marked "Forty Long" and selected a navy blue striped suit.

"Take your time trying it on, if you know what I mean."

Stuart entered the stall and locked the door. Between the wooden slats he could see the young man standing point-blank to it. His voice, slightly muffled, drifted through. "In the late 1880's Brandt College allowed some Iriquois Indians to enroll."

Stuart removed his shoes, unbuckled his pants.

"One of them realized that to make it in the white man's world, he had to have connections, people who owed him, so he started the Totem. Over the years the Totem grew until its members, people from various walks of life, had a powerful network. They deal in *favors,* Stuart. *Important* favors. Do you understand so far?"

"Yes." He put on the navy blue pants.

"The members have already given you an introductory offer, you might say."

"They have?"

"Your 'A+' from a hard professor, for one. A certain young lady asking *you* to the semi-formal this weekend."

"What?" Stuart nearly shouted. "How could—"

"Never underestimate the Totem, Stuart. Perhaps your professor needed a favor. Or *owed* one."

Stuart put on his shoes and slipped the jacket on. "What about the girl?"

"Well, Stuart, maybe the girl is under her father's thumb. Maybe he needed her to do something for *you* so someone would do something for *him.*"

Stuart let all this sink in a moment. "Wow," he said softly.

"And Stuart, your new job at the hospital?"

"That *too?*"

"St. Mary's tends to hire only *local* students, as a rule."

Stuart opened the door, making eye contact with the salesman.

"Very nice fit, Stuart. Why don't we step over by these mirrors and I'll pin the pants."

"Okay, uh . . ."

"Albert. Albert Seligmann."

They went over to the mirrors, Albert dropping to one knee, adjusting the cuffs. "The Iriquois believed in the medicine of animals, medicine meaning 'magic' or 'power'. Members are known by their animal Totem name."

"Do you have meetings?"

"No. It's an invisible, very secret network. It's best for everyone that way."

"And I got all this . . .good luck—"

"It's called a 'Medicine Boost.' How about this length on the cuffs?"

"Up a little. So Albert, do you have to be *into* this Totem stuff?"

"That was true at one time, but no more. How's that length?"

"Good." He smiled mischievously. "Do I get to pick my animal?"

"No, I'm afraid not. They watch you for a while and assign you one, based on the Totem's needs."

"And you're the Lizard."

Albert stood, a sour look on his face. "As I told you, my name is Albert Seligmann."

Stuart was caught off guard by the sudden rebuff. "Oh, you don't actually *say* the names in public."

Albert seemed to nod, then turned his attention to the suit, brushing his hands across the shoulders, tugging slightly at the jacket's hem. "Excellent fit, Stuart. I'm sure Gayle will be impressed."

"How did you know her *name?*" Stuart asked, surprised again.

Albert tilted his head and gave a knowing wink. "Well, shall I put the suit on your account?"

Stuart looked embarrassed. "I don't have an account here."

Albert smiled, patting Stuart's shoulder. "Who's talking about *here?*"

. . .

Stuart Fass sat in a study cubicle of the Ruth Woldt Memorial Library, thinking about the past two weeks. For all his fantasizing about Gayle Roussel, their relationship had quickly fizzled. They simply were not compatible. When he braced himself and suggested that they break it off, she quickly agreed. He couldn't help but notice the *relief* on her face. It was obvious she would have gone out with him against her will for as long as he desired.

For the past week, when time allowed, he looked up information about the Five Nations of the Iriquois, and their animan Totem.

Albert was the Lizard, which stood for the Medicine of dreams; desires. He wondered what Albert dreamed of. "Probably to *own* Messner's someday," he chuckled.

He enjoyed trying to guess which animal's name would be his. But he would have to wait, according to Albert, who had avoided him on return trips to Messner's.

"They'll let you know, Stuart, be patient," he had said. "It's not a good idea to be seen here hanging around me."

"Oh yeah, I didn't think," Stuart said. "Someone might catch on about the Totem."

"No," Albert corrected. "Someone might think we're *gay.*"

. . .

It had been a month since he went to Messner's that first time when he found another envelope in his mailbox. He ran into the snack bar, found a secluded corner, and read it.

> *Welcome to the Totem, Stuart. You are the Antelope, the One of Action. Good things will continue to come your way, by your own efforts, and the Medicine Boosts of the Totem.*
>
> *Here are the requirements. First, you must continue to be an upstanding citizen. There is no place in the Totem for thugs. Second, if the Totem needs you to perform a task, you must do it without question and without failure. You have accepted the fruits of our labor; you must now be a willing participant. Third, most important, you*

must never break the circle, NEVER. You MUST stay inside the Medicine Wheel. Da naho! Wi:yo:h! (It is said! It is good!)

He was a bit uneasy about the strong warning against naming names, breaking the circle of secrecy. But his overriding feeling was one of buoyancy and accomplishment. He was the Antelope. "It is said. It is good," he whispered.

. . .

For five months things flowed smoothly, yet uneventfully. Of all his "Medicine Boosts," the hospital job had been the most beneficial. It gave him 12-20 hours a week, delivering magazines to waiting rooms and doing light cleaning. It allowed him to meet his expenses without tapping heavily into the fund his father had bequested.

Stuart was sitting at his kitchen table studying when the phone rang. He thought it might be his mother, presently reliving the joys of puberty with his thirteen-year-old sister.

"Hello."

"Hello, Stuart. This is the Eagle. The Totem has need of your services." The voice was rich and deep, with a no-nonsense businesslike timbre. Still, he feared a prank by someone who found out about the Totem.

"How do I know this is real, sir, with all due respect?"

"Very good, Antelope. A little caution is well-advised." There was a slight pause. "In October you were given three Medicine Boosts. An 'A+' on a mid-term, a date with a particular young lady, and a job at St. Mary's. Oh, and an expensive suit of clothes from Messner's. Convinced?"

"Yes, sir."

"All right, Stuart. Here is what we need. We want you to be aware of the patient in room 505. He is an older man, about 65. Make sure he's comfortable. Tidy up his room, bring him a magazine, that kind of thing. If he seems busy working, don't pester him. That's all for now, Antelope."

"Sir, am I supposed to—"

"It is said. It is good," the voice said emphatically. There followed a click and the sound of the dial tone.

"It's *said* all right, but I don't like the *sound* of it," said Stuart, as he hung up the phone. They weren't asking for anything more than he might have done anyway, but there was *something* odd about it. What stake did the Totem have in this man? But he knew he couldn't refuse.

. . .

Stuart was helpful to the lone patient in room 505, finding him polite but never openly friendly. Like the Eagle had said, there were times when he appeared busy, folders and ledgers covering his bed and tray table, dictating into a portable tape recorder. Stuart couldn't hear what he was saying, but he wasn't trying to listen.

He did want to know who the man was, though, and what possible interest the Totem could have in a sixtyish executive. It was simple enough to learn his name; he simply read it off the slot on the door: Connard St. George. A few questions to floor nurses brought him the man's occupation. He was Chief Executive Officer of a large corporation, Adirondack, Ltd.

An important man in this neck of the woods, Stuart thought. What did the Totem want with him? Did they want him *dead?* Would they order *him* to do it?

. . .

Stuart Fass and the business section of the paper *never* crossed paths. But two days later, he found Connard St. George's photo staring at him from its front page.

There was a feature article on St. George, whose headline read, "CEO Fights the Good Fight." It detailed the dual battle Connard St. George was engaged in: stomach cancer, and an attempted hostile takeover of Adirondack by another corporation.

It was obvious to Stuart the Totem wanted him out of the way to allow the takeover. St. George was using his last available strength, the article stated, to resist, trying to rally friendly and neutral shareholders. The longer he could hold out, it continued, the better the chance of the opposition weakening.

The expected call came that afternoon. The Eagle's voice had a definite sense of urgency. "Antelope, it's time for decisive action. You will find a vial in your hospital uniform tomorrow. You must exchange it at the desk where medications are kept. You will see St. George's name and a similar vial there. When the head nurse leaves, switch vials. Take the old one and trash it, flush it down a toilet, whatever. *Understood?"*

Stuart's mouth froze.

"Antelope?"

"Sir, I *can't*. The head nurse never leaves her—"

"That's been arranged! Just do as you're told. This is *crucial!"*

"Sir, why—"

"You're our only connection to St. George! I ask you again, Antelope, do you understand your instructions?"

"Yes, sir."

"Do *not* fail in this, Mr. Fass. It is said. It is *good.*" The familiar click sounded.

Stuart found himself shaking as he hung up. Here was the bill, at last. For an 'A+' exam, an arranged date, and a part time job, he was to *kill* a perfect stranger. *Oh, almost forgot,* he scolded himself. *AND a new suit.*

. . .

He fell into a fitful sleep by three A. M., and was too strung out to attend classes. The day was spent watching the clock. His hospital shift would begin at two. At one-forty he drove to the hospital, parked his car, and went in through a staff entrance. He opened locker 76 and changed into his powder blue uniform.

There was a bulge in one pocket. The vial. He didn't dare take it out to look. He would get rid of it at the first opportunity. He left the changing room to report to the fifth floor head nurse, Mrs. Letto.

He approached to find her rushing from behind the desk, struggling with her coat.

"Stuart, there you are. Watch the desk until they can reassign someone."

Stuart noticed her panic. "What happened?"

"My garage is on fire. The house could go next. My neighbor called." She ran toward the elevators, keys jangling.

"Well, here's the "diversion," Stuart thought. *They'll hurt ANYONE, the bastards.*

His final visit with his father jumped into his head. It had taken place in a hospital room miles from here. His father told him to "always stand up and be counted." And he had: environmental groups, the Student's Rights Forum, and other campus activities. He was being urged to run for class president next year.

And now this. He had let down his guard, taken favors under false pretense. And the chickens were coming home to roost. What would Dad have thought of this unholy mess?

Footsteps snapped him back to reality. A nurse he didn't recognize approached. "Okay, young man. I'm here for Nancy Letto." Still half in a pensive daze, Stuart stepped out from behind the enclosure, gazing back at the slotted medication holder. St. George would *still* get to fight the good fight.

"Something wrong, young man?" the nurse asked.

"No, ma'am. Everything's fine, now. Placing his hand on the bulge in his pocket, he hurried off to the men's room.

. . .

On the drive home after his shift, he kept wondering how long. "How long before this hits the fan?" he said aloud. Had he really done St. George a good turn, or did this mean someone disguised as an orderly or nurse would smother him while he slept?

He had no proof of anything. Typewritten letters, long since thrown away, and a voice on the phone were dim evidence. What about Dr. Dante and Gayle? Even if they cooperated, the trail back to the Totem was so diluted with someone doing a favor for someone doing a favor for someone doing . . .and on it went.

These thoughts filled his head throughout the night and all the next day. He couldn't afford to miss two days of classes, so he showed up and sat there, still wondering. If they threatened him, he would go to the police. He could divulge one name, if necessary: Albert Seligmann, the Lizard.

His phone rang at 7:05 that evening. Stuart turned off the TV as he picked up the receiver. "Hello?"

"That was a very stupid thing you did yesterday, Stuart. I thought I made it clear to you—"

"Forget it, Eagle. I don't *do* murder."

"*Murder?*"

"You heard me. I know who St. George is. You want him out of the way so Adirondack can be taken over."

"Fool!" the voice hissed. "You don't have the faintest idea what this is about!"

"It's about killing Connard St. George."

"You presumptuous idiot. We're trying to *save* his life."

"Save it?"

"The vial contained a drug developed in Denmark. It isn't approved here yet, so it's unavailable. With that drug, St. George had a chance for a cure. With *conventional* treatment he won't last two months. *And,* Mr. Fass, do you know what happens when he dies?"

"What?" asked a confused, nervous Stuart.

"His spineless second cousin sells Adirondack, and this region loses over 850 jobs, which affect Totem members and their families."

Stuart swallowed hard. "I'm very sorry, sir. I guess I jumped to an improper conclusion."

"That's not *all* you did, Mr. Fass."

Stuart felt his neck hairs stand on end. "Give me another chance, sir. I'll go back tomorrow and switch vials. There's more of the drug, isn't there?" He could hear panic in his voice.

"Too late!" came the shouted reply. "The conventional drug is now in his system. His body would reject the new drug. They're not compatible. The combination would be fatal within twelve hours." The voice softened. "Mr. Fass, you've helped kill a good man."

Stuart dreaded the question, but heard himself asking it. "What happens now, sir."

His answer was the sound of the dial tone.

. . .

He attended his two morning classes, then drove to the police station, parked in the municipal lot across the street, and went inside, stopping at the window of the desk sergeant.

"Yes?" asked the graying, heavy-jowled officer.

"I'd like to report the existence of a secret organization. I believe my life is in danger."

The officer's eyebrows rose, then he pulled a complaint form from a desk drawer. "Name?"

"The Totem."

The officer exhaled loudly. "*Your* name."

"Oh, sorry. Stuart Fass."

"Address?"

"Eighty-three Osborne Street."

"I'll go get Detective Dellenbeck. He handles these."

Not sure if he had made himself understood, Stuart asked, "These *what?*"

"Gang-related complaints."

"This isn't a *gang*. It's an organization. A secret *society.*"

"Right, a *gang.*"

It wasn't worth it to him to get into a semantics debate with the man. The sergeant returned moments later, accompanied by a tall man with brown hair, graying moustache, and a ski-jump nose.

"I'm Will Dellenbeck, Stuart," he said extending his hand. Stuart shook it gladly. "Why don't you come into my office and we'll talk." Dellenbeck led Stuart into a room two doors down the hallway, where they were seated.

"Sergeant Dunne said some gang has made threats against you, is that right?"

"It's not a *gang*, it's a secret organization."

"Let's do this, Stuart," Dellenbeck said, holding up his hand. "Start at the beginning, and tell your story straight through."

For fifteen minutes, Stuart narrated, starting with the note on his windshield, ending with the dial tone from last night's chilling call. The detective dutifully took notes, his face barely changing expression. When Stuart was finished, he leaned forward, waiting for Dellenbeck to say something. The detective continued to look at his notes. After a few moments, he made eye contact and cleared his throat.

"Stuart, I'd like to be more encouraging, but you haven't given me anything I could use to justify an investigation against this . . . secret organization."

Stuart's jaw dropped. He stared in disbelief.

"Mr. Fass, you're asking this department to investigate a grade you got on an exam, and a girl asking you to a dance. That doesn't sound like police work to me."

"The *phone call*, damn it!" Stuart shouted.

"Were you threatened during this call?"

"No, but—"

"Were obscenities used?"

"No."

Dellenbeck shrugged. "Stuart, I don't even have enough to ask the phone company to put a trap on your line."

"They aren't gonna *call* me again," Stuart screeched, they're gonna *kill* me!"

"Let's assume that this organization—"

"The *Totem.*"

"Let's assume the Totem exists. What you've described is no more than a private club using their so-called influence for nickel and dime favors. They got you a job. They gave you a suit. We can't bother with things like that. We've got *real* problems in this city. Drugs. Gangs."

Stuart's eyes brightened. "Okay, drugs. What about the vial I had?"

"*You* had it, Stuart. Not *them.* And you threw it away, along with the letters. Again, not a shred of evidence."

Stuart dropped his head and spoke softly. "My God, you're really *not* going to do anything about this, are you?"

"Stuart, I simply *can't.* You've given me nothing."

Stuart's head popped up. "I gave you a name. Albert Seligmann."

"Oh yes, the clerk at Messner's. What do I have on *him?* He *gave away* a suit?"

Slowly, Stuart came to the realization that he did, indeed, have nothing. "What do I do?" he asked softly.

Dellenbeck seemed to be thinking. "Well," he began, "you can disappear, go back home, for one."

"I can't do that. I'll get 'F's' in all my courses. Besides, I'm sure they can find my home address."

"You can hire a bodyguard, although that's a bit extreme."

Stuart shook his head in disgust.

"The only other thing I can tell you is to hang in there. If you're threatened, then come back and swear out a complaint."

Stuart rose and reached for the door.

Dellenbeck looked pityingly at him. "I'm sorry."

"Thanks anyway," came the toneless reply.

He quickly left the building and walked to his car. He drove out of the lot, passing the front of the police station.

A hand holding apart the slats of a venetian blind let them slip back. Desk Sergeant Morgan Dunne turned from the window and reached into his pocket, taking out an ornate tie clip. He had removed it, unnoticed, upon hearing the word 'Totem' from the young man. Returning to his desk, he picked up the phone and punched several numbers.

"Sir, this is Morgan Dunne. Sorry to disturb you on your private line. The Antelope has broken the Circle. Yes, he was just here. The Fox or the Hawk, whoever's available. Yes sir, I'll take care of everything. It is said. It is good."

He hung up the phone and shrugged. "Tough shit, Stuart," he whispered.

He held up and admired the tie clip, bedecked with a black onyx bird, its eyes two deep red garnets. Dunne stroked the bird, a crow, the Law Medicine of the Totem.

"ONE GOOD TURN"

As Charlie Edmondson walked up the porch steps to deliver the mail to Ray and Agnes Zaugg, he noticed their dog and cat were not on the porch, and Ray's old Ford was not in the driveway. There was a note taped to the front door. As he read, he could feel his knees shaking and turning to mush.

Charlie, Agnes and I are in the garage. We thought long and hard about this, and we're sure we're doing what's best. Please come in and call the authorities. All the papers they'll need are on the kitchen table.

One last favor, and it means a lot to us. Have the animal shelter ask whoever lives here next if they would adopt Ben and Jerry, so they can live out their days in their own home. I know this is a lot to ask, but we've been friends since we both started at the post office. Thanks again. God bless.

Ray and Agnes had signed the note. Charlie dropped his mailbag and cried quietly into one cupped hand. The Zauggs had been in failing health and owed back taxes. He knew elderly people sometimes did things like this.

He opened the front door and went inside, unfastening the note. In the dim living room he could see into the kitchen, where several papers were laid out neatly on the table.

There was one sharp bark, and Ben, a yellow lab, sauntered over and sniffed his hand, looking for his daily treat. Jerry, the black and white cat, stood in the kitchen doorway. Charlie stroked Ben's head, then sank down on the couch and cried some more.

. . .

It had been a bittersweet relocation for the DiNardo family. Caught in a downsizing movement at work, Doug DiNardo had taken a pay cut and could no longer afford his mortgage. Luckily, he was able to find a new home for a token down payment, and back taxes owed by its former tenants, Ray and Agnes Zaugg. His wife Joyce was able to keep her job as a cafeteria aide, but taking their three children and moving a month into the school year had taken its toll, especially on Steven, age 12, their oldest.

Steven was mad at his father for moving, mad at his mother for getting to see his old school every day, mad at his sister Jessica and brother Corey for adjusting to the new environment, and mad at the rest of the world for just *being there*.

Steven sat slumped in his chair even after having finished dinner. When the phone rang, it startled them. They hardly knew anyone yet. Doug DiNardo answered it. After a few 'I see's' and one 'that's interesting,' he said, "I'm sure they'll be thrilled. Why don't I let you know tomorrow." He hung up, smiling.

"That was the animal shelter. Seems the couple that lived here had a dog and cat, and hoped that whoever lived here next would adopt them." Joyce looked pleased, while Corey and Jessica shouted their approval.

"When can we get them?" asked Corey.

"A day or two, I guess," answered their father.

Only Steven showed no interest, and in fact seemed more disturbed, as though his misery should be shared by the rest of the family. By the time his sister spoke up, he had reached his breaking point.

"I know!" bellowed Jessica. "We could name them after famous *people.*"

"Yeah," Steven offered sarcastically, "the dog can be 'Hitler' and the cat can be 'Mussolini.'" He slumped back down in his chair, looking sullen again.

"Steven, why are you being like this?" Joyce asked.

Steven glared. "You know why. Because of Dad's stupid boss, I end up in 'Nowheresville' away from all my friends." He rose suddenly, knocking the chair askew. "I got the paper route because you made me, but if you think I'm gonna take on some dog and cat, well, forget it!" He dashed upstairs to his bedroom and slammed the door.

Jessica and Corey looked at their father, eagerly anticipating a punishment for their older brother.

"Well, kids," he said mildly, "Steven is still having some trouble adjusting. He'll come around." He smiled at the two younger children. "The dog is a big, friendly lab named Ben. The cat's name is Jerry. Get it? Ben and Jerry. They *already* have famous names."

"Mom, will they be sad because their old masters aren't here any more?" asked Corey.

"Well, maybe a little. But they'll get used to having new people that love them, don't you think?"

"I guess so."

Joyce turned to Doug. "I hope someone *else* starts getting used to new things."

. . .

A week later Joyce and Doug were clearing away supper dishes when they felt someone watching. They turned to find Corey, looking disturbed and uncertain.

"What's wrong, dear?" asked Joyce. "Has Steven been calling Ben 'Hitler' again?" Doug suppressed a laugh at the thought of the big lab wearing a Nazi uniform.

"No," the boy replied. I wanted to know what 'gay' means."

Joyce's eyes widened. "Where did you hear that term, dear?"

"Steven told me some kids said these two old guys on his paper route were gay. What's it mean?"

Doug and Joyce exchanged apprehensive glances. "You want to take this one?" she asked.

"Corey," Doug said, "some people are . . .*different* in the things they like, and the people they like to be with. It's not a bad thing. Okay?"

"Okay."

"Why don't you get started on your homework now, dear," Joyce said.

"All right. Dad?"

"Yes, Corey?"

"Steven *is* still calling the dog 'Hitler.'"

"We'll take care of it. Get going now."

When Corey's footsteps had faded, Joyce said, "Doug, I'm concerned about this."

"Calling the dog 'Hitler'?"

"Having *gay* men on his paper route."

Doug stared blankly at her.

"You *know.*"

Doug's face flashed understanding. "I wouldn't worry about it, Joyce. If these men were into that, I'm sure it would have come to light by now. Besides," he added, attempting to be glib, "why would they bother Steven? They have each *other.*"

"That's not—" She stopped and pointed toward the living room entrance, holding a finger to her lips. The children sometimes eavesdropped on them. She grabbed Doug's arm and tiptoed to the entryway.

They found Ben and Jerry sitting silently at attention in the dusky light of their living room, *staring* at them. Doug turned to his wife. "Is this odd, or what?" he asked, half joking.

"It looks like they were actually listening in," Joyce said.

"Well, they *weren't,* Joyce," Doug said, trying to lighten the moment. "Right, guys?"

Ben and Jerry continued to make eye contact, a solemn, penetrating gaze.

. . .

Small towns have their ways. They take care of their own, even dogs and cats. No matter where Doug or Joyce appeared in town, they were given information on the yellow lab and his unlikely partner.

"They like to sleep out on the porch at night," a clerk at the hardware store informed Doug. Their mail carrier, a kindly gent named Charlie, delivered no only the mail, but a daily bonding session with his pals, Ben and Jerry. It became clear to Joyce that he carried fond memories of the previous residents, Ray and Agnes Zaugg.

Finally she mustered enough nerve to bring up an uncomfortable topic. "Charlie, I was concerned about my son delivering the paper to two older men. I don't know their names, but—"

"Oh! You mean Lloyd and Felix. They're harmless, believe me. Moved here 'bout twelve, thirteen years ago. Share a house on Cochrane Road, half a mile from here. They claim to be best friends from childhood separated for forty years." He laughed softly. "Each one says the other is startin' to get a little soft upstairs," he said, tapping his temple. "You should hear 'um sometimes. Sound like a couple old hens squawkin' at each other."

Joyce hesitated. "What's the town's reaction to . . . their lifestyle?"

Charlie looked puzzled. "Lifestyle? *What* lifestyle? They live in their house and take walks together, if that's a *lifestyle,* Mrs. 'D.'"

Joyce's motherly instincts prevailed. "I was just concerned about the fact that my son Steven delivers the—"

"They aren't *child* molestors, if that's what you're askin'," Charlie interrupted. He picked up his mailbag and tromped off the porch.

Joyce was not accustomed to being spoken to harshly. After Charlie left, her upset, nervous energy prompted her into a cleaning spree of the kitchen. She had decided to rearrange all the cabinets and was in the process of emptying then out, stacking everything on the counter.

Peering inside, she noticed a white index card, its unlined back blending in with the paint. She had somehow missed it when she originally filled the cabinets. As she reached for it, Doug came bouncing in the back door, returned from his errands. He found every piece of kitchenware they owned piled on the counters.

"I thought you were finished with this."

Joyce didn't answer. She was reading the index card. "Doug, look at this. What do you think it means?"

Doug took the card and read aloud. "One good turn, and it's yours." He turned to his wife and shrugged.

"I must have missed it before."

He examined the card again. "It can't have been in there very long. It's not faded."

Joyce frowned heavily. "Doug, Charlie told me the people that lived here before planned everything, left all their important papers out, and requested the new owners adopt Ben and Jerry. Do you think this was intended for *us?*"

"Maybe, but I have no idea what it means. 'One good turn.' What is *that?*"

Joyce's disturbed expression remained. "I don't relish the idea of living in a house where I might find another message from the grave."

Doug's normally calm face showed definite irritation. "You're starting to sound like one of the kids, Joyce. How can we expect Steven to adjust to a change when you can't hack it yourself?"

"You know, Doug, you could be a little more—" She stopped, eyes wide, looking over his shoulder.

Doug turned. Sitting side by side in the living room doorway were Ben and Jerry, staring at them silently. Joyce exhaled in abject frustration. Doug would have liked to make a witty comment, but that part of his mind had just been outvoted.

"What the hell's going on here?" he whispered.

. . .

Steve DiNardo and the three boys who had invited him on their after-school escapade stood outside the five foot wrought iron fence of Roan Lane Cemetery.

"This is where we hang out," said Greg Pinder, a stout boy with a brown crew cut. "You have to climb the bars. It's the rules."

Steven looked at the menacing spiked tips of the black bars, then at the ground, where a slight depression had been scooped. "Can't you just go under? Somebody already dug this out."

Pinder frowned, looking at Bobby Mallory and Leo Clark, who shook their heads. "We never do anything by the book," said Mallory, a tall boy with light blond unruly hair. "We thought you might be okay. You don't seem to be one of those goody-goody new kids. So are you in or not?"

"Here's how we do it," said Leo Clark, a black-haired slight boy with thick glasses. Placing one foot on the bottom support brace, he hoisted himself up, carefully landing his other foot on the top support bar. Balancing, he lifted his lower foot so it, too, perched on the top level, then jumped to the other side. Bobby and Greg climbed over next. Steven went last, taking care not to impale himself on the bars.

"What do you guys do in here?" he asked.

"Lots of stuff," said Leo. "We bring magazines, explore, stuff like that. We take turns sneaking cigarettes from home."

Steven frowned. "My parents don't smoke. I can't sneak any."

"We'll share with you," said Greg. "*If* you're willing to try it."

"Sure. No problem."

As they walked through rows of headstones, Steven noticed two recent graves by the roadside. "Zaugg," read the large, grayish headstone. "Hey, this must be the people that lived in our house before us," he said. They stopped by the gravesite, hardened dirt covering the side-by-side plots.

"That must be creepy, living there," said Leo.

"Any ghosts out in the garage?" Greg teased.

"Nah, It's like any other house. Except for that dog and cat."

"What about them?" asked Bobby.

"They're kinda weird. They just lay on the porch all day. And they're always *staring* at you."

The others shrugged.

"My dad says if you kill yourself, you automatically go to Hell," said Leo. "Hey Zauggs!" he yelled. "Hot enough for you down there?"

Laughter erupted. When it had subsided, Greg nodded to the others and said, "Steve, we got a little initiation for you. To be a part of our group, you got to pull something on the two old faggots on your paper route. You know who I'm talking about?"

Steven seemed uneasy. "Those two guys on Cochrane Road?"

"That's right, Steve-o. Lloyd and Felix. The two queers."

"What do I have to do?"

"That's up to you. You got a week to think up something."

"And it's gotta be something *good,*" said Bobby. "You can't just ring their doorbell and run away. It has to be somethin' really . . .*outrageous.*"

"Destructive, even," said Greg.

"Yeah, destructive is good," agreed Leo.

Greg rose. "Let's go guys. Steve needs to be alone to do some thinking." The three boys made their way towards the woodlands bordering the far end of Roan Lane Cemetery.

Part of Steven DiNardo was convincing himself that this would be no problem. But that loud, annoying part of his conscience was reminding him that the two men had done nothing to him, that he was raised better.

"Still," he told himself, "a guy's got to have friends, especially when he's the new kid." It was a question of mind over matter. He would spend the next week working up an imagined hatred for Felix Velder and Lloyd Farnham. He sneered. "Who cares about a couple of old queers?"

. . .

Steve DiNardo was having a tough time. His mom could be overprotective, and his dad a bit wishy-washy, but they *had* fostered in him a precise code of right and wrong. He still called their adopted pets 'Hitler' and 'Mussolini', though. They were always *standing there* when you turned around, like they'd been spying. And they took off together most nights. He was surprised there were no complaints from neighbors.

That thought led him to the main problem. He was supposed to come up with a nasty prank to pull on Mr. Velder and Mr. Farnham. Each day he delivered the paper to the quaint two-story house on Cochrane Road. Often he would see them sitting on the porch reading or talking.

Lloyd Farnham was a tall man with white hair and moustache, and usually wore a straw hat. Felix Velder was short, with glasses and a neatly-trimmed white beard. He always wore a Notre Dame baseball cap. Steve had braced himself for the worst, expecting to find them engaged in some disgusting display of affection, but had not. They didn't seem like lovers, as kids at school said, but more like old friends.

Today, as he approached their porch, there was no sign of them. For some unknown reason, he crept quietly up the steps. He peered through their screen door. The afternoon sun illuminated the two men perfectly. Both sat on the couch, Lloyd's head towering over Felix, watching a late afternoon game show.

Their right hands were clasped together, and Felix had one arm affectionately draped over Lloyd's shoulder. Steven DiNardo's stomach did a flip. In his mind, he was witnessing the most revolting display imaginable. Shocked and disgusted, he slipped the paper into their mailbox and snuck off the porch

That did it. Problem solved. Whatever nastiness he devised, they deserved it.

. . .

"Hitler's got something in his mouth," Steve announced, as the family was finishing dinner that evening.

"Steven," Joyce said, "I thought we agreed that—"

"Okay, okay. *Ben* has something in his mouth."

The dog stood off to one side, a patch of white protruding from his lower muzzle.

"What you got, boy?" asked Doug, going over to him. He removed a white card from the dog's mouth. "It's that three-by-five card you found in the cabinet last week, Joyce. The *mysterious* secret message."

"What secret message, Daddy?" asked Jessica.

"Nothing, honey. Mom found a card in the kitchen cabinets when she was cleaning."

"Maybe there's buried treasure in the back yard!" shouted Corey.

"What a jerk," mumbled Steve.

"Steven, that's enough of that. I'm sure there is no buried treasure in our yard, Corey, and I'd better not find any holes out there," Doug warned.

The children departed to their rooms for homework time, Ben trailing behind. Joyce's expression, familiar now to her husband, was half bewilderment, half concern.

"*Now* what?" he asked.

"I put that card in the top drawer of my dresser, and haven't touched it since."

"Oh God, Joyce. First you have them spying on us, now you've got them opening *drawers.*"

"I might have left it open a little," she said softly.

"Joyce, a dog might pick up something in its reach, but *how* in the name of God did he get in that drawer? And *why,* Joyce? Animals have *reasons* for doing things."

Joyce held up the card. "Because it's *the card,* Doug. It's the message left behind by the Zauggs."

Doug's expression went from disbelief to astonishment. "Joyce, you *can't* be serious! Are you implying that this ... *dog* took something out of a drawer he couldn't possibly reach in the first place *with* the intent of calling it to our attention? *Are* you?"

Joyce DiNardo looked resolutely at her husband. "Yes, I *am.*" Hurt by her husband's tone and close to tears, she tramped upstairs to their bedroom, where she slammed the door behind her. She sat on their bed, turning toward the dresser. A patch of black and white stood out from the light brown finish of the wood. Jerry was sitting motionless on the dresser. The top drawer was a mere two inches below the cat's perch, partially open.

. . .

Moments after the final bell at the Deerfield Consolidated School, Steve DiNardo was walking toward Cochrane Road, accompanied by Greg Pinder, Leo Clark, and Bobby Mallory.

"Today's the day, Steve-o," said Pinder, slapping him on the back. "You all set?"

"All set."

"I'll be going with you just to make sure." He turned to the others. "Meet you guys later." They headed off towards Roan Lane.

"Good luck," one of them called back.

Greg and Steve continued toward Cochrane Road. It was an unseasonably warm day for October, the dry air rich with nature's changing-of-the-guard aromas.

"Well, Steve, what's it gonna be?"

"How about I set a fire?" he replied, pulling a book of matches from his pocket.

"Impressive. Set fire to what?"

"I been scouting around on my paper route. They got piles of leaves and bushel baskets all over the back yard."

"That's great! We can watch from the woods behind the house."

Within ten minutes they circumvented Felix and Lloyd's house, and crouched behind bushes that bordered the back yard. Steve surveyed his various targets and pulled out the matches again.

"Careful, now," warned Greg. "Don't want to be seen."

"Don't worry," Steve replied, with disgust in his voice. "If I know those two, they're on the couch, *holding hands!*"

He checked the windows one last time, then rushed forward and began setting fire to leaves piled on the ground and inside bushels. Greg watched approvingly as Steve darted from pile to pile. Several piles combined into larger fires. His task accomplished, Steve ran back to their hiding place, panting with the adrenalin rush.

"Way to go," said Greg. "Now starts the *real* fun."

Inside, Felix Velder was in the bathroom, dressing following his shower. His sixty-six-year-old sense of smell didn't detect a thing. But Lloyd Farnham and *his* sense of smell had been in a house fire, fifty-five years earlier, when he was twelve. That fire had crippled his mother, his younger sister dying of burns a week later. For Lloyd, fire was the most terrifying sight on earth. He was a human smoke detector, and even upstairs on the opposite side of the house, it was recalling for him the worst experience of his life.

"Fire, there's a fire! Call 9-1-1, Felix!" he screamed, as he ran out their back door in the direction his senses pulled him. What he found drove his panic to a frenzy. The *entire backyard* seemed to be burning. There must have been a dozen fires, all of them threatening, he felt, to race towards the house and engulf it, like the house fire so many years ago.

He screamed uncontrollably, his heartbeat and blood pressure skyrocketing. Twenty yards away, screened by bushes, one boy stifled laughter, while his companion realized, too late, what a dangerous deed had been perpetrated.

Seconds later, Felix Velder emerged, horrified. He ran down the steps to the nearby garden hose and began spraying water in a 180-degree arc. His back to Lloyd, he was unaware of his friend's panic. Lloyd Farnham collapsed onto the ground, flames a few feet from his head.

"Holy shit!" hissed Greg Pinder. "I'm gettin' the hell outta here." He sprinted into the woods.

Steve DiNardo continued to watch, terrified that his "prank" had become a life-threatening situation. He *wanted* to run, but his feet seemed cemented to the ground.

Felix had gotten much of the burning under control, and when he turned to reassure his friend, found him lying on the ground, eyes closed. He shrieked so loudly it actually hurt Steven's ears. Felix sobbed, cradling Lloyd's head in his lap. "Oh my God!" he wailed. "My only friend in the world. Please God, don't do this!"

For Steven, it was the "moment of truth," that instant when your humanity forced its way past whatever had temporarily won out. Steven knew CPR, knew it well. And no matter what this man might be of his own choosing, he was a human being whose life stood on the brink. He rushed from the bushes, covering the ground in seconds. "Call an ambulance!" he shouted, as he knelt beside the men. Felix got halfway up the steps, then dashed back down, grabbing the hose.

"Oh, my God, the fire's not out yet," he babbled. "I've got to—"

"Never mind that! Call an ambulance!"

Felix dropped the hose, running up the steps like a confused chicken.

As Steven initiated the life-saving technique his teachers and parents had drilled into him, a ridiculous scene was playing in his head. Greg, Leo, and Bobby were laughing at him. The imaginary Greg was saying, "Hey, DiNardo, heard you gave mouth-to-mouth to a queer." The other boys laughed uproariously.

Steven tilted Lloyd Farnam's head to the proper angle, forced his mind to clear, and began CPR.

. . .

Joyce and Doug were clearing away the dinner dishes. The children had departed for their after-dinner routines, which included homework, and for Jessica and Corey, exploring the attic.

Steven lay on his bed, thinking, something he had done a lot of in the past three days. He had been locally acclaimed as the boy who saved Lloyd Farnham's life. Teachers and kids in school congratulated him. Their phone rang constantly with complete strangers calling to add their praises. *Life in a small town,* Steven thought.

He had gotten lucky, too. Greg Pinder, afraid that he would get in trouble, hadn't told how the fire started. But the strangest thing was the behavior of Felix Velder. Once everything was under control, the firemen asked Felix what happened. He told them he may have left some leaves smoldering when he went in the house. Steven knew that was completely false. There had been no attempt to burn the leaves before he himself had set them afire.

When everyone had gone, Velder shook his hand, bubbling his thanks over and over. But Steve knew other boys had played pranks on them. Felix had to have at least *some* suspicions. But he hadn't even said anything to him in private.

In the paper, it said that Lloyd Farnham had a "mild episode," and would fully recover, thanks to *his* quick, decisive actions.

Through all his soul-searching, Steve had come to realize a few things. People were what they were, and you didn't have the right to judge. And throwing in with guys like Greg would eventually lead to big trouble. And one thought prevailed:

Felix had been willing to keep him out of trouble in gratitude for something he would have done anyway.

His thoughts were interrupted by his brother and sister running down the attic stairway, shouting. "Mom, Dad, come quick!" Steve poked his head into the hallway to find everyone rushing to the attic, followed by Ben, loping behind them with a decided limp. He had been limping for nearly a week, although the vet could find no injury. Steve followed the procession to the attic.

"What's wrong?" Doug asked.

The children explained that Jerry had gotten caught behind some loose boards in back of an old bookcase.

Doug moved the heavy bookcase enough to squeeze behind it. "Cats don't usually get into places they can't get out of," he mused. "C'mon Jerry, c'mon girl," he coaxed.

As the DiNardos watched, a white leg appeared. With seemingly little effort, the rest of Jerry followed. It seemed obvious that she was not really "stuck." A thin, hardback book slid from behind the boards, possibly jarred loose by the cat's movements. Doug braced his shoulder against the bookcase, reached in, and retrieved it.

"Maybe there's a treasure map inside!" shouted Corey.

"What a jerk," mumbled Steve.

Doug opened the book, whose cover was a deep blue, with ornate gold etching. The cream-colored, unlined pages were empty. "It's some kind of journal, but it's blank," he said. He turned to the inside cover. "'Property of Raymond T. Zaugg,'" he read. He flipped to the first page. A three-by-five card slid out, but Doug caught it. Silently he read it. "'One good turn, and it's yours,'" he said softly.

Joyce DiNardo covered her mouth.

Doug lifted his shoulders in resignation. "Maybe they *did* leave this for us, and Ben and Jerry led us to it."

"Led us to *what?*" asked Steven. "An empty book?"

Doug flipped through the pages again, all seemingly blank. But halfway back were several cellophane wrappers. Inside were stamps, not the ordinary variety, but odd-shaped, colorful commemorative ones. The remainder of the pages all contained cellophane packets of stamps. Most wrappers gave information on the stamps' identification. "A stamp collection," Doug said, showing it around.

"Think it's worth anything?" asked Steven.

"I doubt it. These people owed back taxes and medical bills. They could have sold these if they had any value."

"Wow! *Nazi* stamps," cried Jessica, looking at the page her father had turned.

Doug examined the page. "My God, these look like real stamps issued by the Third Reich. There's a collector in town that might know something about these."

The family somehow ended up focusing on Ben and Jerry in the attic doorway. Jerry's tail curled back and forth on the floor, snakelike. As if on silent command, the two turned and exited down the stairs, the cat gliding, Ben limping.

. . .

"Heard about your good luck, Mrs. D.'," said Charlie Edmondson, handing Joyce the mail while holding a dog biscuit out to Ben. He snapped it up and sniffed Charlie's hand.

"Thanks, Charlie. Hard to imagine the Zauggs owing taxes and doctor bills while they had a stamp collection worth nearly fifteen thousand dollars."

Charlie smiled wryly, scratching Ben's ear. "Well, that was Ray for you. I guess he was determined to leave something behind."

"He could have sold it and gotten out of debt."

"He could have, but he was a stubborn old goat, wanted to go out on his own terms."

"I guess."

"Your husband told me how you found one card in a cabinet, and the other with the stamps. Maybe your son saving Lloyd's life was the 'one good turn'."

"It's so . . .*weird*, though."

"Well, Mrs. D.', who knows. Maybe some people don't really die a hundred-per-cent." He laughed softly. "If *anybody* could find a way to stick around *after* they were gone, it'd be Ray Zaugg."

Joyce pointed at Ben and Jerry. "It's like they *knew* everything and were waiting for the right time."

Charlie picked up his mail sack. "Mrs. D.', some things just don't stand up to explainin'." He turned and headed down the steps. "You have a nice day, now."

. . .

It had been several weeks since Lloyd Farnham's close call. In the cool dusk he was taking his customary walk down Cochrane Road, accompanied by his best friend in the world, Felix Velder. Lloyd was recovering, but he forgot things more often, and sometimes got confused about everyday information. Felix had given up trying to set him straight. Filling in every detail for Lloyd had lost its charm.

As they headed home, two four-footed shapes passed them, heading in the opposite direction. Lloyd looked over his shoulder at the animals.

"Dog looks familiar," he said. "Isn't that Ray Zaugg's lab?"

Here we go again, thought Felix. Try as he might, he could *not* get Lloyd to process the fact that Ray and Agnes were gone, their pets adopted. "*No,* it's *not* Ray Zaugg's lab," said Felix impatiently.

"Ohhh." Lloyd paused, thinking. "Sure looks like him."

"But it's *not.*"

Lloyd paused again. "It's got Ray's *limp.*"

Felix nodded grudgingly. "True enough, it's got Ray's *limp.*"

The two walked on in silence, hand in hand. Lloyd turned over images in his mind until a familiar one entered. He turned to Felix. "Come to think of it, that *cat* looked familiar, too."

An exasperated Felix Velder slammed his Notre Dame hat onto the road.

"Was that Ray's—"

"No!"

Lloyd looked curiously at his friend, then shrugged. "Sure looked like her."

In ultimate frustration, Felix proceeded to kick his hat down Cochrane Road. Lloyd, thinking he had forgotten an everyday routine, threw *his* hat to the pavement and began kicking it down the road, trying to keep pace with Felix.

A quarter mile away, by a small turnout, the yellow lab and his Angora partner stood by the wrought iron bars of Roan Lane Cemetery. The cat slipped easily between the metal spikes, as the canine belly-crawled under the fence's bottom brace, his body filling the depression he had dug weeks earlier.

Inside, they trotted towards the familiar gravesite, one with a prowl, the other with a limp.

"THE MAN IN 3-C"

From the moment I first saw him, I sensed something . . . different about the man in apartment 3-C. He reminded me of a squirrel, the way they look at you, with their body turned so they can run if necessary. They're *used* to people, but don't trust them completely.

Yes, John C. Franklin reminded me of a squirrel. My father would have rolled his eyes and said, 'Claire, you're a sixteen-year-old girl with an overactive imagination.'

My whole life, I've been fascinated with "big" mysteries. My favorites are the Bermuda Triangle and UFO sightings, but I'm also into conspiracies and secrets. And now this: John C. Franklin, who rents an apartment in the building my father owns and manages.

It's an old three-story building that Dad inherited from Grandpa when he died a couple of years ago. He had to hire a custodial service, but he does all the repairs himself. He's still employed as a carpenter, but not full time any more.

I go with him to the apartment regularly, depending on schoolwork. It's just the two of us. Mom died of cancer when I was eight.

We live here in Marston, California, thirty miles south of Fresno. We do all right, for the most part. To Dad, I'm the girl with the far-out ideas about who killed John Kennedy and Martin Luther King, and the *real* reason things disappear in the Bermuda Triangle.

But back to Mr. Franklin. He seemed to be in his late sixties. He was civil, but not much more. There was a controlled nervousness in his manner whenever I saw him or even said hello. Two things: he never talked about himself. Not one story about the "good old days." The other thing was his eyes. They had a jumpy, nervous quality to them.

My first theory was that he was a German war criminal. Too young, probably. Then I thought he might be a retired double agent or government hit man. Those people are all over. You'd never suspect who they are, either.

I listed dozens of possibilities. None of them seemed to fit, but neither did "ordinary lonely old guy." So I started investigating. Since Grandpa was gone, I began with my father. "Dad," I asked, "how long has Mr. Franklin lived there?"

"Geez, let me think. Since before Grandpa had his first heart attack when I started to help out. At least ten years, probably longer. Why?"

"There's something strange about him."

Dad held up a warning hand. He had been down *this* road before. "Now hold it, Claire. I don't want you bothering him with another one of your 'theories.' He's not Hitler, and I'm sure he wasn't in on Kennedy's assassination."

"Dad, the Russians buried Hitler in a secret grave, for your information, and I don't think he's an assassin. But there's *something* that he's hiding. I can tell."

"Well, let me tell you something, young lady. His rent is part of our income, which we need. Especially if you're going to college someday. Besides, he doesn't bother anyone and he's entitled to his privacy. Are we understood on this?"

"Yes, Dad." I gave him a "Daddy's little girl" smile. They still come in handy. "But, if he *wanted* to be friendly, and talk or something—"

"Claire, you're a sixteen-year-old girl. What have I told you about—"

"Dad, Mr. Franklin's an *old man!*"

"Still, you should always be careful."

"I will, Dad. I promise. But I *can* be friendly if it's not a bother, right? We want our tenants to be *happy,* don't we, Dad?"

He sighed. I was wearing him down, as usual. "I guess we do."

. . .

With that settled, I began the next phase of my plan. I walked over to the apartments after school while Dad was still at work. Since I seldom go there without him, I needed a cover story. I had lost a schoolbook and thought I may have left it somewhere in the building. I planned to ask all the tenants on the third floor if they'd found it. I brought my cat Mickey along in my backpack. He likes it there, and I thought he could be useful in making conversation with Mr. Franklin.

I started with Mrs. Bridge in 3-A. She's a widow, lived in England much of her life. She's okay, *sometimes.* She said she would keep an eye out for my book, but seemed a bit annoyed that I'd lost it in the first place.

Next were Mr. and Mrs. DiMaria in 3-B. They're older, Italian, and always cooking and offering me food. You could gain ten pounds just knocking on their door. Also, Mr. DiMaria was forever requesting repairs. They hadn't seen my book, and then asked how I could even *carry* any books, I was so skinny. I should eat something. I managed to get out of there with Mr. DiMaria calling after me, "Claire, ask you father to come look at my toilet. She's not a-workin' so good."

Then came apartment 3-C. I took Mickey out of my backpack, holding him in one arm as I knocked. I could hear a game show on television, then nothing, then shuffling steps.

The door opened, and there he stood , wearing a plaid shirt, old pants, and slippers. His eyes jumped from Mickey to me.

"Yes?" he asked.

"I'm Claire Jessup, Mr. Franklin. The super's daughter."

"Yes. What can I do for you?"

"I think I left my history book in the building. I was wondering if you'd seen it."

"No, I haven 't. I'm sorry."

There was an awkward silence. I had to stretch out this encounter, somehow. I thought of something quickly. I recoiled sharply and dropped Mickey. "Ow! Darn cat scratched me." Good old Mickey had no sooner hit the floor when he scampered inside Mr. Franklin's apartment. Just what I was hoping for.

Mr. Franklin seemed flustered, then said, "I guess you better come in and get him." Mickey was circling the perimeter of the kitchen, which opened onto a living room.

I overacted sneaking up on him, all the while scanning the apartment. The furniture was beat-up, out of style, and sparse. Not a single photograph of anyone. The only decoration was a poster of the Golden Gate Bridge. At the same time, I was grabbing at Mickey and *missing* him, of course. Finally, he circled back to the door, which was still open a crack.

"He won't run out, will he?" Mr. Franklin asked.

"No," I said, as I came alongside Mickey, who had finally stopped. I knelt to pick him up and that's when I noticed what had been carved into the bottom of the door, so small you'd actually have to be at floor level to have seen it.

"Guess I'll get going," I said. "Sorry to have bothered you."

"That's okay."

Another awkward silence. As he held the door for me I asked, "Do you like cats?" How lame!

He paused, as though thinking about it. I thought *that* was pretty odd. Either you *like* cats or you *don't.*

"I . . .*admire* them."

"You admire them?"

"Yes, they go their own way."

I had no idea what *that* meant.

As I stepped into the hallway, he said, "I hope you find your book."

"What book?" Stupid! "Oh, the uh . . ."

"History book you lost," he finished.

"Yes," I said, jabbing my finger for emphasis. "I better check the basement." I scurried off. It was time to start making a list of clues and theories. I was convinced now that Mr. John C. Franklin was a man with a secret.

. . .

Most people wouldn't have suspected anything from my brief "visit" to Mr. Franklin's apartment, but I did. I already mentioned the way he acted nervous, like a squirrel, his jumpy eyes, and how he didn't ever talk about himself. I found it odd that he had no pictures of anyone in his apartment, just that poster of the Golden Gate. You don't just put up a picture of a *bridge* in your home.

And that cat thing. He 'admires' them. 'They go their own way.'

And the tiny number 109 carved into his door. It wasn't anything done by a manufacturer. It could have been done by carpenters during installation. But wouldn't they have just penciled it in? My dad is always making marks on pieces, but he doesn't *carve* them in permanently. A person *living* there did that, but *why?*

Whatever he was being secretive about was none of my business, but it's in my nature to want to know everything. Especially if it's a secret.

. . .

During the next three months I took every opportunity to go to the apartment building with my dad. Twice a year dad gives every unit a complete efficiency and safety check. The times I was in Mr. Franklin's place he acted his usual self: polite, but jumpy. Dad hardly seemed to notice him.

Part of me is this regular kid in school, but then I go home and explore these mysteries. I've been taping a lot of specials off cable, shows on political conspiracies and assassinations, the real reasons wars were fought, the Lindberg kidnapping, and the Roswell incident. I was getting quite a collection.

Then I taped a program on great prison escapes made into movies. The first segment re-enacted a famous escape made by British pilots from a German POW camp during WWII. Then they showed how this American escaped from a Turkish prison that was pretty close to being hell on earth.

The point was that you can't break some people, no matter how tightly they're caged. The human spirit, the urge to be free, will somehow prevail. It was inspiring, in an odd way.

The next segment was about these three men who escaped from Alcatraz in 1962. They chiseled away at decaying cement in back of their cells where their air vents were, making them wide enough to squeeze through. Then they made plaster dummies of their own heads to put in their bunks so guards wouldn't see they were missing. Using various rigged-up devices, they unscrewed a ventilator covering and got onto the roof.

To get across a mile of bone-chilling water, they glued raincoats together with contact cement and inflated them to make a raft. Some of their personal effects washed ashore on nearby Angel Island. It was assumed they drowned.

Then they showed photos of the three. John and Clarence Anglin, brothers, were shown together. The next picture was the man behind the escape attempt, Frank Morris. I paused the picture and stared in disbelief. I could feel the hair on my neck tingling. That face! Those eyes! Even in a still picture, they looked jumpy.

It was Mr. Franklin. He was thirty-five years younger, but the likeness was too similar to be a coincidence. I let the tape continue. There were more details on the escape, and how they closed Alcatraz less than a year later. Then they showed the cells they inhabited. Frank Morris's cell number was *109.*

The same tiny number I found carved into his door, where no one would ever see it. No one except me. Why, though? Did he still feel like a prisoner after all these years? The lone decoration on his wall made sense *now.* In the background of that picture is Alcatraz.

When that segment was over I stopped the tape. I was shaking. Tears were rolling down my cheeks.

Old Mr. Franklin had been a rough character in his youth. A convicted bank robber, maybe worse. A man who broke out of one prison after another until he was sent to Alcatraz, an escape-proof island fortress in the middle of San Francisco Bay. And yet he had done the impossible. His ingenuity and an odd type of courage had spurned him and two others to succeed at what no one else had, before or since.

The tragic irony was he couldn't share his greatest accomplishment with a living soul. I was crying out of sadness and pity. A lonely old nobody marking time until he died. Yet to me, he was a hero.

. . .

I didn't tell my father when he got home. Provided he believed me, he would have gone straight to the police, I'm positive. An escaped felon gets turned in, even if he could no longer hurt a fly. Even if he had pulled off one of the most ingenious endeavors in the history of the human race. Most likely, I would have gotten the overactive imagination speech, and probably banned from setting foot in the building again.

Neither of those possibilities were going to do me any good, so I spent that evening in my room, thinking about what I should do. I know he's a wanted man, but thirty-five years have passed. Time had left him behind long ago. In my opinion, he achieved the ultimate victory of the human spirit over its worst enemy: loss of personal freedom. Like I said, to me, he was a hero.

. . .

It was the last day of school before Christmas vacation, so we got out at noon. I rushed home and grabbed the tape on great escapes, and unhooked our VCR. I hadn't seen one in his apartment.

I had no idea how he would react to the news that I knew who he really was. He might get violent, or threaten to call the police, but that would only draw attention to himself. But I was prepared for a long session of him denying everything. I just had to convince him that he was in no danger from me.

When I got to the apartment building I took the back stairs so no tenants would see me and mention it to my father. I stopped in front of apartment 3-C, my heart racing as much from nervousness as exertion. I knocked. After a moment the door opened. He looked bigger to me now, stronger, unconquerable. This was the man who escaped from Alcatraz. I smiled in pure adoration.

He seemed surprised. Then his eyes narrowed and he looked like a squirrel ready to break for the nearest tree. "Did you lose another book?" The unpleasantness in his tone made me even more nervous.

"No, I . . ."

"Did your cat run away again?"

"No, I have to talk to you privately. It's important."

"We can't talk privately in the *hall,* can we?"

I stepped inside and took off by backpack containing the tape and our VCR. My eyes were drawn to the poster on the wall.

"Did your father send you?"

"No. He doesn't know I'm here. I don't think he'd approve of what I'm doing."

"Well, neither do *I.* "

"What do you mean?" Fear and nervousness oozed from my voice.

"From the first time I saw you, you seemed to be staring at me, like you're *studying* me."

I looked down, embarrassed.

"Then, you knock on my door with a story about a lost book, you pretend your cat scratches you and you go after him, all the while checking out my apartment."

My mouth hung open like a fish pulled from water. "How … how did you know?"

"I may be old, but I'm very observant. The cat never touched you. And you forgot your own lie when I said I hoped you found your book. You were casing my home like the common thief I thought you were."

"But I wasn't. I'm not a thief, I just—"

He silenced me with a wave of his hand. "I know that *now.* A real thief would have returned to make their score." He paused and looked me in the eye. "But there *is* something you want, isn't there? That's why you're here now without your father's knowledge."

I nodded meekly and unzipped my backpack, taking out the video tape.

"What's that?" he demanded.

"It's a show I taped off TV. It's about great escapes." I watched his face. He didn't flinch.

"Yes, so?"

"It's got Frank Morris and the Anglin brothers' escape from Alcatraz." I didn't imagine it. He recoiled noticeably, then tried to compose himself.

I felt so many emotions at that moment. Like a fool, my voice cracked and tears welled in my eyes. "It's okay. I know who you really are. I just wanted you to know I would *never* tell. You have no idea how much I admire what you did. It was one of the most heroic things I ever heard of." I was really blubbering by the time I finished. He didn't try to comfort me, though. He just stared at me until I'd composed myself.

"So that's what this is all about?" he asked. "You think I'm some guy that broke out of Alcatraz? Sorry to disappoint you, but—"

"Yes you are!" I insisted. "Do you want to see your picture on this tape?" I ran over to the door. "How come Frank

Morris's cell number is carved into your door?" I walked over to the poster, tapping the prison in the background. "Cats go their own way," I said softly, "and so did you."

He looked stunned and scared now. I walked over to him by the couch. "Don't worry. You'll never have to go back. You *deserve* to be free." I could actually see him shaking, and he sagged down on the couch and covered his eyes, crying softly. My greatest moment; I solved a mystery. Watching him cry, though, I felt like a pile of crap.

He looked up and wiped his eyes. "How...how?" he asked plaintively.

My voice shook. "Something in your eyes, the way you looked at people. You always seemed like you were ...*hiding out* instead of *living.*"

For a minute or two he kept shaking his head. "A girl," he muttered over and over. "A *teenager.*"

"I'm interested in stuff like this," I replied. "I just *knew* you were somebody."

He stood up next to me. He was a giant once more, invincible. "What's your name, again?"

"Claire."

"What do you want, Claire?"

I shrugged. "We can be friends, but it's up to you. Either way, I'll never tell. I swear."

He seemed lost in thought. "Is that it?"

Of *course* that wasn't it. I hesitated. "Could you tell me about that night?"

"I've never actually told it *aloud,*" he mused. "Always to myself."

"You can skip the preparation stuff," I said. "It's on the tape and that Clint Eastwood movie."

"Clint Eastwood," he said contemptuously. "That son-of-a-bitch owes me lots of money." He smiled devilishly. "What *do* you want to hear about?"

I was nearly breathless in anticipation. "The part no one else knows about." To see the look on his face, I almost regretted having asked. But he began immediately, as though it had been bursting to be heard.

"We inflated the raft, lay across it, and started paddling. There was barely room. Water so cold it made you cry. Halfway across, Clarence panicked. Couldn't feel his arms or legs, he said, and slipped off. He was a few yards behind us when John went back for him." He paused and lowered his voice. "I kept going."

"You *did?*"

"We agreed beforehand. Whoever was on the raft had to keep going. We knew we only had so much time before hypothermia set in."

"What happened?"

"I could hear Clarence crying out and John trying to calm him down. A boat went by about thirty yards away. I couldn't hear over their motor. The water got choppy, and it was all I could do to hang on. After it passed, I looked behind me and listened. Not a sound. I called out, but . . ."

He dropped his head and choked up a little.

"I was so furious that they had gone through all this and drowned anyway. It wasn't fair. I guess that's what kept me going. I wasn't gonna be cheated. I couldn't feel *my* arms anymore, either. I had to keep looking at my hands to make sure they were still on the raft. I just kept kicking and paddling until I reached shore." He paused. "And that's it."

My mouth hung open. "You were the only one . . ."

"Far as I know. The way I figured it, one man could never propel a raft that far until he froze or drowned. I don't think I would have made it without them. That's why I took the name John Clarence Franklin. John and Clarence for the brothers, and Franklin so I'd have a *little* of my old self."

I was half in a daze, hearing this firsthand. It was better than anything I had on any tape. "How did you manage to avoid capture?"

"Don't forget, everyone thought we *all* drowned, so none of the Feds were looking for me after the first couple days. I was experienced, too. I knew what an escapee had to do."

"Like what?"

"I destroyed the raft. Currents would have carried it out to sea if we'd all drowned. Then, of course, I had to get civilian clothes. Luckily, I found a Salvation Army bin."

"What about money, food, and shelter?"

He shook his head. "No problem. I looked like just another wharf rat. There were mission churches that took care of people before you had homeless shelters." He winked. "And I knew where to look for people to set me up. New identity. A job."

"Wouldn't they want *money* for that?"

"I traded. *My* services for *theirs.* "

"You had to—"

"I'd rather not say anything more, you understand. As soon as my debt was paid, though, I went straight. Now I live off my pension like any other sixty-seven-year old."

"What brought you *here?*"

"West coast was the only part of the country where I wasn't known, but I had to get out of San Francisco. Too cold." His face turned grim. "After that night in the bay, I vowed never to be cold again."

He became silent. I looked at my watch. "I better get home, Mr. Morris, before my—"

"It's Mr. *Franklin,* Claire. John C. Franklin."

"Right. Sorry." I picked up the tape. "Maybe you'd like to have this."

He shook his head. "I watch TV, Claire. I've seen myself a few times over the years. But I left Frank Morris behind long ago. You understand."

"Sure."

He walked me to the door and held it open. I smiled proudly. "See you around, Mr. Franklin."

He put an index finger to his lips and smiled back.

. . .

In all the excitement, I had forgotten about our annual drive to Los Angeles to spend Christmas with my Aunt Judith and Uncle Henry. We've done that every year since Mom died. I walked in the door to find Dad taking care of last-minute details and making sure I got packed for our week in L. A. He didn't even ask where I'd been.

I had an enjoyable week with Aunt Judith, Uncle Henry, and my cousins Caroline and Bill. But the whole time I was preoccupied with thoughts of my amazing discovery, a discovery I could never share with anyone.

We got home on a Saturday night, and I helped unload the car and collected Micky from Mrs. Wells next door. When I came back Dad was asleep on the couch. That long drive had wiped him out. There was one message on our answering machine, so I played it back.

Mr. Jessup, this is Mr. DiMaria, apartment 3-B. I rolled my eyes. Another repair job.

Mr. Jessup, the man in 3-C, Mr. Franklin. He gets a U-Haul the other day anda moves out. He left me the key anda two envelopes, one for you anda one for Claire. I went in anda looked around, you know? Seems okay, but I'm sure you wanna come anda check for yourself. Anda could you have a look at our kitchen sink? She's not a-workin' so good. There was a click. Through my tears, I managed to hit the 'Save' button.

. . .

"You're quite the somber one, Claire," Dad observed, as we were getting ready to go to the apartments the following morning.

"I was sad to hear about Mr. Franklin," I replied. "I didn't even get to say goodbye."

Dad was staring at me. "Claire, you didn't uh, *pester* him, did you? We talked about that."

"*Now* who's got the overactive imagination?" I said, trying to put a false cheeriness into it.

" I *hate* when people move with no advance notice. I lose a month's rent. You never know what they've done to the place."

I nodded absently, but was too absorbed in sadness and guilt.

Mr. DiMaria answered our knock and gave Dad the key.

"What about the envelopes?" I asked, trying not to sound too anxious. He handed one to each of us.

Dad opened his and read the one-page note. He nodded approvingly. "His older brother is very sick, and he moved back east to take care of him." He discovered a check inside the envelope. "How *about* that. He paid up for January so I wouldn't be stuck. See, Claire? Some people *are* honest, you know."

Mr. DiMaria cleared his throat. "Maybe before you go you can take a look at the kitchen sink. She's not a-workin' so good."

Dad winced. "Claire, here's the key. I'll meet you next door when I'm finished."

I was so grateful to get out of there. I didn't want to read his letter in front of anyone. I hurried down to 3-C. It still seemed like this was his sanctuary and I was invading it. But I'd *done* that already. I unlocked the door, went inside, and took a long look around. Everything was gone, but it didn't have that messy look apartments do when people move. My eyes were drawn to the wall where the poster had hung. Empty wall. Empty apartment. I hurriedly opened the envelope and read his note.

Claire, I'm sorry about this. I know you meant what you promised, but at my age I can't take any chances. Things happen, despite the best of intentions. Who would know that better than me? I won't be communicating with you again, you understand. I left you a souvenir under the loose tile by the window. I figure you'd appreciate it.

Best always,
John Clarence Franklin
P. S. Destroy this.

I rushed to the corner and pried up the tile. Under it was a three inch square piece of something. It was greenish-black, frayed and rotting; some kind of plastic or rubber.

The raft! It was a piece of the raft. Probably his most prized possession. I started getting teary-eyed, but heard my father coming. I pocketed it and the note and wiped my eyes.

Dad stood in the doorway, looking the place over. "Not bad. Slap a coat of paint on and she's all set. What did Mr. Franklin say, Claire?"

"He thanked me for being nice to him, that's all." I managed a smile.

"Okay, we're out of here."

When we got in the pickup, he turned to me. "So who is Mr. Franklin, *really?*"

"What?" My heart nearly stopped.

He smiled the way he did when he made fun of my theories.

"He's nobody, Dad. It was just my overactive imagination."

He nodded happily and patted the check in his shirt pocket, a gift from John C. Franklin.

I reached into my pocket and wrapped a hand around a little piece of history, a gift from Frank Morris, the man in 3-C.

"SOMEWHERE THEY CAN'T FIND ME"

I'm twenty-seven now, so it's been almost twenty-five years since Dad's plane went down in the Gulf of Mexico. Sometimes the hardest thing to take is the way some people look at me, like they expect that if I'd just *try* a little harder, I could *become* him.

My famous father was Ricky Coates, a singer-songwriter with a six-string guitar who came out of Indiana in 1971 and took the top forty by storm with songs that seemed to tell everybody's story at once.

Dad was just starting to hit it big, like so many other rock stars, when it ended. Of course, there's one big difference with my dad. He's alive. He faked his death.

I still don't know how or why he did it, but he *did.* Who helped him, and how did they keep the secret all these years? I know Mom is in on it, but what does she get out of it? It can't be money. At the rate Dad was going, he would have made double yearly what the insurance policy on him paid out one time.

No one in that plane could have survived, so my guess is Dad never even got on board. The Cessna exploded about a minute after takeoff, broke apart, and plunged into the Gulf of Mexico about three-hundred yards off shore.

The rescue party recovered what they believed to be six bodies; the three guys in the backup band, Dad's road manager Tommy Lyons, and the pilot. So who was the sixth? Or were the victims so blown apart that they made six bodies out of five sets of remains? It's gruesome, I know, but I'm sure this is how he got away with it. Namely, there was no way of identifying a *face*. But Mom flew right down there and identified him anyway. That's one reason why I think she was in on it.

I've had my doubts, but then I examine things I learned secretly. I've become quite a snoop over the years, especially after I discovered evidence that Dad was alive and hiding out somewhere.

The record company made a fortune off their "dead" rock star. America had a new hero to mourn. My mother got to be a celebrity, once removed. She got to work with music people and TV producers who did documentaries about my dad. She opened a restaurant/nightclub here in Indianapolis, which I manage. It combines good entertainment and great cuisine with a sort of museum to the "late" Ricky Coates. On display are some of his guitars, music awards, rough drafts of hit songs, all that.

The way I see it, the only real loser was me. I grew up without a father. It was an ego trip occasionally to be pointed out to some girl I liked that I was Ricky Coates' son, but that didn't make up for him not being around. I came to hate him, sort of. I mean, the guy would rather play dead than be a father to me.

. . .

Proof. Of course. You can't claim anything unless you've got proof. I do, sort of. What happened was at age sixteen I needed a copy of my birth certificate for some school activity. It was in a wall safe Mom had in her bedroom. I already knew the last number of the combination because she always left the dial on it from the previous use. I stood over her shoulder when she was getting my birth certificate and watched her get the first number, then made a big production of turning around and announcing I wasn't peeking while she got the other two numbers.

One day when she wasn't home I kept trying second numbers, and sure enough, on the twenty-fourth try, the safe opened. I had always been curious about what was in there, and I *did* feel guilty about what I was doing. When I was little she said she had a handgun in there for personal protection. Right after my father "died" we were hounded by record agents looking for posthumous deals, curiosity seekers, obsessed fans, you name it. Anyway, there was no gun in the safe. Either she had gotten rid of it, or kept it somewhere else.

All the safe held were insurance policies, my birth certificate, some other odds and ends, and a typed envelope addressed to Mom. I pulled a single sheet of paper from the envelope. There were two lines written on the page, in my father's handwriting, which I had seen on first drafts of some of his songs. The lines read,

"I will be living quietly,

Somewhere they can't find me."

The postmark on the envelope was from someplace in Louisiana, dated about a month *after* the plane crash. And just like that, after fourteen years of growing up with a legend instead of a father, I realized what he had done. My head snapped up, my body stiffened. "You bastard," I whispered.

. . .

The way I figure it, that was his signal to Mom to let her know that the plan was in operation. I never told her I knew. I could have taken the letter to some investigative reporter, but I didn't.

I was so outraged, I figured I'd pay them back by having a secret from *them*. My secret being that I knew *their* secret.

I felt in control, like the director of some bizarre movie, and they were acting out these strange parts. That's what you do when you're a slightly neurotic sixteen-year-old.

About those two lines on the letter I found: they were from my dad's first hit single, "Closed For the Season." It's about this shy teenager who gets the nerve up to ask this pretty, but real snooty girl to go to the drive-in with him. She agrees, but on the night they go, the drive-in had shut down. They find a sign out front that says "Closed For the Season." The girl makes him feel like the world's biggest idiot. Then she blabs it all around school. Pretty soon everybody is laughing at the poor kid. He's so devastated that he becomes a social dropout after that, a loner.

It's a catchy tune, but I don't see why it was so popular. But then, nothing about the 70's makes much sense to me.

. . .

The years went by, as they say. Next month, May twelfth to be exact, will be the twenty-fifth anniversary of the plane crash that ended his career. *How* and *Why*. That's all I really care about any more. If he were to turn up on my doorstep tomorrow I swear I wouldn't tell anyone. But I really would want to know, for my own sanity, *how* and *why*. The rest is all yours. You can have him.

I guess it's time. I'm taking a drive to Washburn, Louisiana, a little town on the Gulf of Mexico. Mom thinks I'm meeting friends in New Orleans and spending a week there. *I* can lie, too. I got an out-of-state friend to call the club when Mom was there and invite me to New Orleans. He's really from Texas, but agreed to do the fake invitation, no questions asked.

When I get to Washburn, I'm gonna look up a man named Frank Vanderkellen, who I'm sure was Ricky Coates in his "previous life." I didn't tell anyone or confront my mother when I found that letter, but that doesn't mean I didn't take *any* action.

I did my share of snooping the past eleven years. Some days, it was all I looked forward to. Other days I was too busy living. Over the years I've found unmailed letters in Mom's pocketbook, addressed to Frank Vanderkellen of Washburn, Louisiana.

I imagine she's been writing him all these years, maybe sending money, as well. For all I know, she's sent him photos of me and updates on my semi-normal life. In a way, I almost hope he *hasn't* loved me from afar. I've worked hard to build up this hatred.

. . .

I found Washburn on my third day of driving. It was small, but you could tell it hadn't escaped the fallout from progress, such as an ATM right next to Hank's Bait and Tackle Shop. I headed for the Pelican All-Night Diner out on Airport Rd. That's where Mom sent the letters. It seemed *odd* that Dad would be using a *diner* as his mailing address. Is there *anything* about this whole mess that *isn't* odd?

Washburn Municipal Field was bound to be out here somewhere. That's the airport the plane took off from that night in 1973. The airport and diner were nearly together, one across the highway from the other. I'd always pictured the airport as some tiny hole-in-the-wall operation, but it, too, had grown over the years.

I parked in the small lot adjacent to the diner and headed inside. A sign on the door said, "F. L. Vanderkellen, Proprietor." Hard to describe the tight feeling in my chest, seeing that name. So, he *owned* the diner. I thought that it was kind of strange he wouldn't have put more distance than *this* between himself and the airport where his career ended. Maybe it was supposed to be symbolic, I don't know.

There were two older guys sitting together at the counter, and a family of four at a corner table. In my mind I was seeing the picture of Ricky Coates that everyone has; huge, bushy head of hair, brown beard, about five-nine, one-fifty. I kept reminding myself, he'd be forty-eight years old now.

The man behind the counter looked to be in his forties, and was about five-nine. But even without the beard or mop of hair, he didn't look anything like Dad. He wore horn-rimmed glasses, his hairline started on *top* of his head, the hair itself thin and graying. Maybe twenty-five years of "living quietly" wasn't so easy.

I took a stool a ways down from the two men, my heart pounding as he walked over and nodded pleasantly.

"Frank Vanderkellen?" I asked, my throat just about dried up now.

He nodded again. "Yes."

It was my voice I heard, but it seemed as though someone else was working it. "Could I just call you Ricky Coates?"

His mouth fell open, his eyes widened like dinner plates, and he *examined* every inch of my face for at least thirty seconds. His words were unbelieving. "Oh my God." At the corner table everyone was looking in our direction.

How many hundred times had I planned what I would say if I ever found him? They were always insults to make him feel like scum for deserting me. All I could do, though, was stare at him with a triumphant sneer. "Hi, Dad," I said. "Long time no see."

. . .

My mind must have been swimming with emotion, because it didn't register what he was saying as he shook his head. Finally it did, though. "I'm not your dad, fella."

I had been preparing myself for all the denial, so I wasn't surprised, just angry.

"I'm not Ricky Coates," he said, lowering his voice and looking around. "I'm Frank Vanderkellen."

"Then why did you look at me like that? You *know* who I am, right?"

He sighed. "Yeah, You must be his son."

"Whaddaya mean, *his* son? Who are *you?*"

"I told ya, I'm Frank Vanderkellen. Keep your damn voice down."

I glared at him. "Okay, *Frank.* Why does my mother write to you if you aren't my father?"

"Everything okay, Frank?" asked one of the customers at the counter, a grizzled man in his late sixties. He looked at me suspiciously.

"It's fine, Bud."

"Me and Petey be headin' out, then. See ya."

Both men ambled toward the door, Bud looking back once. Frank checked the family in the corner, who had lost interest in us.

He leaned toward me. "Take a good look at me. Do I look *anything* like your father? Even the *slightest* resemblance?"

"No," I admitted. "So why *does* my mother write you? Are you a messenger or something?"

He shook his head in resignation. "No. She sends me money. Two-hundred bucks a month."

"For what?"

"To keep quiet."

"To keep quiet that he's still *alive?*" We locked eyes. Neither of us moved a muscle. I wasn't even *breathing*. It all came down to this moment.

"That's right," he said. "He's still alive," he whispered. "Two-hundred a month is what your father and I agreed on that night." He smiled slightly. "That was good money at one time. I was only twenty. What did I know? As it is, half the time I feel like a blackmailer, except that it was *his* idea."

Even though it confirmed what I had believed for years, this whole conversation had just blown my circuits. "So who knows about . . . where exactly *is* my—"

"Hold on," he interrupted. "I'll be out back about ten tonight when the night guy relieves me. I'll tell you the whole story. I guess I owe you that much. What you do from there is your business."

I looked at him in near disbelief. "You've kept a secret like that for twenty-five years, and you're gonna give it up just like that?"

"Yep. Told your dad I'd keep shut until the law or his son come lookin' for him. That was part of the deal, too."

"You *actually know* where my—"

"Like I said, come around back at ten, and I'll tell ya' everything. Agreed?"

I looked at my watch. "After all this time, I guess another six hours won't matter."

He smiled. "I guess."

. . .

Those six hours seemed like yet *another* twenty-five years. A movie, miniature golf, McDonald's, the strip mall; I covered every inch of Washburn, Louisiana. You don't know how tempting it was to call Mom and tell her who I'd just talked to. But I was actually worried she'd get in touch with my dad and he'd take off. Can you imagine, having to constantly count your own mother as an *adversary?*

Somehow, the time finally passed, and I headed back to the Pelican All-Night Diner. Just as he promised, Frank Vanderkellen was sitting on the steps in back, looking tired yet contented. I stood facing him, too tense to sit.

"My father owned the diner then," he began. "I was just a twenty-year-old working for him, not headed anywhere, I guess. We was across the street, right *in* the airport. This town was barely a speck on the map."

"No offense," I interrupted, "but why was my dad even *playing* here? He was pretty famous by then."

"It was a makeup date from before he hit it big. We got him for his old price, too. I doubt he even cleared expenses, what with his band and everything."

I looked at him impatiently. He got the hint.

He exhaled deeply. "Okay, here we go." The story he told took thirty-five minutes. I ended up learning as much about Frank Vanderkellen's *life* as I did about what really happened.

As it turned out, things were coming undone for my dad, despite his success. His marriage was just about shot because of all the time spent away. The record company was hounding him about his contract involving quotas on singles, albums, and concert dates they required. There were major problems with guys in the band and Tommy, his manager. Dad was hitting the bottle and the weed pretty hard. It was the classic self-destruct trip.

After the concert, as arranged, Frank's father took him to the airport to cook for the guys, then left. Everything else was closed. So Frank was out there about one-thirty A. M. and took care of the band, Tommy, Dad, the pilot, and one other guy.

According to Frank, everybody was ready to kill each other. Dad got into it with the band, then ripped into Tommy for adding another guitar without consulting him. That's who the other guy was. He wasn't in the show that night, he had just met them there. Tommy started in with the *pilot* about something, no one knew what, then the band started screamin' at Tommy about the new guy, both of whom were screamin' back.

When the smoke cleared, Dad decided there was no way he was getting on a plane with these people. He told them to leave without him, he'd charter another plane later. No one objected. So they all headed out, and Dad stayed behind, telling his problems to poor Frank, who's just a twenty-year-old country nobody. He told Frank at the rate things were going he'd be dead from an overdose or suicide within a year.

The plane took off, and less than a minute later there's a big explosion. Dad and Frank ran outside and watched the plane go down a few hundred yards off shore. It was obvious there were no survivors. Frank rushed inside, and as he got to the phone there's my father right behind him, yanking on his arm, saying, "Don't mention my name, *please.*" Frank didn't really understand, but all he did was report a plane crash, not a passenger list.

As soon as he hung up my father told him what was going through his mind. It was his chance to get out—alive. No one except Frank knew he wasn't on board. It had come out during all the arguing that the new guitarist was something Tommy did on his own. *No one* knew the guy was there to join them. With the tremendous explosion and crash, Dad realized no one on board would be even slightly recognizable. They would find six bodies, and assume one of them was Dad's—until it came time for identification.

Dad needed two things. He needed Frank to keep his mouth shut. And he needed Mom to come and identity his body, which of course was the new guy. And luckily, he was not well-known or family-connected. I'm not sure if or at what point anyone even missed him. Kind of sad, really. Dad struck a deal with Frank on hush money. Frank wasn't the kind to lie or cheat an insurance company, but he honestly thought he was saving Dad's life.

Under normal circumstances, he would have been on that plane. In a way, he had gotten to watch himself die, and come out alive on the other side. For Ricky Coates, it was time to live quietly, and be glad you could live at all. He called Mom right from the airport before the police and everyone else arrived. Imagine, calling your wife to tell her *you're* dead.

He spelled out to her what she'd have to do, and that she would be financially taken care of and was free to remarry. The last thing he told her was he would contact her as briefly as possible, to confirm the plan, and start paying off Frank. I assume that was the note I found.

Somehow, I was overlooked in all the discussion.

The amazing thing was everything worked. Why would anyone think Ricky Coates wasn't on his own chartered plane, right? Mom played her part to perfection. She and Frank turned out to be the world's best secret-keepers. Frank even told me about hiding Dad in the loft of an abandoned airport utility shed, shaving off his hair and beard, bringing him food and stuff. Eventually Mom paid Frank to get Dad a professionally-done fake I. D. It sounded like some spy thriller or escaped convict story.

And then came the unhappy ending to the whole mess. When Frank was finished I naturally asked him where my father was now.

"Sorry," he said. "That's *not* part of the deal. "I only agreed to own up that he was still alive."

"Wait a minute!" I shouted. "I didn't go through all this just to—"

"Calm down!" Frank shouted back. "Stop and think. If your father were to surface now, do you think he'd have another moment's peace for the rest of his life?"

"I guess not."

"And insurance fraud is pretty serious. He could end up in a Federal penitentiary."

"I wasn't gonna *tell* any—"

"These things *always* get out once the cat's out of the bag. Listen to me! He's *alive.* He's as content as he's ever *gonna* be. But here's the thing you *gotta* understand. He *doesn't want* to be *found.* "

There must have been a stunned, wounded look on my face. Frank stood and put a hand on my shoulder. "I'm serious. He doesn't want *anyone, ever* to find him. Treat it like he *was* on that plane, like people think. It'll be best for everyone, believe me."

I stood there silent for a moment or two. "He's *that* determined to hide?"

"Yes," Frank said somberly.

"The hell with him then," I whispered.

"I'm really sorry," Frank offered.

I waved my hand like it was no big deal, but it really was. When it all came down to it in the end, it really was.

Frank seemed uncomfortable and looked at his watch. "Getting' late. Got a place to stay?"

"Who said anything about *staying?*" I replied bitterly. I thanked him, shook his hand, and headed for my car.

I thought about what my dad had done, and why, and what it must have taken to stay "dead" all those years, living quietly where they couldn't find him. My eyes burned as I pulled out of the parking lot. Through clenched teeth I hissed, "Stupid!"

. . .

Franklin Louis Vanderkellen watched the car pull out some hundred feet away in the darkened lot. Seated again, he reached behind himself without looking and knocked lightly on the back door, which opened onto an alcove behind the diner's kitchen.

The door opened about a foot. Behind it was a man in his late forties, bald, wrinkled, and dressed in a cook's white uniform. He removed his wire-rimmed glasses, wiping his reddened eyes.

Without turning, Frank said, "You get a good look at him?"

"Yeah, I did."

"Nice-looking kid."

"Sure is."

Frank turned his head halfway, a smile appearing. "I assume he looks like his Mom, then."

A soft, mournful laugh sounded behind him. "I guess so."

Frank hesitated, then said, "I thought I was doin' the right thing that night." He paused purposefully. "Now, I don't know."

The door closed slowly, footsteps faded behind it. Frank looked down, shaking his head, and muttered, "Stupid." He raised his head and looked down Airport Road, where a single set of taillights embedded themselves in the darkness.

"A WALK ON THE MOON"

I've been in institutions most of my adult life—as an orderly. The politically correct term for 'orderly' now is 'Resident Assistance Specialist'. Me, I prefer 'orderly'.

It's not glamorous or well-paying, but it has managed to keep me occupied since I quit college back in 1967.

Nineteen sixty-seven. Where has the time gone? I'm married now with two grown daughters. My wife is a waitress at an Italian restaurant here in Mitchel, Indiana. I am presently employed at the Crabtree Hill Institute, a state-run facility for the mentally disturbed.

We've got them all at Crabtree: schizophrenics, psychos, the severely retarded, the delusional, everything. Every day I come in at 8 A. M. to relieve "3J" in C-wing. "3J" is Darius Jackson, the night orderly, a burly, even-tempered black man in his late twenties whom I've gotten to know in my three months here.

. . .

Elliott Sandersford, age 49. Room 7-C. One of ours. He's what we call a "Bouncer," having been in and out of various care facilities since he was twenty. He's as close to being totally sane as anyone, but there's something in the real world that sets him off, he goes on one of his rampages, and ends up back inside. In the seventies his parents had him committed, later on it was his wife. The past three times it was of his own choosing.

You would think that a doctor could communicate with him, possibly isolate the causes of his violent behavior. But that was the thing about Elliott that fascinated me. For twenty-seven years he equivocally refused to talk about *anything* remotely related to his violent episodes.

He was nice about it, almost like being a good sport. You would think that by now some hotshot psychiatrist could have tricked him into revealing *something*. You have to admire a guy that could withstand all those medical experts and hold onto whatever it was he was holding onto.

And there's the catch. I *knew* that Elliott knew *exactly* what his problem was. But he kept it to himself, as though all he needed was to be out of life's mainstream for a while. But sooner or later out there, something triggered him, and he ended up back inside.

. . .

I couldn't resist. I started asking "3J" questions about Elliott. "Where did all this start?"

"Way back in 1969," "3J" answered. "He was in a bad auto accident that summer, spent a week or two in a coma, then some more time heavily sedated. He had a lot of painful injuries."

"But I never noticed any—"

"3J" was waving a hand in my face. "Nope. No permanent damage. Everything he broke healed up just fine."

I tapped my temple, looking questioningly at him.

"Nope," he repeated. "Can't find any permanent damage. And they keep lookin'."

"How could there be no brain damage, and yet *after* this accident all his trouble started?"

"3J" raised his arms in perplexity. He paused a second. "Look at his life outside the bad spells. He's a tax accountant, works for a big firm, has a wife and kids, and they've all stood by him."

"He's able to keep a *job?*" I asked.

"His employer is very progressive. Me, I would've fired his ass years ago."

"You're a hard case, "3J"."

"Well, he's lucky. His wife's a big-time consultant for some high-tech companies. She could buy and sell us a few times."

I was quiet for a moment, then decided to say what was on my mind. "I'd love to have a talk with him."

"3J" looked puzzled. "You talk with him."

"No, not *conversation*. A *talk*. About what get him in here."

"Don't go *there*, man," "3J" shot back. "He won't fall for it, and you could get in big trouble. You don't belong inside his head. *He* doesn't even want to go in there."

"He *needs* to, though. If the right person were to—"

"Whoa! Hold it right there, Jeremy. What makes *you* the right person?"

"Well, we're about the same age, for one."

"We got plenty of doctors his age. And they ain't got a sniff of what makes this guy tick. Where you get off thinkin' he'll talk to you?"

"Just a feeling."

He looked at his watch. "I got to get home. Look Jeremy, I like you, so I'm gonna say this: the guy is where he needs to be. Even *he* knows that. Leave it alone."

. . .

Elliott Sandersford spent much of his time in Crabtree's library. He liked to read magazines, claiming that his best friend from high school was the Research Deputy for *People.* He was conversant on sports, politics, current events, you name it.

And there I was, trying to probe where trained experts had failed time and time again. I decided to use the direct approach. "Elliott, you seem like an intelligent, stable person. What is it that lands you in here?"

He smiled up at me from the *People* magazine he was reading. "You too, Mr. Coard? Are you on the case now?"

"Not really, I'm just curious." He looked like he was considering an answer.

"Mr. Coard, I think every person in the world has a soft spot, a little piece of reality that they just can't handle, no matter how hard they try. When my soft spot comes up, I fly into a rage, destroying everything I can get my hands on. I've already told the doctors that, so save yourself a trip."

"I know that. And you've never harmed a single person during your rages."

"That's right. It's a *controlled* rage. Since you're playing doctor now, what's that tell you?"

"That you really don't want to hurt anyone?"

"Hooray for me."

"You were completely normal before your auto accident, Elliott."

He feigned a surprised interest. "Ahhh, the 'accident theory' again. Do you know that there is no evidence of any lingering physical, mental, or emotional damage from my accident?"

"Of course I know that. But everything points to that being the turning point."

"Ahhh, the 'turning point'theory again. Look, Mr. Coard. I know you mean well, but you can't help me. Thank you for your concern, but my soft spot is part of me. I've lived with it as best I can since 1969. If you'll excuse me, I'd like to get back to my *People* magazine. Did you know that my best friend from high school is the Research Deputy at *People?*"

"Yes, I did."

He looked up at me admiringly. "Gee, Mr. Coard, you know *everything.*"

. . .

So much for the direct approach. Elliott had not only made a fool of me, but he told me later that I didn't have to worry, he wouldn't be informing my superiors of my "indiscretion." "Good orderlies are hard to come by," he added, with a wink.

The "soft spot" he'd lived with since 1969. It *had* to have been something to do with the accident. He had his first violent episode in November of that year, some weeks after his release from the hospital. That, I knew had to be my starting point. But first I had a phone call to make, to Mr. Alfred Gauger, the Research Deputy of *People* magazine.

. . .

After a couple of tries, I finally hooked up with Elliott's high school best friend, Alfred Gauger. I introduced myself, and told him I was calling on behalf of Elliott Sandersford. He seemed pleasantly surprised, until I told him about Elliott's accident and his many stints in and out of care facilities.

"Are you his doctor?" he asked.

"No," I admitted. "I'm a . . .Resident Assistance Specialist at Crabtree, where he currently resides. I . . .we're trying to get a fix on what sets off his violent episodes."

"I don't think I can help you there. I graduated a year after him. Then I went to Colby College, up in Maine. I ended up living there for over twenty years, working in research in various libraries before I got lucky and landed this job."

My face dropped in disappointment. "So you haven't seen him since *graduation?*"

"That's right. Kind of sad, really, but neither one of us was the type that wrote or called. Wish I had, now."

"Is there anything you could tell me that might shed some light on why he goes off the deep end, *and* won't tell anyone *why?*"

"I don't think so. He was a regular guy in high school. We were in band together. He came up our cottage in the summertime. He was pretty normal, from what I remember."

"Yeah, the accident must have messed him up, but all his brain tests come up okay."

"How strange."

"July eighteenth and November nineteenth of 1969."

"Excuse me?"

"July eighteenth was the date of the accident, and November nineteenth was his first violent episode, at his parents' home while they were at work."

"What were *they* able to tell you?" he asked.

I could have slapped myself. "His parents?"

"Yes. You said he was at their home when the first episode occurred. Are they still alive?"

"I honestly don't know," I said, embarrassed. "I never checked."

"Mr. Coard, speaking as a research person, you always start with the closest source. For my money, that would be his parents."

"Yes, I'll check that out. Speaking of research, I wonder if in your capacity as Research Deputy you could find something for me."

"Look Mr. Coard. We're very busy here. There's nights I'm still working at eleven."

"For your high school best friend?"

There was a pause. "All right." He exhaled impatiently. "What do you want me to find?"

. . .

I was beginning to think there was hope, after all. I checked Elliott's records again. His father had died back in 1981, but his mother, now eighty years old, lived at a rest home a few miles from here.

Something else in his file caught my eye, Shortly after being admitted here, he demanded a room change. As a matter of fact, he had another of his episodes in the process. He was quickly moved from the south side of the building to a room just across the hall, facing the north side. That satisfied him. The two rooms aren't more than twenty feet apart. They both looked out on open grounds with trees and roadways in the background. I filed it away for further reference.

Although Alfred Gauger agreed to my request, he reiterated that it might be weeks before he got back to me. What the heck. After nearly thirty years, what was another few weeks?

. . .

The Schofield Retirement Facility was located about halfway between Mitchel and Crabtree Hill. I called and found that it would be convenient to visit Mrs. Leona Sandersford any Saturday morning. That next Saturday, I drove over.

A receptionist had me sign in, take a visitor's badge, and pointed to an open veranda in back where a group of residents were sunning themselves. An aide introduced me to Mrs. Sandersford, sitting at a small table with another elderly woman. They had large glasses of lemonade in front of them.

"Do I know you?" Mrs. Sandersford asked.

"No, ma'am. My name is Jeremy. I'm from Crabtree Hill Institute."

She frowned. "Crabtree Hill. That sounds familiar."

"That's where your son Elliott lives."

Her face brightened . "I have a *son* named Elliott. *He* lives in a home, too."

I nodded politely. "Mrs. Sandersford, I was trying to find out a little bit about his background. Maybe we can help him better if we knew more."

She seemed to be only half-listening. She pointed at the glass in front of her. "You haven't touched your lemonade, young man."

"That's *your* lemonade."

She covered a smile, looking at the woman next to her. "That couldn't be *my* lemonade."

"It couldn't?"

"Of course not. I don't *like* lemonade."

"But—never mind. Mrs. Sandersford, what was Elliott like as a youngster?"

Like many elderly people, Leona Sandersford was fuzzy on things that happened ten minutes ago, but with amazing clarity could describe Elliott's lucky shirt from fifth grade, or the license number of his first car, a 1963 Chevy Nova.

"What did he like, what was he interested in?" I figured I had to get lucky eventually, but even her specific answers left me grasping at thin air.

"He loved science, exploration," she said finally, in response to nothing in particular. "I thought he might grow up to be a scientist, but then the car accident happened that summer, in 1969."

She continued musing. I let her go, hoping by chance she might mention something important.

"That was awful, those first days after the accident. We didn't know if he would live at first, then we didn't know if he'd come out of the coma." She sighed and shook her head. "His dad and I spent weeks at the hospital. We ate there, slept there." She laughed. "We had the TV on in his room all the time like the doctors told us. They were hoping he'd respond to *something*. That's where my husband and I watched them walk on the Moon that night, two days after the accident."

"Yeah," I said, remembering, "that was incredible."

"Elliott was so looking forward to it." She shrugged, and suddenly fixated on the nearly-full glass of lemonade next to her. "You still haven't touched your lemonade. Is there anything *wrong* with it?"

"It's not—I guess I'm not that thirsty."

She turned toward the other woman and whispered loudly, "He could at least make an effort."

I had obviously hit another dead end. Wishing her well, I said goodbye.

. . .

Alfred Gauger called me at home, two weeks after our first conversation.

"Mr. Coard, I looked up the major headlines for the two days you gave me."

"Great. What was happening on July eighteenth?"

"The big story was that Senator Edward Kennedy was involved in an auto accident on Chappaquiddick Island, off Martha's Vineyard. Mary Jo Kopechne, his passenger, drowned when the car went off a narrow bridge into a tidal pool. Kennedy did not report the accident until the next day."

"Yeah, I remember. I doubt if that's anything, though. What else?"

"Well sort of an ongoing story. The Apollo 11 astronauts were on their way to the Moon."

I remembered that Elliott's mother had said he was looking forward to the Moon landing, but missed the entire event because of his accident and coma. "Anything else that day?"

"Not really."

"Okay, what about November nineteenth?"

"An interesting coincidence, Mr. Coard."

"What have you got?"

"Apollo 12 *landed* on the Moon early that morning."

The *Moon* again! "That can't be a coincidence, Mr. Gauger." I began thinking out loud. "If Elliott was looking forward to the Moon landing and then *missed* it because of his accident, wouldn't he be *thrilled* when he finally got to see a lunar landing and moonwalk?"

"You would think so," Gauger replied, "except for one thing."

"What?" I asked.

"Very early on, one of the astronauts pointed the TV camera at the sun while adjusting it, and the sun's rays burned it out. There were essentially *no* TV pictures of Apollo 12's moonwalk."

There was dead silence at both ends. "Are you still there, Mr. Coard?"

. . .

Yes, it seemed far-fetched for Elliott to come unglued over something so vicarious, but I was convinced that was it.

At the next opportunity, I switched shifts with another orderly, taking the four-to-midnight block. When it was dark out I checked the view in rooms on both sides of the corridor in Elliott's wing. Guess what? You can see the Moon on the south side, where Elliott's first room was, but not on the north side, where he demanded to be moved.

I found him sitting on the bed, playing solitaire. He looked up and saw me standing in the doorway. "Evening, Mr. Coard. Taking the night shift, I see."

I paused and took a deep breath. "Too bad you're on this side of the corridor, Elliott."

"Why's that?"

"Beautiful Moon out tonight." He looked at the cards on his bed, face tense, one hand in a fist. "Did you hear me, Elliott? I said there's a—"

"Yes, I heard you," he snapped.

"I'm sure Jonathan across the hall wouldn't mind if we went in his room to look. Whataya say?"

"No thank you, Mr. Coard." The tone was controlled , but his facial expression and body language showed obvious tension.

"It's about the Moon, isn't it, Elliott?"

"Just be quiet, please, Mr. Coard." The voice quivered now. There was no eye contact. His hands messed the cards. He made an elaborate production of picking them up.

"You missed the first Moon landing because of your accident, so the second one meant everything to you."

Elliott became even jumpier, tossing cards around and mumbling.

"But one of the astronauts ruined the camera, and there *was* no televised moonwalk."

He jabbed a finger at me from where he sat. "You need to shut up now, Mr. Coard."

"It was just too much for you. The disappointment overloaded your circuits during the course of the day, and you blew. Your parents came home to find the living room nearly destroyed."

He was standing on the bed now, like a six-year-old having a tantrum. "You . . .*shut up.!*"

I rushed out, heading for the Director's office. I had a story to tell her.

. . .

I got in trouble for what I did. A written reprimand was put in my file. I could have been suspended without pay or even fired. I also received the somewhat amazed thanks of Dr. Ruth Winoski, head of our facility.

She thought it best, however, that I have no further contact with Elliott, so I was transferred to the other wing. That was okay, but not nearly as interesting. All the patients on that side of the building were *normal* crazy.

I did call "3J" on the orderlies phone occasionally to find out how things were with Elliott. With the new information they had, they were trying to get him to acknowledge his problem and deal with it. "3J" said they were making slow but steady progress.

A few weeks later, to my surprise, Alfred Gauger called me and asked about Elliott. He was pleased to learn that the information that he had found turned out to be the root cause of Elliott's problems. When he hung up, I figured that would be the last I ever heard from him.

But a week-and-a-half later I got a package from him. It was a two-and-a-half hour video tape of the Apollo 11 moonwalk. "I don't know if this will help Elliott," he wrote, "but he might like to have it anyway. It probably was the greatest thing that happened in our lifetime. Tell him I send my best and hope that someday he is able to put all this in a healthy perspective." I turned the tape over to Elliott's doctors.

Things were routine for a few weeks. Then one morning I got a call from "3J" as I clocked on.

"Get your ass down here, Jeremy," he said. "Someone wants to see you." He wouldn't give any details, but he was laughing a little, so I figured I wasn't in trouble this time. When I got over to C-Wing, "3J" was getting ready to leave.

"I got to go, but you should stop in Elliott's room."

My face tensed. "3J" handed me a paper with permission from Dr. Winoski and Elliott's doctors to enter his room and talk about anything of *his* choosing.

"This ought to be interesting," I said.

"Nothing to worry about, "3J" said. He clapped me on the shoulder. "It was Elliott's idea, and he got it approved. Enjoy." He walked off down the hallway.

I walked down to Elliott's room and peeked in. He was sitting on the bed, facing the doorway. "Come in, Mr. Coard."

I entered tentatively, and as I did Elliott stood and extended his hand. We shook.

"No hard feelings, Mr. Coard. I know you were trying to help me. I'm glad you didn't get fired."

"Me too," I said, returning his smile.

He walked over to his TV, which had a VCR hooked up. "I'd be honored if you'd watch this with me, Mr. Coard."

I knew what it was, but asked, "Watch what, Elliott?"

He beamed. "Mankind's finest hour." He pressed the 'Play' button, and a grainy black-and-white picture appeared. A blurry metal leg stood in the foreground. A ghostlike shape filled the screen, descending the rungs of a ladder. Neil Armstrong, *man*, was about to take a walk on the Moon.

Elliott tapped my shoulder. "Too bad you're not working the night shift."

"Why's that Elliott?"

"Beautiful Moon out tonight."

I laughed, remembering my own words. On the TV screen a man named Armstrong stepped onto the Moon.

CPSIA information can be obtained at www.ICGtesting.com
Printed in the USA
BVOW030022190613

323690BV00001B/3/P